DIAMOND
IN THE
ROUGH

Joyce Byers Hill

Yakima, WA

Books by Joyce Byers Hill

A PLACE CALLED HOPE series:

Diamond in the Rough

JC's Hope

Building Dreams

Dedication

I dedicate this book to my daughter, Chereé Lyne Hill, without whose insightful collaboration and constant encouragement this book might never have been finished. She always told me I should write a book. When I had doubts, she offered support and encouragement. When I wondered if it would be good enough for people to want to read it, she assured me it would be. She has been a never-ending source of inspiration and pride. I am so fortunate to be able to claim her as my daughter, and even luckier to be able to call her my friend. I love you to the moon and back, kiddo!

I also dedicate this book to my amazing nephew, Sean Christopher Byers, whose life was cut far too short at a mere twenty-three years. Sean always had a missionary's heart and lived his entire life as a true disciple of Christ. The world was a much better place because of his short time on earth. I miss your smiling face, buddy. Rest in peace, Bubba. I love you.

And finally, I would like to thank God for blessing me with a talent for writing. It is a true gift and has given me many years of enjoyment. Thank you, God, for all my blessings.

Chapter One

Meghan Maxwell stood in the middle of an empty, weed-infested vacant lot with a smile on her face. She loved a good challenge, and this was most definitely a challenge. Yes, this was by far the biggest project she had ever attempted, but it also provided a much-needed diversion from her recent troubles. Divorce is never easy, but hers had been particularly ugly, taking an immense toll on her not only emotionally, but financially as well.

Living in an apartment had never suited the free-spirited Meghan, but she was a survivor and always managed to do what needed to be done to survive. Being stuck in an apartment in town for the past three years after divorcing Danny was one of those things she had to suffer through while she made other plans. Or, rather, while God patiently unfolded His plans for her.

God. Where would she have been without Him in her life for the past several years? Chills ran down her spine as she shuddered at the thought. The sun provided welcome warmth, but she was suddenly chilled. Shaking her head in an attempt to ward off a dark mood, Meghan said a silent prayer that those days were now behind her. No, she wasn't about to let this day be swallowed up by wallowing in the past. This day was too important.

With an easy smile once again adorning her face, she

surveyed the one-acre piece of property that now belonged to her. Well, to her and the bank. By scrimping, saving, and working two jobs, she had managed to come up with the down payment required to purchase the piece of property. Sure, it didn't look like much now, but she could envision the future in her head. Plans constantly swam around in her head, sometimes making it difficult to sleep at night. But knowing what the future could be provided the motivation she needed to keep up the struggle; that and her daughter.

Stealing a quick peek at her watch, Meghan knew she still had an hour before she needed to pick up Kaci from school. She could hardly wait to tell her the property was finally theirs. Now they could begin working on their dream. She didn't know how long it would take, but eventually they would have a home of their own. A home where they could paint the walls any color they chose and put nails in the wall wherever they wanted. No more clearing everything with a landlord. No more tiptoeing around a husband where everything was either his way or the highway. This piece of property represented not only a dream, but it was a fresh start. Independence.

The next hour flew by quickly as Meghan took some measurements and laid out some preliminary stakes. She knew exactly where she wanted to build the house. It had to be far enough back from the road so that traffic wouldn't be a constant irritation, yet not so far back that it looked hidden. After staking out the location of the house, she stepped back toward the road and let her mind go to work.

It wasn't difficult to envision what the modest two-story farmhouse would look like. She had gone over the details so many times in her mind that it seemed to be permanently engrained. The house would be painted in a soft blue, with white trim. And there would be plenty of windows. Sunlight was as necessary to

Meghan's survival as air, and she wasn't about to skimp on windows. Large bay windows that would invite the morning sun to warm the home. And, of course, there would have to be window seats at the bay windows. Kaci spent hours with her nose in a book, and she had always wanted a window seat where she could curl up with a good book.

There would be a large wraparound porch that came from the dining room at the side of the house, all the way around to the front, and ran the length of the house. The porch would be wide enough to be able to have a porch swing, a couple chairs, and maybe a small table. The perfect spot to be able to spend evenings watching the sun fade into darkness. She could feel it. It already felt like home.

* * *

As Meghan pulled into the parking lot of the high school, she silently chastised herself for running late. She had spent a little longer at the property than she intended and was now nearly fifteen minutes late. Putting the Jeep Cherokee into park, she quickly looked around for Kaci, hoping her fifteen-year-old daughter wouldn't be upset. A smile crossed her face as she spotted Kaci sprawled out on the grass, reading a book.

Now why doesn't that surprise me, Meghan thought, as she got out of the Jeep and headed across the parking lot toward Kaci.

"Hey, kiddo!" Meghan greeted her daughter, "Is that a new book?"

"Oh, hi, Mom," Kaci replied as she tucked her bookmark into the book. "No, it's the one I'm finishing up for lit class."

"Sorry, I'm late. It's been a busy day."

"No problem," Kaci stated with a smile. "You know me, as long as I've got a book to read, waiting is not a problem."

Meghan laughed as she gave her daughter a hug, then they started for the Jeep. "Do you have much homework tonight?"

"Nope. Got it all done in study hall. Well, actually I finished my geometry during English, did my biology during history, then finished my ELS project during study hall. Bottom line, I get the night off."

Meghan chuckled as she gave her daughter another hug. "I don't know how you manage to keep everything straight, but I sure do like the results."

Kaci knew her mom was referring to her most recent report card that, once again, reflected straight As.

As mother and daughter got into the Jeep, Meghan asked with a smile, "Have I told you lately how much I love you?"

"Just this morning, in fact," Kaci replied, "but I never get tired of hearing it."

"And I never get tired of saying it," Meghan smiled genuinely. "Hey, do you want to stop and get something to eat? Then we could swing by the property. I signed the papers today."

"That's great, Mom!" Kaci said enthusiastically. "Why don't we stop at Subway and get sandwiches? Then we could go have our first picnic at our new home."

"Well, it's not exactly a home yet, but I think that's a great idea."

After making a quick stop at Subway, the Maxwell girls headed out of town toward the site of their future home. It was a short drive since the property was located only a couple miles outside of town, but Kaci took advantage of the time to fill her mom in on the happenings of her day. They turned off the pavement and drove in toward the center of the lot just as Kaci finished recounting a volleyball mishap during P.E. class. Kaci laughed as she told how a classmate hit the ball off the pole holding the net, then the ball ricocheted, bouncing off the head of the P.E. teacher.

Meghan suppressed a grin as she said, "Lucky for you guys Mr. Harper is a good sport."

"You're right," Kaci quickly said. "He didn't get mad or anything. He knew it was an accident. But you should have seen the surprised look on his face!"

As Kaci grabbed the sandwiches, Meghan opened the back of the Jeep and relished seeing the happiness in her daughter once again. Kaci had become so sullen and withdrawn after the divorce, but she gradually returned to the happy, fun-loving teenager Meghan enjoyed spending time with. They sat side by side on the back of the Jeep, savoring their favorite sub sandwiches, each lost in her own thoughts.

Kaci gathered up the sandwich wrappings and napkins, while Meghan closed the lift gate. Just as Kaci tossed the trash into the litter bag in the Jeep, she noticed the wooden stakes pounded into the ground.

"Hey, Mom," she asked, pointing to the stakes, "what are the stakes for?"

"I'm glad you asked," Meghan responded after an unsuccessful attempt to put her arm around her daughter's shoulder. Kaci's five-nine frame meant that was no longer a comfortable position for Meghan, who was now dwarfed by at least four inches by her teenage daughter.

Kaci smiled as she easily put her arm around her mom's shoulder. With a mischievous smile, she said, "No, really, shorty, what are the stakes for?"

Meghan tried to act indignant at the reference to her short stature, but her attempt fell short, as usual. "I don't think I want to tell you now. You've insulted me."

"Sorry, shorty," Kaci laughed. "I promise it won't happen again."

"Like I haven't heard that before," Meghan doubted. Ever since Kaci passed her mom's five-four height just before her twelfth birthday, it had been a running joke between them.

"Those stakes, oh great tall one," Meghan indicated, "show the location of our future home. What do you think?"

"Great spot, Mom," Kaci said. "I like the way it sits far enough back from the road that we won't be bothered by noise."

"Ah," Meghan nodded. "Great minds do think alike. That was my exact intention."

Meghan marveled at how much her daughter resembled her. Not only in looks – they both had hazel eyes and sported matching auburn ponytails – but also in their ideas and way of thinking. They were kindred spirits. And if they had not been mother and daughter, Meghan was very sure they would have been great friends.

Chapter Two

Travis Harmon had been sitting in his pickup for more than half an hour, just watching. He had washed his late-model Ford pickup earlier this morning, but wasn't the least bit concerned that it was now covered in a light film of dust. Even when he was a small boy, he had been attracted to construction sites. That fascination with building had never left him, and rarely could he pass a construction site without a familiar longing tugging at him. He could easily spend an entire day watching something being built, even though he preferred to be doing the building rather than the watching.

He knew he should get on into town. He had a long list of things waiting for his attention at the church he pastored. There were a few of his parishioners he planned to visit today, and his sermon still needed some work; but it was hard to be inside on a nice spring day, especially if there was construction going on outside.

Travis never got tired of seeing a rough piece of property being cleared in preparation for building. It was easy and satisfying to see progress. That's something that isn't always visible in his line of work. You can watch the daily work on a home being built and see the transformation from a pile of building supplies to a finished structure. The transformation in people is rarely that obvious. Maybe that was why he enjoyed working with his hands. He took great satisfaction in the pieces of furniture he built, but he took immense pride in the homes he constructed. Even so, he recognized his true calling. All the beautiful homes he had designed, planned, and built over the years could not hold a candle to the burning passion he had for leading souls to Christ.

For nearly an hour, Travis sat transfixed, watching the bulldozer clear the large lot. Whoever was operating that dozer obviously had a lot of practice. It was like watching an artist work on a masterpiece. The dozer was not just plowing haphazardly through the land, knocking down whatever happened to be in its path. It worked the ground with finesse, until it coaxed out of it just the right look. Yes, that dozer operator was definitely a master at his craft.

Finally, the bulldozer came to a halt, the engine was shut down, and the operator climbed out of the seat. Travis watched as the man dusted off his blue jeans and flannel shirt, then removed his hard hat and shook the dirt out of his hair, revealing a ponytail. Travis did a double-take but wasn't too surprised. Long hair on construction workers was very common today. The thought made Travis reach up and tug at the end of his wavy brown hair now touching his shirt collar. One more thing to add to the list. He needed to get a haircut before the weekend.

Well, enough daydreaming. He had work to do. Travis started the engine on his pickup and was about to shift it into gear when he realized the bulldozer operator was heading his way. Well, there goes another half an hour. He knew once he started talking construction, it would not be easy to pull himself away. Maybe just a few minutes of shoptalk then he'd be on his way.

Travis turned off the engine of his truck as the bulldozer

operator walked across the vacant lot. Before the construction worker reached the road, Travis realized that, blue jeans and flannel shirt or not, this dozer operator was most definitely not a man. He was used to seeing long hair, even ponytails, on construction workers, but the fact that this particular heavy equipment operator was a woman certainly took him by surprise.

Meghan made a cursory look for traffic before crossing the rural road toward the pickup. As she neared the truck, she slapped some more dust off her Levis then tucked her hands in the front pockets.

"Hi," she said with a smile as she approached Travis. "I noticed you parked over here and wondered if there was something I could do for you."

Travis had gotten out of his truck as Meghan approached and greeted her with an equally warm smile.

"Actually, you've just caught me at one of my favorite pastimes," Travis confessed. "I'm a sucker for construction sites. I could sit and watch for hours. Very few things fascinate me as much as watching things being transformed."

"I know just what you mean," Meghan nodded. "There's a lot of satisfaction in watching buildings go up and bare pieces of ground being recreated. It's like watching art in progress."

"Watching art in progress…" Travis considered. "I like that. That's a pretty good description of the way I look at building projects."

Travis reached out his hand in greeting, "By the way, I'm Travis Harmon. I didn't mean to interrupt your work."

Meghan shook his hand as she smiled. "I'm Meghan Maxwell, and you didn't interrupt my work. If the truth were known, you probably rescued me."

Travis looked at her quizzically. "What do you mean I probably rescued you?"

"Well," Meghan began, "I'm sometimes my own worst enemy. I get started on a project and never seem to know when to quit. I don't know how many times I've worked through lunch without even realizing it. Although that does seem to be a pretty effective diet plan," she added with a laugh.

They shared an easy laugh, as Travis consulted his watch. "Then I must agree that I probably did rescue you. It's already twelve-thirty."

"That's what I mean," Meghan replied. "If my curiosity hadn't gotten the best of me, I'd still be out there, working through lunch once again."

Travis grinned as he rationalized. "All good construction workers, and from what I've seen this morning, that certainly includes you, need nourishment to keep their strength up. Why don't you take a break, since I've already interrupted your work, and grab some lunch."

"I suppose I should," Meghan said.

"Would you care to join me for some pizza?" Travis asked hopefully. "There's a great pizza place just at the edge of town."

"I see you know your pizza," Meghan replied with a grin. "Luigi's is my favorite pizzeria, and one of my biggest weaknesses."

"A construction worker with a weakness for pizza?" Travis laughed. "Now that's a surprise!"

Meghan joined in his laughter as she considered the lunch offer. "Okay, sure, pizza sounds great. But I need to drive my own car. If I put off gassing up the Jeep any longer, I'll have to push it home!"

Thrilled that he wouldn't have to eat another lunch alone, Travis quickly agreed. "Not a problem. I need to get to work right after lunch anyway. Let's just meet at Luigi's."

"Sounds good," Meghan responded as she started across the

street toward her Jeep. "I'll see you in a few minutes."

* * *

After making a pass through the salad bar, Meghan and Travis found a table and sat down.

"Would you mind if I asked a blessing on the food?" Travis asked.

"Thank you," Meghan responded, "that would be nice."

Following a short prayer, the two began to eat their salads as they waited for the pizza to arrive.

Travis was the first to break the silence. "So, how long have you been doing construction work? I know it's becoming more common, but it's not every day you see a woman operating heavy equipment."

Meghan laughed as she replied, "You're right. It's not exactly a typical occupation for a woman. But then, I'm not exactly a typical woman either."

Travis had to agree with her as he looked into her hazel eyes. He was certainly beginning to believe that he had not stumbled onto a helpless damsel in distress.

"I've grown up in the construction business," Meghan explained. "While most little kids played with Tonka trucks, I grew up climbing around on the real McCoy. My dad owned his own construction business. In fact, I work in the family business. Well, I work for my brother now. He took over the business after Dad passed away."

"That would certainly explain your obvious expertise on the bulldozer," Travis commented.

"Thank you," Meghan said appreciatively. "I'll take that as a compliment."

"I'm glad," replied Travis, "that's how I meant it."

The pizza arrived just as they finished their salads. "Boy," said Meghan as she grabbed a slice of pizza, "I didn't realize I was so hungry. This smells incredible."

"It doesn't look too bad either," Travis agreed, taking a slice loaded with mushrooms and olives.

"Okay," began Meghan, "your turn."

"My turn for what?" Travis asked.

"What do you do for a living? Are you into construction too?"

"Well," Travis replied, "I am a carpenter by trade, but that's only my hobby now. It's what I do to relax."

When he didn't continue, Meghan questioned him further. "So, if that's what you do for fun, what do you do to earn a living?"

"I'm a pastor," Travis explained as he watched a surprised look cross her face.

"Hmm," Meghan mused, "a carpenter who spreads the gospel. What a unique idea."

Travis smiled as he continued to marvel at this interesting lady. "Well, I wasn't exactly the first to come up with that combination of occupations."

"I seem to recall there may have been another one before you," Meghan said with a grin. "You're in the same business, maybe you've heard of Him."

"I do believe I have heard His name a time or two," Travis replied as he grabbed another slice of pizza.

"So, where do you pastor?" Meghan asked.

"I'm the senior pastor at Hope Community Church. It's over on Fremont, just past the grade school."

"You're kidding!" Meghan exclaimed in surprise. "You're our new pastor?"

"Well, I'm not exactly new. I've been there for over six months."

"Ouch. I knew I hadn't been very faithful in my attendance recently, but I had no idea it had been that long. I knew the church had hired a new pastor, but that was the last I heard. Sometimes life gets pretty busy, but that certainly shouldn't be an excuse."

"Well," Travis replied good-naturedly, "now that you have discovered the error of your ways, you can work on correcting them.

"What did you say your last name was again?"

"Maxwell," Meghan replied.

"Meghan Maxwell," Travis said knowingly. "I thought that name sounded familiar. You have a daughter too, don't you?"

"Yes," Meghan answered hesitantly. "How did you know that?"

"I have good connections," chuckled Travis, as Meghan smiled. "Actually, your names are on my list of people to contact. Since I'm still new in the area, I'm trying to make a point of getting to know all the members of our church. I've gone through the church directory and have made a list of the names I don't recognize as having met them at church. Then I'm contacting those people to arrange a time to meet with them.

"So, Meghan Maxwell, when would be a good time for me to stop by and introduce myself?"

Meghan chuckled at his sudden seriousness. "Well, Pastor Harmon, I believe any evening this week would work for me, so you can work around your schedule. And I assume you already have my phone number, so you can just give me a call once you decide on a time."

"Okay," Travis agreed. "I'll probably call you tonight to set up a time. In the meantime, I'd better let you get back to your work and I had better get back to mine."

Meghan glanced at her watch and was surprised at how late it had gotten. They continued talking as they walked to their vehicles. As she reached her Jeep, Meghan shook hands with Travis. "It was nice meeting you, Pastor Harmon."

"And it was nice meeting you, Meghan Maxwell," he said seriously. "But, please, you can call me Travis."

"Well, Travis," she said agreeably, "I look forward to your phone call."

Chapter Three

Kaci had just finished helping her mom tidy up the living room when she looked at the clock and beamed proudly, "I believe that's a record. We've had dinner, cleaned up the kitchen, and tidied the living room in less than an hour."

"Wow," said Meghan, "and we still have nearly half an hour before they get here."

"Who do you think Pastor Harmon is bringing with him?"

"I'm not sure, but he said it would probably be one of the church elders."

Meghan had told her daughter last night about meeting the new pastor. After the glowing report from her mom, Kaci was looking forward to meeting him. She knew that her mom felt lacking in her duties because their attendance at church had fallen off. She also understood how difficult it must be for a single parent to juggle all the responsibilities of raising a teenager, managing a house, and working two jobs. Then you add everything she's gone through in the past six months trying to put together the land deal, Kaci could easily see how church had gotten pushed to the back burner, even though neither of them felt good about it.

"Does Pastor Harmon drive a pickup, Mom?" Kaci asked as

an unfamiliar truck pulled into an empty parking space at the apartment complex.

"Yes, he does," replied her mom.

"I think that may be them," Kaci stated as she pointed to a pickup on the other side of the parking lot.

Meghan joined her daughter at the window and replied, "That does look like his truck, so it could be."

As two men exited the pickup, Kaci spotted her former teacher. "Mom," she said excitedly, "look, it's Mr. S!" Rick Sanders was one of the most popular teachers at the junior high school, and most of his students called him Mr. S.

"Boy," Meghan said as she shook her head with disappointment. "We really need to get back to church. I had no idea Rick had been made an elder."

Just then the doorbell rang, and Kaci just about tripped over her backpack getting to the door. She managed to regain her dignity before she pulled open the door with that familiar Maxwell smile adorning her face.

"Hi, Mr. S!" beamed Kaci.

"Hi, Kaci," he replied. "It's good to see you again."

"You, too. How are Jayme and Hailey?" Kaci asked, referring to his two young daughters.

"Growing like weeds," he laughed. "I think it's time to stop feeding them!"

"I see you two need no introduction," observed Pastor Harmon with a chuckle.

"Oh, sorry," Kaci apologized. "You must be Pastor Harmon."

Meghan had arrived at the door and was standing behind her daughter, smiling at the exchange. "Why don't we invite them in, so they don't have to stand out on the porch?"

The girls stepped back and allowed the men to enter the living room.

"Pastor Harmon," Meghan began the introductions, "this is my daughter Kaci.

"Kaci, this is Pastor Harmon."

"Hi, Kaci," Travis greeted, shaking her hand. "It's nice to meet you."

"Hi," replied Kaci.

"And I believe you both already know Rick Sanders," said Travis, stating the obvious. "Rick is my newest elder."

"Hi, Rick," greeted Meghan, reaching to shake his hand. "Nice to see you again. Congratulations! I had no idea you were made an elder."

"I'm still getting used to it myself," he said with a smile. "It just happened a couple of weeks ago."

"Come on in and sit down," suggested Meghan. "Make yourself comfortable and I'll get the refreshments I have in the kitchen."

"I'll give you a hand, Mom," offered Kaci as she headed to the kitchen. "That way it won't take two trips."

"Thanks, kiddo."

The two men settled in on the sofa, as Travis took in the surroundings. He had always believed that the way a person decorated their living area said a lot about them, and he had no trouble matching Meghan's décor to her personality. Her apartment appeared to be modestly but tastefully decorated. There was an assortment of trophies on the entertainment center, most of which looked to be either softball or archery trophies. Travis smiled as his eyes landed on a shelf of baseball memorabilia that included a pennant from the 1954 World Series.

As he scanned the pictures adorning the walls, Travis was pleased to see how important family was to Meghan. Nearly all the pictures were either of Kaci or other people who shared a family resemblance. The only other items on the walls were framed prints or plaques that had Christian themes. It was encouraging to see evidence of her faith, and he hoped to be able to discuss that very topic in the near future.

Meghan returned to the living room carrying a pitcher of lemonade and a tray of glasses, followed by Kaci bearing a plate of chocolate chip cookies.

"Hey, how did you know chocolate chip were my favorite cookies?" Travis asked seriously.

"I didn't," replied Meghan with a warm smile. "You just happened to luck out because they're our favorite cookies."

Rick laughed as he said, "You thought you were getting special treatment, didn't you?"

"Special treatment or not," Travis replied, "it still looks like I get chocolate chip cookies!"

The girls joined in the laughter as they got comfortable on the loveseat.

"Rick," Meghan began, "would you mind asking the blessing on the refreshments?"

"Of course," he replied.

"Dear Heavenly Father, thank you for the opportunity to visit with the Maxwells. We pray that You will guide our discussion this evening and point out any areas where we may be able to assist them. We ask that You bless these refreshments and the hands that prepared them. We ask these things humbly in the name of Jesus. Amen."

"Don't be shy," Meghan said with a grin as she began pouring lemonade. "Dig into that plate of cookies. I'd hate for Kaci and I to be forced to eat them all!"

"I'd hate to see that too," laughed Travis, grabbing a cookie. "I'll do my best to prevent that from happening."

Getting right down to business, Travis suddenly became Pastor Harmon. Meghan noticed the slight change in demeanor, but it was so natural that it could have been easily missed. She halfway expected him to begin with "the purpose of our visit," and was pleasantly surprised when he asked Kaci what grade she was in at school. After a brief discussion of her daughter's favorite and least favorite classes at the high school, she was surprised when the pastor asked Kaci if she planned to go into the family construction business.

"You've got to be kidding!" Kaci exclaimed with the indignity only a teenager could master. "I mean, I like to build things, especially with Mom, but that's not what I plan to spend the rest of my life doing."

Pastor Harmon tried unsuccessfully to hide his laughter. Rick didn't even bother with an attempt.

"Pastor, you've got a lot to learn about Kaci," Mr. S said through his laughter. "It's a little difficult to operate heavy equipment while your nose is stuck in a book!"

"I can see how that could be a bit dangerous," Pastor Harmon agreed as he tried to regain his composure.

"So, tell me, Kaci, if you don't plan to have a hard hat as part of your work attire, do you have some idea what you want to do?"

Kaci glanced over at her favorite teacher and smiled as they seemed to share a secret. "I'm going to be a teacher," she stated as if there were never any doubt. "I want to teach third and fourth grade at my old school."

"Well, that occupation would certainly be safer if your nose were in a book!" the pastor nodded in agreement.

"I'm not sure Kaci could survive without books," Mr. S explained knowingly. "She's a teacher at heart, and she's great with kids. It's a perfect fit."

Pastor Harmon marveled at the easy camaraderie Rick and Kaci shared and could tell they shared a passion for teaching. "So how long have you wanted to be a teacher, Kaci?"

"Forever," she replied excitedly. "It's all I've ever wanted to do. Well, there was that time when I was three and I wanted to be a paleontologist, but I outgrew that pretty quickly."

"A paleontologist! I don't know many three-year-olds who even know what a paleontologist is! It appears that your mom isn't the only person in the family who isn't typical!"

Mother and daughter exchanged knowing glances and smiled. If he only knew how many times they finished each other's sentences!

Rick watched the exchange with a smile on his face as their new pastor got to know this remarkable family. Having known the Maxwells for several years, he had gotten to be close friends with them, especially after Kaci was in his class at the junior high school. He knew some of their background and the struggles they had faced in the past few years. He became a surrogate father to Kaci after her parents divorced and enjoyed seeing both her and her mother blossom as a team. It always amazed him to be able to see how God worked in people's lives to turn painful situations into something positive. Meghan and Kaci had always been close, but their bond became even tighter during the breakup of the marriage. In fact, it seemed at times that they could read each other's thoughts.

* * *

Meghan smiled as she watched their new pastor get to know her daughter. She saw how easily Kaci was able to tell him about her dreams, and how animated she became when he asked her questions. It always amazed her how quickly Kaci fluctuated between being a typical teenager and being a serious soon-to-be adult. Even when she was a precocious five-year-old, Kaci always seemed to be a grown up in a little kid's body.

Because of Kaci's rocky relationship with her dad, she had never really gotten along very well with men. Other than Rick Sanders and family, Meghan had never seen her daughter open up to another man like she was to Pastor Harmon. Here was a man her daughter could really bond with. And she definitely needed a good male role model in her life.

A soft chuckle from Pastor Harmon interrupted Meghan's thoughts and brought a surprising blush to her cheeks.

"We thought we had lost you," the pastor said with a smile in his voice. "You were certainly deep in thought."

"Sorry," Meghan said. "I hope I didn't miss anything too important."

"Not at all," joked Pastor Harmon. "We just solved all the problems of the modern world and came up with the meaning for life. But other than that, you didn't miss much."

"A pastor, a carpenter, and a comedian," laughed Meghan. "You must stay pretty busy!"

"As a matter of fact, I do," Pastor Harmon laughed. "And besides, a sense of humor always comes in handy when you're dealing with people!"

Hearing a chime from the grandfather clock in the corner of the room, Travis glanced at his watch and realized it was getting late. Still smiling at Meghan, he said, "It's beginning to get late, and I don't want to keep you ladies up past your bedtime, so we'd better get going."

As the two men stood up, Rick gave both Meghan and Kaci a hug. "It was sure good seeing you two again," he said sincerely.

"It's great seeing you again too, Rick," replied Meghan. "And congratulations on becoming an elder. I'm sure we'll be seeing you in church again real soon."

"And don't forget, Mr. S, my babysitting offer still stands. Any time you need someone to watch Jayme and Hailey, just let me know."

"I'll do that, Kaci, thanks."

"It was nice meeting you, Kaci," said Pastor Harmon, shaking her hand. "I think I'm really going to enjoy getting to know you and your mom."

"It was nice meeting you too, Pastor Harmon," replied Kaci.

"Oh, I just thought of something. Since you enjoy working with little kids so much, Kaci, have you ever thought of helping out in the kindergarten or primary class at church?" asked Pastor Harmon.

"No," responded Kaci, "I really haven't. But that would be fun."

"I have a feeling you'd be a natural. Why don't you check with Mrs. Jackson at church? I'm sure they could use your help."

"Thanks, I'll do that."

"Well, Ms. Maxwell," began Pastor Harmon.

"Please," Meghan interrupted, "call me Meghan."

"I stand corrected," he replied with a smile. "Thanks for your hospitality, and especially for your chocolate chip cookies. They were great!"

"I'm glad you enjoyed them."

"Trouble is," Pastor Harmon began seriously, "you're now one up on me. You know one of my biggest weaknesses, and I'm sure you plan to take advantage of that knowledge. You do plan to take advantage of my weakness, don't you?" he asked hopefully.

"Oh, but you're mistaken," Meghan began in mock seriousness, "I know two of your biggest weaknesses."

"Oh, really?"

"Have you already forgotten that I'm aware of your fondness for construction sites?"

"Touché," he laughed.

"Maybe I'll just have to invite you out to the construction site for some chocolate chip cookies."

"That, my dear Ms. Maxwell, is an invitation I would not refuse."

Chapter Four

Dave Marshall felt like an intruder as he stood in the doorway of the pastor's office at Hope Community Church. The pastor sat at his desk among a pile of books, but he was staring out the window, seemingly deep in thought. It was obvious from the assortment of books and papers on his desk that Pastor Harmon had been working on his sermon. But something had taken his mind away from his task. Dave followed the pastor's line of sight, hoping to see what had captured his attention, but saw nothing except the normal menagerie of squirrels and quail that seemed to forever grace the lawns of the church. God's little creatures could certainly be entertaining, but the pastor seemed to be looking right through them, not noticing their constant antics.

Dave had been the head elder of this church for many years and had seen more than a few pastors come through the doors. All had become his friends, and a few had taken a piece of his heart with them when they moved on. He knew that Travis was one of those special ones who would become much more than just a pastor to him. He was truly a man of God who lived and breathed according to God's will. Everything about the man was genuine. There wasn't a phony bone in his body. What you saw was what you got. And what you got was an amazing Christian character that seemed to bring out the best in everyone around him.

Yet here he sat, staring out the window, deep in troubled thought. And Dave knew a troubled pastor when he saw one. People tended to forget sometimes that members of the clergy were real people, with real problems, just like them. And occasionally they needed to be ministered to as well.

"Everything okay, Pastor?" Dave asked quietly.

Startled, Travis turned toward the door. "Hi, Dave. I didn't hear you come in."

"Sorry, didn't mean to sneak up on you," Dave replied with a grin.

"That's okay," Travis replied. "I guess I was lost in thought."

"Yeah, that's what it looked like. Either that, or you were avoiding your work."

Travis chuckled as he surveyed the mess on his desk. "I have to admit that I can understand how it would look that way. Come on in and sit down."

Dave took a seat in his favorite chair, off to the side of the pastor's desk. "So, is the sermon giving you a hard time? Or is that gorgeous spring weather the culprit?" Dave knew how much Travis loved the outdoors and had to occasionally force himself to work inside.

"Am I that transparent?" Travis asked with a smile.

"No," Dave replied. "I just happen to agree with you. It's hard to be inside on a day like this."

"Amen to that."

"So," Dave began, "is cabin fever really the problem, or do you have something on your mind?"

Travis looked at his friend and smiled. He had bonded right away with his head elder, and they spent a lot of time together outside of church. He had a lot of respect for Dave, and had learned quickly that his instincts were usually pretty close to the mark.

"What if I told you I had nothing on my mind?" Travis baited.

Knowing he was taking the bait, Dave jokingly replied, "Then I guess I'd have to agree with you, since you should know your empty mind better than anyone."

The two men shared a laugh. Dave tried to come up with another angle to find out what was bothering his friend. It was at times like these that Dave envied the gift Travis had of drawing people out.

"How are the congregational visits going?" Dave asked, referring to Travis's desire to get to know everyone in his congregation.

Travis seemed to perk up a bit as a small smile tugged at the corners of his mouth. "They're actually going quite well. I've managed to meet several people in the past week that I haven't seen at church since I've been here."

"That's great. Sometimes people stay away from church for reasons that aren't obvious, and they would gladly return if they thought they were missed. That's one reason I really appreciate your proactive stance on absentee members. People want to belong, but they also need to know that they're wanted and missed."

"You're right."

"There have already been several families who have returned to church since your visits with them. In fact, it still amazes me that you were able to get the Turianos back. They haven't been to church in over five years."

"It's hard for people to return after they've been gone for that long. But they were ready to come back. They just needed to feel welcome," explained Travis.

"I hate to see anyone fall away, no matter what the reason," he continued. "God can't help anyone if they keep shutting Him out. And just like any other relationship, it will shrivel up and die if it's not nurtured."

Dave loved seeing the passion Travis felt for people. He sincerely wanted everyone to have a personal relationship with their Savior. And he wasn't shy about expressing his beliefs. When Travis talked about how God could work in people's lives, it wasn't just rhetoric; he believed it to the very core of his being. That's what made him so effective in ministering to his flock.

"What do you know about the Maxwells?" Travis began. "Do you know how long they've been away from church?"

"Meghan and her daughter?"

"Yes," confirmed the pastor. "Rick Sanders and I met with them a few days ago."

"Well, let's see," Dave considered. "You've been here a little over six months, and I know they stopped attending shortly before you arrived. So, I guess it's been seven or eight months."

"Do you have any idea why they drifted away?"

"Not specifically," Dave replied, "but I know they've had a tough time of things for the past several years."

"In what way?"

"Meghan's marriage had been pretty rocky for a long time. Her former husband had a huge alcohol problem and refused to get any help. As Kaci was growing up, things became more and more difficult. Eventually, Meghan decided that she didn't want Kaci growing up in an alcoholic home, so she left and filed for divorce."

"How long ago was that?"

"I think their divorce has been final now for about three years."

"Was her husband a member of the church?"

"No, he never attended church at all, as far as I know. And I know that was the source of some of their problems as well."

"Oh?"

"Meghan grew up in a Christian home and has always had pretty strong beliefs. Danny, that's her ex-husband, never attended church with her and Kaci, and didn't respect their beliefs. Toward the end of their marriage, he made it pretty hard for them to attend church. In fact, Meghan and her daughter even stayed away for a while, hoping to salvage what was left of the marriage. Pastor Wilson and I counseled her on more than one occasion about the dangers of being yoked to an unbeliever. But she wanted to do everything she could to save the marriage. And if you get to know Meghan at all, you'll soon discover that she's not a quitter."

Pastor Harmon smiled, "From what I've seen, that doesn't surprise me at all!"

"Yes," Dave smiled in agreement. "She's quite a gal. She's been through a lot, but Meghan's a survivor. It takes a lot to get her down, but I've never known her to stay down for very long."

"I've already figured out that she's not a very typical woman," Travis remarked.

"That's for sure," Dave laughed. "Typical is one word that could never be used to describe Meghan Maxwell! You should see her operate heavy equipment!"

"As a matter of fact, I *have* seen her operate a bulldozer. That was certainly an eye-opening experience!"

"I should have known!" Dave roared in laughter. "If there's a construction site within fifty miles, you've probably been to it!"

"Okay, okay," Travis said as he held his arms up in mock surrender. "I'm guilty as charged. So, I happen to have a weakness for construction sites. That's not so bad, is it?"

Dave couldn't help but chuckle. "No, I guess there are a lot worse hobbies you could have."

"So, did Meghan and her daughter return to church after the divorce?" asked Travis.

"Yes, they did," replied the head elder. "They attended nearly every week until the past few months. I honestly think part of the problem is that Meghan tends to spread herself a bit too thin."

"What do you mean?"

"Ever since the divorce, she's become almost a workaholic. She was working two jobs, trying to save up money for a piece of land to build a house on."

"So that piece of property she was working is hers?" Travis inquired.

"Hers and the bank's. She managed to save up enough for the down payment, and she's getting a construction loan to build the house," Dave explained. "But she's been raising a teenage daughter on her own, plus working two jobs. And she spent a lot of time in the past few months looking for property and jumping through the bank's hoops to get financing. Then, of course, she spends every free minute getting the property ready for building. Like I said, I think she has spread herself too thin and I think church attendance is what got squeezed out."

His eyes lit up, and the wheels began to turn as Travis said, more to himself than anyone, "Maybe I can find a way to help."

* * *

Driving home from the church later that day, Dave thought about Pastor Harmon. The pastor was always so good about helping others, but he certainly didn't make it easy for anyone to help him. Dave had not been able to find out what was bothering his friend, and he knew that Travis would never come right out and tell him. But Dave prided himself on being able to read people, and in the time he had known the pastor he had learned that Travis's eyes were quite often a window to his emotions. His eyes had revealed that he was struggling with his emotions earlier today.

When he and Travis were discussing Meghan Maxwell, Travis's eyes would light up, then just as quickly cloud over. That confusion is what he had seen in the pastor's eyes earlier. Had he been thinking about his previous visit with the Maxwells and trying to figure out how to help them? Dave suspected there was more to it than that. He knew it wasn't frustration or indecision he saw in the pastor's face – it was sadness.

Chapter Five

Travis had hoped that a hot shower after his short hike would be relaxing and help him concentrate. He was frustrated that he was having so much trouble focusing on his sermon, but nothing he tried seemed to help. As much as he enjoyed being outside on a beautiful spring day, he had to admit that cabin fever was not the culprit. Thinking he needed a change from the sandwiches that had become his usual dinner fare in the past few weeks, he had stopped by the supermarket on his way home and picked up a steak and salad makings.

After slipping into his favorite pair of Levis, Travis pulled a T-shirt over his wet hair as he headed to the back patio, grabbing the butane lighter on his way through the kitchen. He carefully lit the barbecue, then closed the lid to keep the heat in, and went back into his apartment to make a small salad and get a potato ready to nuke in the microwave. As he grated cheese for the salad, he tried, without success, to think about his sermon.

"Maybe I'll think better on a full stomach," he said aloud, going back outside to put the steak on the barbecue. As the steak grilled, he set his place at the table, opting not to eat in his recliner again tonight.

Before long, the smell of the nearly cooked steak began

rumbling sounds in the pit of his stomach as he remembered that he had forgotten to eat lunch again today. *Maybe if I'd eat more regular meals*, he silently chided himself, *I'd be able to focus a little better.* He could hear the microwave ding as he took the steak off the grill and shut off the propane to the barbecue. Once seated at his small dining room table, Travis bowed his head and said a short, heartfelt thanks to God.

Feeling a bit better after the satisfying meal, Travis put his dishes into the dishwasher, grabbed his Bible, and settled himself into the recliner to work on his sermon. After twenty minutes of staring at the same page without really seeing it, he quietly closed his Bible.

Lord, he pondered, *why am I having so much trouble keeping my mind on my work? You know that nothing makes me happier than preaching Your word and ministering to Your flock. I just don't understand why I feel so restless.* Travis paused in mid-plea, almost hesitating to give voice to his thoughts. *Why do I feel so empty?*

Give it time. But it's been almost three years, God. *It takes time to heal.*

Almost instinctively Travis's eyes went to the picture hanging predominantly on the opposite wall. "Angela," he said softly. "I still miss you, sweetheart." The pretty blonde face stared back at him wordlessly. Like so many times over the past three years, his mind went back to the afternoon his world turned upside down. He could still see the ashen, tear-streaked face of his head elder standing in the doorway of his office at the church. A policeman stood behind him. Angela… drunk driver… killed instantly… lost the baby… Angela. The words tumbled through his brain and ripped their way through his heart.

I loved her so much. How can I move on without her? How can I possibly move on without the son who never had a chance?

How? *It takes time. Allow your heart to heal.* How long, Lord? How will I know when my heart is healed? *You'll know.*

* * *

With his face buried in his hands, and his heart in turmoil, Travis couldn't stop the ringing in his ears. He jerked his head up suddenly, popping his neck, when he realized the ringing in his ears was actually the doorbell.

"Coming," he said groggily as he tried to shake himself back to reality. "Just a minute."

Travis opened the front door and was greeted by the concerned face of his head elder. "Hi Dave," Travis said by way of greeting. "You look worried. Is something wrong?"

"You tell me," Dave replied anxiously, studying the disheveled face of his friend. "When you didn't show up at church for our meeting, I tried calling you. There was no answer, so I thought I'd better swing by here in case you were having trouble with your pickup or something."

"Oh, Dave, I'm sorry," Travis apologized as he nervously ran his hands through his hair. "I completely forgot about the meeting. Why don't you come on in and we can discuss the air conditioning budget now."

"I've got a better idea. The air conditioning budget can wait a few days. Why don't you tell me what's bothering you."

"What do you mean?"

"Travis, you're my friend," Dave began gently. "I knew something was bothering you this afternoon, but I couldn't get it out of you. Sometimes you lock yourself up so tight no one can reach you. I didn't want to pry earlier, but I'm prying now."

When his friend made no move to speak, Dave reached out and touched Travis's shoulder and made contact with his tortured eyes. "I want to help, Travis. I'm here to listen."

Travis looked away, and Dave followed his line of sight to the picture hanging on the wall. "It's Angela, isn't it?" Dave inquired sympathetically.

"It's been almost three years since they were killed," Travis began as the two men walked into the living room, stopping in front of his wife's picture. "Most of the time I do okay. But sometimes…" his voice trailed off.

Dave knew that his friend's wife and unborn son had been killed by a drunk driver. In fact, that was one of the reasons Travis requested a transfer to a different church. He felt he needed a change of scenery to help heal his broken heart. Dave felt it was a blessing for Hope Community Church to have gotten Pastor Harmon; he was one of the most sought-after pastors in the conference. In fact, Dave had been on the interview committee several years ago when Hope Community first tried to hire Travis for their small congregation. He had met Angela and had been very impressed with her devotion to both God and her husband's ministry. But the timing wasn't right, and God had impressed upon Travis to remain where he was for the time being.

"Do you ever regret leaving Montgomery and moving here to Hope?" Dave asked.

"No," Travis replied honestly. "I know this is where God was leading me. In a way, I couldn't get out of Montgomery fast enough. The intersection where Angela was killed was one I drove through every day. It was actually a relief when I felt God called me to minister in Hope. Even though it was difficult leaving the home we shared, I built that home for Angela, I knew that God had other plans in mind for me."

Dave admired his friend's unwavering faith in God. "Can I ask you a personal question, Travis?"

"Sure."

"Were you ever angry at God?"

Travis paused before answering, his eyes wet with unshed tears. "You know," he began, "I don't know how to explain it, but I've always been surprised that I wasn't angry at God. I'm not trying to sound self-righteous or anything, but I never even considered blaming God for what happened to Angela. Oh, I had a lot of anger to deal with for a while, but it wasn't directed at God. I was angry at the intoxicated driver. I was even angry at the inventor of alcohol for a while. But what really hurt was when I realized one day that I was angry at Angela for dying. . . and for taking my unborn son with her. That was hard. I had never once been angry at her when she was alive, and yet I was mad at her for dying." Travis shook his head. "Makes no sense."

"Grief does strange things to people," Dave replied by way of understanding. "So, do you think things are getting any easier for you?"

"You know," Travis replied, "even though it doesn't seem like it at times, I really do think things are getting better. I lean on God a lot. Although I don't understand it, I know that this is all part of God's plan. And most importantly, I know that He will give me the strength to get through it. Like I said, most of the time I do okay. Don't get me wrong, I still miss her so much at times that I just ache, but each day it's a little less painful. I often wonder what my son would be like. . . who he would look like. Would he look like me? His mother? That really hurts. I know that Angela would want me to move on with my life. I just don't know if I'm ready to do that."

"Do you think that may be what's causing you so much anxiety and confusion?"

"What do you mean?"

"Maybe you're afraid to move on. Maybe you want to move on, and you think you're ready to, but you're afraid it would be disloyal to Angela's memory."

"I don't know," Travis said slowly. "You could be right. Sometimes I feel like I'm in the middle of a tug-of-war that has no winner. I know that I can't change the past, as much as I'd like to. And I also know that I can't live in the past. But I just don't know if I'm ready to move into a new future, one without Angela."

Dave's heart ached for his friend, a person who was always so strong for everyone else, and yet so vulnerable. "Well, my friend," Dave said, "you look like you could use a good night's sleep, so I won't keep you up any later. But before I leave, if it's okay with you, I'd like to have prayer with you."

"I would really appreciate that, Dave."

The two men knelt in the middle of the room and put their hands on each other's shoulders. "Dear Loving Father," Dave began, "I would ask for a very special blessing upon your faithful servant Travis. You understand his heartache better than anyone. You know his heart and what it will take to heal it. You brought him to us to serve Your purpose, and in time You will help him understand what that purpose is. You don't expect him to forget about his precious wife, Angela, but you do expect him to follow the promptings You put in his heart. You will know when his heart is healed sufficiently to move on, and You will show him the way to his new life. I pray that You will gently move him in the direction You desire for him, and that You will help him see Your plan when his heart is ripe. Please be with him tonight, comfort him, ease his pain, and give him rest. In Jesus's precious name we pray. Amen."

As the men stood up, the unshed tears in Travis's eyes began making their way down his cheeks. "Thanks, Dave," Travis said as he embraced his friend in a bear hug. "You're a good friend."

"Now I expect you to call me if you need anything," Dave

admonished, his own eyes wet with emotion. "And next time, don't make me drag it out of you!"

Travis laughed as he wiped his eyes. "Okay, okay, I think I got the message."

As they walked to the door to say goodbye, Travis gently slapped his friend on the back. "Thanks, Dave."

"Not a problem. Take care of yourself, and call me if you want to talk. Now go get some sleep."

Travis closed the door and headed to his bedroom with an appreciative smile gracing his face.

Chapter Six

As the cement truck was being hosed down at the back of the property, Meghan slowly walked around the freshly poured footings of her new home with a sense of satisfaction. The past few days had been a whirlwind of activity as she worked to get the footings framed in time for today's scheduled arrival of the cement truck. With promises of a good home-cooked meal for her bachelor brother, she had managed to enlist Todd's help in framing the footings. Even though her fiercely independent streak wanted to build every aspect of her new home by herself, she knew that that was an unrealistic dream. Some things very simply required more than one set of hands. And try as she might, she had never been able to squeeze more than the allotted twenty-four hours into a day.

So, although it went against her nature to accept help, she realized that her dream would never become a reality if she didn't swallow her pride and accept help when she needed it. It was an undeniable fact that she would need to contract out certain aspects of the construction because she either didn't have the expertise necessary to do the work herself, or it was a job that required more than one person. Pouring the cement footings was one such job. It was too much for one person to do alone.

Inspecting the fresh cement as she worked her way around the perimeter of the home, Meghan couldn't help but smile. "It's really happening," she whispered in amazement. "The building of my dream has finally started. One day this foundation will have a house on it where Kaci and I can build memories."

Meghan waved at the driver of the cement truck and yelled her thanks as he drove off the property. She immediately returned to her inspection of the footings, visualizing each room in the house as she worked her way around to what would become the main living area. She knelt down beside the framework, pulled a sixteen-penny nail out of her shirt pocket, and carefully began scratching the date and her initials into the wet cement.

"That's yesterday's date, in case you're interested."

Startled by the sudden voice behind her, Meghan lost her balance and nearly put her hand into the wet cement. She was about to launch into a tirade about how rude it was to sneak up on someone when she looked up into a familiar set of hazel eyes.

"Travis," she said in mock seriousness, "you nearly made me a permanent fixture in my home's foundation!"

"Sorry." He laughed as he reached out to help her up. "I didn't mean to sneak up on you. Well, okay, that's not entirely true. I did intend to sneak up on you. I just didn't mean to startle you."

"I'm not sure I buy that either," Meghan replied skeptically, as she playfully slapped him on the arm.

"Okay, so I admit the look on your face was priceless." Travis brought his free hand from behind his back and handed Meghan a sack. "How about a peace offering? I brought lunch."

Meghan accepted the Subway sack, appeared to consider the peace offering, then shook her head regretfully. "Sorry, I'm just not hungry enough to eat two sandwiches."

Travis watched as a mischievous smile crossed Meghan's

face. "I have an idea," he suggested. "Why don't you share the other sandwich with me?"

"Well, I suppose that could work. But only if you'll share the chocolate chip cookies I brought."

Travis reached out to shake hands, "You've got yourself a deal."

"Well, in that case," Meghan began, "let's eat lunch. I'm actually hungry enough that I could probably eat both sandwiches!"

"Oh, no you don't," Travis retorted. "You shook on the deal! I get one of the sandwiches and some of the cookies. Besides, you said you were going to invite me out to the construction site for chocolate chip cookies. You actually came out ahead on this deal because I brought the sandwiches."

Meghan laughed as she reached into the back of the Jeep and pulled out a water jug. Handing the jug to Travis, she instructed, "Pour some water over my hands, if you would please, and I'll wash up."

Travis took the jug and raised it above her shoulders.

"My hands, not my head, or there will be no cookies for you!"

"Yes, ma'am," Travis humbly replied like a little boy who had been caught with his hands in the cookie jar. "I hope you like tuna. I wasn't sure what kind of sandwich you might like, but tuna's my favorite so that's what I got."

"I love tuna sandwiches. In fact, I usually put black olives on mine and people think I'm crazy."

"Really? That's not so crazy." Travis watched as Meghan unwrapped her sandwich, revealing the black olives scattered along the top of the tuna.

Meghan looked at Travis in amazement, but said nothing. He shrugged his shoulders and replied, "That happens to be the way I like my tuna sandwiches too."

Meghan asked God's blessing on the food, then they settled into a comfortable silence as they enjoyed lunch seated on the back of the Jeep.

* * *

After polishing off the last cookie, Travis looked over at Meghan and saw that she was staring off into space, seemingly lost in another world. "Judging by the smile on your face, I'd say that whatever thoughts you're lost in must be good ones."

Meghan turned toward Travis, still smiling. "Sorry, I guess my mind wandered a bit."

"You seem to make a habit of that when I'm around," joked Travis. "What's wrong? Don't you think my charming personality is captivating enough?"

"Yeah, right," Meghan laughed as she nudged him with her shoulder. "It has nothing to do with you."

"Boy, what a relief!" Travis replied as he theatrically wiped his arm across his forehead. "For a minute there I thought I was going to have to develop an inferiority complex."

"That, I've got to see!"

"So," Travis began, "what brought that smile to your face if it wasn't my engaging personality?"

Suddenly feeling shy, Meghan ducked her head a bit before replying. "Oh, it's nothing really. No big deal."

Still sitting together on the back of the Jeep, their shoulders lightly touching each other, Travis became acutely aware of her presence and sensed her insecurity. "Hey, you can tell me. I'm a pastor, remember?"

The smile returned to her face as she raised her head and looked into Travis's eyes. "Oh, yeah, that's right. I have such a hard time thinking of you as a pastor."

Travis grinned at her innocent comment. "Why is that?"

"I don't know. Somehow you just don't seem to fit the mold."

"Well, you know, I could say the same thing about you."

"Oh?"

Travis looked at her with a twinkle in his eyes. "Let's just say you don't look like any construction worker I've ever seen!"

"Touché!" Meghan laughed.

"So, if you have a hard time thinking of me as a pastor, why not think of me as a friend," suggested Travis. "And as your friend, I'd sure like to know what put that smile on your face."

Still, Meghan hesitated.

"Oh, come on!" Travis urged. "You'd tell a friend, wouldn't you?"

"Okay, okay," Meghan agreed. "But don't blame me if you discover my thoughts weren't earth shattering."

"Agreed. No expectations of earth shattering thoughts."

Meghan laughed as she replied, "You really are a nut, you know that?"

"Guilty as charged," Travis replied with a grin.

"I was just thinking about my property. I know you probably won't understand because you seem to have all your ducks in a row."

"Trust me, Meghan," explained Travis as his smile faded a bit. "I've got some ducks of my own that not only aren't in a row, but aren't even in the pond."

Meghan watched as Travis's face quickly clouded over, then almost as quickly returned with a smile.

"Tell me about your property, Meghan," Travis encouraged. "I can tell how important it is to you. It's a nice piece of property."

Meghan relaxed a bit and seemed to gather her thoughts. "It is important to me. But it's not the piece of ground so much as it's what it represents."

"It represents a dream, doesn't it?" Travis guessed.

Meghan stared at him in disbelief. "You're right, it does represent a dream. But how did you know that?"

"We all have dreams, Meghan. Dreams are what keep us looking to the future. Dreams are what give us hope."

Silence settled in around them for a moment as they became absorbed in their own thoughts.

"Travis," Meghan broke the silence. "Have you ever had a dream that meant so much to you that just the possibility of it not coming true made your heart ache?"

"Yes, I have," answered Travis as he thought about the empty spot in his life. Not comfortable with being the topic of discussion, Travis turned the conversation back to Meghan. "Tell me about your dream, Meghan."

"It's kind of a long story," hesitated Meghan.

Travis grinned as he looked mischievously at Meghan. "Hey, I've got lots of time. After all, I'm just sitting here watching the cement dry."

Meghan stood, put her hands in the pockets of her Levis, and began walking toward the recently poured footings of her dream house. Travis followed her; anxious to hear her story, but also realizing that he simply wanted to be near her.

"I don't know how much you know about me, Travis," began Meghan. "I was married for many years to a man who wanted to control every aspect of my life. He wouldn't let me make any decisions about our home. I couldn't even put pictures up on the walls unless it was his idea. Even then, they had to be pictures he wanted on the walls. He decided where we were going to live and where we went on vacation. He even chose our friends. I never had a voice in anything."

Meghan paused as she collected her thoughts. When Travis didn't comment, she continued. "He was an alcoholic. He still is, in fact. I grew up in a home without alcohol, so I wasn't really prepared for how difficult life could be living with an alcoholic." Meghan drew in a deep breath and then continued her story. "When Kaci was born, I began to see his alcoholism from a different perspective. I began to see how growing up in an alcoholic home would affect our daughter. I tried to get him to stop drinking, and he actually did for a while, but it was always short lived.

"I grew up in a Christian home and wanted my daughter to grow up with Christian beliefs as well. Danny refused to go to church with us. In fact, he even tried to prevent us from attending. Kaci and I stopped attending church for a couple years; hoping things would get better at home. They never did. Eventually it became obvious that divorce was the only answer. I don't believe in divorce, so that was a tough pill to swallow. I felt like a failure. But with God's help, I made it through the divorce.

"You know, Travis, you don't have to listen to all of this if you don't want to."

"But I do want to," Travis assured her. "Go on. What happened after the divorce?"

"Kaci and I moved into an apartment in town."

"Is that where you live now?" asked Travis.

"Yes, it's where you and Rick came to visit us.

"I began working two jobs, trying to save up enough money to buy a house. Before long I realized that, with my connections in the construction business, it would make more sense to buy a piece of land and build my own home. So, I spent every waking hour working toward that goal.

"Almost a year ago I found this piece of property, and Kaci and I fell in love with it. I knew that this was where I wanted to build our home. So, I became a working fanatic. When I wasn't working at one of my jobs, I was working on buying the land and obtaining financing for building the house. Purchasing this property meant I would finally be free from Danny's control. I could design and build the house the way Kaci and I wanted it, not the way Danny said it had to be."

"So, buying this property not only represented your dream," Travis said as he stooped down to inspect the curing cement, "it also represented your freedom."

"So, you do understand," Meghan replied in amazement.

"Yes, Meghan, believe it or not, I do understand. Many of us are searching for freedom from something. There are a lot of things in this world that control us. Sometimes, as in your case, it's a person. Sometimes it's greed, envy, jealousy, or other things of this world. And sometimes it's demons from our past. But no matter what's controlling our lives, there's only one way to really find the freedom we desire."

"You mean God, don't you?"

"Yes," Travis nodded. "I mean God."

Meghan was silent for a moment before admitting, "I haven't been to church in a long time."

"I know," Travis replied with a look of understanding. "I'm your pastor, remember?"

They looked at each other and smiled, remembering their little inside joke. Meghan turned serious as she admitted, "I haven't talked to God in quite a while. Life has been so busy. I know that's not a good reason. But there are only so many hours in a day and, being a single parent, there's always so much to do. God probably wouldn't even recognize my voice anymore."

Travis gently took Meghan by the shoulders and turned her to face him. "Are you trying to tell me that God has a lousy memory?"

Meghan couldn't help it – she giggled. "See what I mean? I've never heard a pastor talk that way. Pastors usually say things like 'God doesn't forget' or 'God is all-knowing.' But 'God has a lousy memory?'"

"Okay," Travis replied, unsuccessfully trying to hide his grin. "We've already established the fact that you don't think I'm a typical pastor."

"I'm sorry. We were having a serious discussion, but that just struck my funny bone."

"You're a funny lady, Meghan Maxwell."

"Sorry."

"No need to apologize. God also has a sense of humor, you know."

"He would have to have a sense of humor," Meghan commented. "Can't you just picture God sitting up in heaven, knowing how everything is going to turn out, and watching all of us down here actually trying to control our lives? We must provide Him with a lot of entertainment."

"I'm sure we do," Travis chuckled. "But we also provide him with a lot of joy."

Turning serious once again, and suddenly realizing he was still holding Meghan by her shoulders, Travis dropped his hands as he said, "But back to your comment about God not recognizing your voice. God knows all His children, and each one is special to Him. You are as important to God as if you were His only child. And no matter how long it's been since you've talked to Him, He's always anxious to hear from you."

"You're right, of course," Meghan answered.

"Talk to Him, Meghan. He misses you." Then with a wink he added, "And coming back to church couldn't hurt either."

Chapter Seven

Meghan sat in her Jeep in the parking lot of Hope Community Church and made no move to get out of the vehicle. After several minutes, Kaci said, "Well, Mom, are we going in or not?"

Jerked back to reality by the sound of her daughter's voice, Meghan quietly replied, "We're already here, so we might as well go on in."

They both had mixed emotions about returning to church after being absent for so long. Meghan wondered what people would think. Would they feel welcome? Would they be ostracized? Kaci was a bit nervous as well, but she tended to look at things from a teenager's perspective. She very simply wanted to reconnect with her church friends, many of whom she didn't see on a regular basis because they attended a different school.

Without warning, Kaci threw open her door, looked at her mom, and said, "Last one in is a rotten egg!"

Kaci always knew how to get her mom to spring into action. Meghan bolted from the Jeep and easily caught up with her daughter halfway across the parking lot. She put her arm around Kaci with a smile and suggested, "We probably shouldn't run into church. I'm sure that wouldn't look very reverent."

"I don't know, Mom," replied Kaci with a teenager's logic.

"I'd bet God would be thrilled to see people running into church."

Meghan, feeling much more at ease, nudged her daughter in the ribs and replied, "You know, you're probably right."

* * *

As the congregation stood for the final hymn, Meghan realized there was no chance for a quick retreat to the parking lot. Several of her church friends had already made eye contact with her, and each gave her a warm smile. Kaci returned the hymnal to its place on the back of the pew in front of them and leaned over to whisper to her mom. "Is it okay if I go visit with my friends for a little while?"

"Sure," Meghan said. "It looks like I'll probably be tied up for a while visiting anyway. Go. Bond with your friends."

"Thanks, Mom. I'll meet you out in the lobby in a little bit."

"No need to hurry, enjoy your visit. Just make sure you're not holding up someone's parents."

"Mom," Kaci replied with an appropriate amount of exasperation.

"I know, I know," Meghan laughed. "Parents can be such bores."

Kaci gave her mom a quick hug then joined a mixed bunch of teenagers hanging out in the lobby.

Meghan watched her daughter and her friends for a moment as they laughed and talked, silently thanking God for the great bunch of kids they were. They were all good solid Christians, many of whom had already gone on various mission trips around the world. They were typical teenagers in so many respects, yet it was obvious they shared a very special bond.

Meghan heard someone call her name and turned to see Doris and Ellen headed her way. The two women were in their mid-seventies, but had been close friends of Meghan for many years.

Reaching Meghan just ahead of Ellen, Doris wrapped Meghan in a hug that belied her small stature. "Meghan, dear, I am so glad to see you!"

"It's great to see you too, Doris," Meghan said with a smile as she returned the sincere hug. "It's been a long time."

Ellen managed to squeeze in a hug between tears of joy. "How have you been, Meghan?"

"I've been just fine," replied Meghan. "I've been very busy, much too busy if the truth was known, but I've been fine."

The next twenty minutes flew by as Meghan visited briefly with many of the members of her church family. They all welcomed her back to church with open arms, hugs, and sincere smiles. She began to wonder what she had been so worried about. She had known most of these people for many years, and knew what kind of people they were. She knew that she would be hard pressed to find a more loving group of people anywhere.

Thinking it was probably time to pry Kaci away from her friends, Meghan reached over to grab her purse and Bible from the pew and turned just in time to see a beaming Travis headed down the aisle toward her.

* * *

Travis had to admit to himself how difficult it had been not to barge in on the reunion Meghan was enjoying with her church family. But he was so overjoyed at seeing her and Kaci walk into the sanctuary just before the service started that he had a hard time focusing on his sermon. In fact, he had had a difficult time focusing on much of anything in the past few days. Whenever he attempted to work, thoughts of Meghan popped into his head. She was not an ordinary woman, and he found himself completely intrigued by her. And, he realized, a bit protective of her as well.

But now the lobby was beginning to empty out as people headed home for lunch. He didn't want to miss the opportunity to talk with her before she left. People had been hugging her for the past twenty minutes, and he had to resist the urge to walk up and give her a big hug himself. It would not have seemed a bit out of place – Hope Community was a church full of huggers – but somehow he just wasn't comfortable with it. He suddenly realized that he didn't want Meghan to see his hug as just one more hug from a group of people.

Travis reached out to shake hands with Meghan while, at the same time, putting his other hand lightly on her shoulder. "Well," he began with a sincere smile, "I see you made it."

Meghan returned his smile without hesitation. "Yes, we made it. I loitered out in the parking lot for a while trying to work up the nerve to come in, but we made it."

"I'm glad. So, you apparently were dreading coming back. Was it as bad as you expected?"

"No," Meghan admitted honestly. "I was very pleasantly surprised. I was constantly reminded of what a wonderful, loving church family we have here. It was pretty easy to settle back in."

Travis looked across the lobby at the dwindling group of teenagers. "Well, it appears that Kaci had no trouble fitting back in either."

Meghan laughed as she replied, "Those kids are such a tight group of friends that I'm sure they could be apart for years and pick back up right where they left off!"

"I have no doubt about that," Travis agreed. "Normally when a group of Christian kids grow up together they become their own support system by the time they're teenagers. It's nice to see that in today's world. They tend to look out for each other and help keep each other grounded."

"It certainly makes a parent's job a bit easier, that's for sure."

Meghan and Travis watched the teenagers for a moment as the group continued to break up, each of them finding their way to the parking lot.

"Do you happen to have any plans for lunch?" Travis asked.

"You know," Meghan replied honestly, "when we left home, I was so worried about returning to church that Kaci and I never even discussed lunch. We'll probably just head home and grab a sandwich."

"I have a better idea," Travis offered. "Why don't you and Kaci join me at Luigi's for pizza?"

"I've got to admit, that certainly sounds better than a sandwich."

"Great! Why don't you give me a couple minutes to put things away and close up my office, then I'll meet you out front."

As Travis headed to the pastor's office, Meghan joined Kaci in the lobby where the last of the teenagers were saying their good-byes.

"So, Mom," Kaci began as she put her arm around her mother's shoulder, "what's for lunch? I'm starved."

"How does pizza sound to you?"

"That's a pretty silly question, Mom. Have you ever known me to say no to pizza?"

Meghan laughed at her daughter's serious tone, knowing full well that Kaci could likely survive on pizza if she needed to.

"Pastor Harmon invited us to join him for pizza at Luigi's. Is that okay with you?"

"Sure," Kaci quickly replied. "I like Pastor Harmon. There he comes now."

"Hi Kaci," Travis greeted, as he shook her hand. "So, are you ladies ready to eat some pizza?"

"Absolutely!" they replied in unison, shaking their heads and laughing as they once again had the same thought.

Still chuckling, Meghan suggested, "Why don't we take my Jeep, and we can all ride together. No sense taking two cars."

* * *

After ordering their pizza and making a trip through the salad bar, the girls slid into a booth as Travis slid in on the opposite side. Offering to ask a blessing on the food, Travis reached for Meghan's hand as the three joined hands in prayer. Meghan looked up at Travis after the blessing, her hand lingering slightly in his as their eyes met.

"Thank you for inviting us for pizza, Travis."

"Yeah, thanks Pastor Harmon," added Kaci. "This is our favorite pizza place."

Travis smiled in reply, "It seems to me I've heard that before."

They enjoyed their salads in silence for a few minutes before Travis asked, "How's the house-building project going, Meghan?" He loved the way her eyes lit up whenever she talked about the house.

"We're ready to start framing. Todd is rounding up a couple of his buddies from work to help with the initial framing." Meghan chuckled as she added, "He promised them that I'd barbecue some steaks in exchange for their labor."

Travis laughed as he said, "I hope you jumped on that offer. Framing is hard work. I think you got the better end of that bargain."

Meghan joined in his laughter, "Yeah, I know. Todd knows it too. He just likes to think that he's pulled one over on me."

"Todd is your brother, isn't he?"

"Yeah, he's my little brother. He runs the construction

company now." Meghan paused for a moment before adding, "You should meet Todd someday. You two are a lot alike and I think you'd like each other."

"Most definitely. I have great respect for anyone who can finagle a barbequed steak dinner out of someone. When are they going to get together to begin the framing?"

"They're going to start on Friday morning, then work some this weekend and see how much they can get done."

"Can they use some extra help?" Travis offered.

"There's no such thing as too much help," Meghan replied with a smile. "Who did you have in mind?"

"In case you had forgotten," Travis said, trying to appear offended, "I am a carpenter by trade."

"I seem to vaguely remember that. But do you have any experience?"

Travis enjoyed this playful side of Meghan. "My dear lady, I have no less than a dozen custom-built homes to my credit."

"Well, I suppose we could give you a chance, if you're sure you're qualified."

"Oh, I'm qualified. And I expect to get in on that barbecued steak dinner, as well."

"Boy, here you are already stating demands and I don't even know if you're any good."

"I guess you'll just have to wait and see then, won't you?"

"You can bet I'll have my eye on you. I work with Todd and the boys, so I know the kind of work they do. But you, I'm just not sure about, so I'll have to keep close tabs on you."

"Let me guess, you're the foreman on the job?"

Meghan laughed at his mock surprise. "That's right, buster. And I run a tight ship."

"I'll just bet you do! Don't worry, boss, I won't let you down."

Chapter Eight

Meghan was at the construction site before the sun peeked over the horizon, anxious to get a start on the day. The framing phase of construction projects was one of her favorites because you could begin to see the building take shape. She hadn't slept well last night, nervous with anticipation. Each day her dream was sneaking a bit closer to reality. If it were possible, she would spend all her time at the site, thinking that would make things move along a bit quicker.

"Do you always get such an early start on the day?"

The pleasant sound of Travis's voice behind her made her heart skip. Was spending the day with him part of the reason for her nervousness this morning?

"You know, Travis," Meghan began as she turned to face him, "you're beginning to make a habit of sneaking up behind me."

Travis chuckled as he reached out and put his hand on her shoulder. "Well, at least there's not any wet cement around for you to fall into this morning."

"Very funny. I had forgotten you were also a comedian. By the way, what are you doing here so early? Todd and the boys probably won't be here for another half an hour."

"As you know," Travis replied with a smile, "it's hard for me to stay away from construction sites, especially if I get to be involved in the actual construction."

"I know just what you mean. I can't wait to grab a hammer and get to work."

"So, you're a working foreman, huh? Why doesn't that surprise me?"

Meghan simply smiled, content in the knowledge that Travis understood, and shared, her passion for creating.

Glancing past Travis toward the road, Meghan's excitement began to grow as she saw two pickup trucks pull onto the property. Todd, her six-three little brother, emerged from the first pickup about the same time two other muscular construction workers got out of the second truck. All three workers donned their hard hats as they walked toward Meghan and Travis, with Todd carrying an extra hard hat in his hand.

Travis knew instantly which of the men was Meghan's brother; he recognized the familiar smile that must run in the family. Travis stepped toward Todd, reaching out to shake his hand. "I'm Travis Harmon," he greeted by way of introduction. "You must be Todd."

Todd smiled as the two men shook hands. "Picked me out of the crowd, huh? My sister must have told you a little something about me."

"Well," Travis admitted, "she did mention that you were her little brother, but you've got to be at least six-three. What really gave you away was your smile. It must be a family trait."

"Guilty as charged," Todd confessed, giving Travis a friendly pat on the back.

"I want you to meet a couple of my buddies. John, Randy, this is Travis, the friend of Meghan's I was telling you about. He's going to give us a hand today."

The men shook hands, instantly taking a liking to each other.

Todd handed a hard hat to Travis, saying, "I brought an extra hard hat for you. One hard-and-fast rule I have is that everyone wears a hard hat on any of the sites we're working, even the volunteers."

"I couldn't agree with you more," Travis replied. "I did bring my own hard hat in the truck, though, so I won't need yours. Thanks for thinking to bring it along."

"Well," Todd chuckled, "if you've got your own hard hat, you must not be a novice to the construction business."

"No, not exactly a novice. I've actually been a carpenter by trade for nearly twenty years. So, I guess you could say I know my way around construction sites."

"That's good to know," Todd stated with respect. "Volunteers are always great when you're working for free, but volunteers with experience are even better."

Meghan playfully slapped her brother on the arm. "I take offense to the 'working for free' comment. You know full well that you're in this for the barbecued steak dinner."

"Yeah, yeah." Todd laughed as he pulled on his sister's ponytail. "Only because you grill steaks even better than Dad did."

Looking at Travis, Todd stated the obvious. "I assume you managed to talk your way into the steak dinner as well, didn't you?"

"Absolutely, it's why I'm here," Travis agreed with a smile.

"Okay, okay, boys, enough with the small talk," Meghan said, pulling her ponytail out of her brother's hand. "It's time to get to work."

"What do you mean small talk?" Todd objected. "Discussing a steak dinner is very serious business."

"Yeah, yeah," Meghan retorted, "and so is building my

house."

Todd held up his arms in surrender. "Looks like the boss has spoken, guys. That must mean it's time to get to work."

* * *

Since the subfloor had already been completed, the crew was able to start right in with the framing. Even though Travis had never worked with this crew before, he fell right into the swing of things as they all worked together like a well-oiled machine. He was surprised, although he knew he shouldn't be, by how well Meghan kept pace with the men. It was obvious that she was an experienced carpenter. They worked side by side throughout most of the morning as Travis fought to keep from being distracted by Meghan's nearness. He couldn't help noticing the faint aroma of her perfume, mingled with the smell of fresh sawdust. He realized it was a combination he didn't mind at all.

By late morning, the rough outline of a house was beginning to emerge from the landscape. They had made good progress. Rooms were beginning to take shape, and door and window openings began to appear. Meghan stepped back to survey their progress as she yelled for the men to take a break.

"Let's break for lunch, guys," she suggested. "I wouldn't want my hardworking volunteers to become malnourished."

The men began to put down their tools and make their way toward Meghan, slapping the sawdust off their jeans as they walked.

"I've got a cooler full of sandwiches, fried chicken, and potato salad in the back of the Jeep," Meghan said as she opened the tailgate to her Jeep. "There's also plenty of cold water, sodas, and iced tea in the other cooler."

Todd walked over to the Jeep to survey the situation. "You're not trying to tell us, little sister, that your fried chicken, although it's very good, is in place of our steak dinner, are you?"

Meghan gave Todd a playful slug on the arm. "You're such a goofball, Todd. Like I could ever get away with substituting cold fried chicken for a steak dinner. A steak dinner indicates that it will be served at dinner time, not lunch."

Travis enjoyed seeing the playfulness and camaraderie Meghan and Todd shared. It was easy to see that they were a tight-knit family.

"Just in case there are any other time-challenged workers in the group who don't know the difference between lunch and dinner," Meghan began, staring right at Travis, "the sandwiches, salad, and chicken are for lunch. That would be the meal we're planning to eat here very shortly. Later, when we call it quits for the day, we will have dinner, at dinnertime. I already have potatoes baking in the roaster on the other side of the Jeep, and the barbecue is set up over there as well. Kaci will be dropped off here later, and she will have a tossed salad and some garlic bread. So, I believe dinner is covered, and all you starving volunteers will get your steak dinner. But for now, why don't we wash up and have some lunch."

Todd grinned as he jabbed Travis in the ribs with his elbow. "I just love jerking her chain occasionally. But she's a real take-charge kind of person, so I know nothing falls through the cracks. And she's a pretty great cook too."

"I'll have to remember that," Travis said, surprised that he actually said it out loud.

Everyone settled in on the tailgates of the pickups, with Meghan joining Travis on the back of his truck. After Todd asked the blessing on the food, the hungry workers dug in with a vengeance as the pile of food rapidly disappeared.

"Hey sis," Todd called out. "You didn't happen to bring any

of your chocolate chip cookies, did you?"

"Maybe," Meghan replied. "Who wants to know?"

"Come on sis," pleaded Todd. "You know nothing finishes off a meal better than your chocolate chip cookies."

Travis bumped shoulders with Meghan as he whispered, "You know he's right."

"Okay," Meghan laughed. "They're in the cooler in a plastic container. Help yourself. But you have to share!"

"All right!" exclaimed Todd with the excitement of a little boy. "I knew you wouldn't let me down."

Meghan chuckled as she shook her head. "You are so spoiled, Todd. It's no wonder you're not married. There's probably not a woman alive who would put up with you!"

* * *

Framing continued at a rapid pace throughout the afternoon. There was little conversation as each of the workers seemed to instinctively know what was needed. Whenever a completed wall was ready to be raised, everyone automatically stopped what they were doing and assisted with raising the wall. Once the wall was braced into position, the workers quickly returned to what they had been doing. Travis was amazed at the lack of flared tempers on the site. He had worked in the construction industry long enough to know that inflated egos and hot tempers were the norm more often than not. It was a pleasant surprise to see how well these people got along with each other.

Another surprise that brought mixed emotions to the surface was how comfortable he was working alongside Meghan. Their easy banter never once interfered with their progress, but certainly made an already enjoyable task even more so. At times he felt almost guilty being so comfortable with her nearness. If he were totally honest with himself, he would have to admit that he was beginning to see Meghan in a way he never thought possible after his wife's death. It was both a frightening and entirely too pleasurable predicament.

By late afternoon, a car pulled onto the property and parked next to Meghan's Jeep. Kaci bounced out of the car and waved enthusiastically to her mom, then turned to remove some things from the backseat. Meghan slipped her hammer into her tool belt and walked over to give Kaci a big hug.

"Hey, kiddo," Meghan greeted her daughter with a hug. "Did you have a good day at school?"

"Yeah, I guess you could say that. I aced my chemistry test."

"I'm not a bit surprised," Meghan responded with a high-five.

"Hi Becky," Meghan greeted her friend. "Thanks for picking up Kaci from school and bringing her out here. I really appreciate it."

"Not a problem, Meg. I needed to drop Kayla off at gymnastics, so I was practically next door to the school anyway."

"And thanks for swinging by the apartment so Kaci could pick up the rest of the food so I can feed these hungry men."

Becky looked toward where the men were still hard at work. "Wow! You guys have sure made a lot of progress today. That's amazing!"

Meghan smiled in agreement. "Things have really gone smoothly today. We haven't had any problems at all. Knock on wood!"

Becky gave her friend a quick hug as she looked at her watch. "I'd better get going. Kayla will be finishing her gymnastics class in about twenty minutes. See you in church this weekend."

"Thanks again, Beck."

"Any time. Bye Kaci."

"Bye. Thanks for the ride."

Meghan took off her tool belt as she headed for the water jug to wash up. "Kaci, would you mind setting up those two tables and the chairs while I get the grill fired up?"

"Sure thing, Mom."

As Meghan got the grill going and checked the baked potatoes in the roaster, Kaci set up the tables and chairs, then Meghan helped her pop up a portable canopy over the tables.

Meghan walked back toward the house to get the guys' attention. "Anyone ready to call it a day?"

Power tools and hammers came to a screeching halt, a good indication that it had been a long day.

"If you guys want to wrap things up and get washed up for dinner, I'll go ahead and throw the steaks on the grill."

"You won't get any argument out of me, sis," Todd replied as he dropped his tool belt into the back of his pickup. The other three men didn't waste any time following suit as they abandoned their tools in favor of dinner.

Travis walked over to where Meghan was manning the grill and offered his assistance. "Need any help?"

Meghan looked up from the steaks and smiled, "No, I think I've got it under control. Maybe you could see if Kaci needs any help finishing up with the tables."

"I don't know," Travis replied good-naturedly. "These steaks smell a lot better than those construction workers do."

"I'm sure neither of us smells much better than they do!"

"I don't know about that, but I'll go see if Kaci needs any help." Travis laughed as he headed over to the tables, arriving at the same time Todd did.

Kaci had just finished putting paper tablecloths on the two tables, along with a glass jar filled with wildflowers.

Todd walked up behind her and threw his arm around her shoulders. "Hey, munchkin, what's with the fancy table setting?"

Kaci playfully poked him in the ribs as she grinned. "Oh, Uncle Todd, you're such a guy."

"Guilty as charged," he laughed.

"You know, Uncle Todd, just because we don't have any power or running water out here yet doesn't mean we have to eat like savages!"

Todd hugged his niece tighter as he replied, "I knew I could count on you to keep me civilized!"

"Todd," Meghan called out from her spot at the grill, "why don't you come take the potatoes out of the roaster for me? And Travis, if you'll bring me that platter, I'll take the steaks off, and then we'll be ready to eat."

In just a matter of minutes, everyone was finding a place at the tables. Travis appeared behind Meghan and pulled her chair out for her, while Todd did the same for his niece.

"Thanks, guys," Meghan said in appreciation.

"Well," began Todd by way of explanation, "as my niece so appropriately pointed out, just because we're roughing it doesn't mean we have to eat like savages."

"Maybe there's hope for you yet, Todd," Meghan laughed lovingly. "Travis, would you mind asking the blessing on the food?"

"It would be my pleasure," he said, as they joined hands.

"Dear Loving Father, we are so thankful for the many blessings you bestow upon us. You have blessed us today with the ability to work with our hands to help Meghan and Kaci see their dream come true. And you have blessed our souls today with friendship and camaraderie. As you continue to feed our souls with an appreciation of your love for us, we ask that you also bless this food so that we might feed our bodies as well. I ask a special blessing for Meghan and her daughter, that You continue to guide and direct their hopes and dreams so that they will always see

Your love in their new home. In Jesus's name we humbly pray. Amen."

In no time at all, the hungry volunteers were digging into their well-earned dinner. "Well, sis," Todd said between bites, "I think you've outdone yourself again. You always did grill the best steaks in the family, but I think these are the best of the best!"

Meghan smiled in appreciation. "It's nice to know they have earned the Todd Byers seal of approval."

"I've got to agree with your brother, Meghan," Travis added. "This is, without a doubt, the best steak I've ever tasted. And even the baked potatoes have a unique flavor to them. What is it that gives the potatoes that special taste?"

"Before I bake them, I coat the potatoes with some olive oil then spread Parmesan cheese over the skins."

"Of course!" Travis said in understanding. "That's the taste I couldn't quite identify."

Travis felt very comfortable sharing dinner with his new friends. Everyone enjoyed the wonderful food while conversation flowed easily throughout the meal. It was obvious why Meghan and Todd shared a special brother-sister bond. They had so much in common, had many of the same personality traits and, at times, even seemed to have the same thoughts. It was almost as if they could read each other's minds. It was a bit spooky. But Travis had seen the same mental connection between Meghan and her daughter. He considered it one of God's greatest gifts, having someone you loved so much that your brains as well as your hearts appeared to function as one organ. It wasn't difficult to recognize God's hand at work in the lives of Meghan and her family.

Travis's private thoughts were interrupted by a playful elbow in his ribs as Meghan looked at him with a grin. "Someone was certainly deep in thought."

Travis grinned sheepishly. "I guess I was. Sorry, did I miss something?"

"It depends on how hungry you still are. I've only asked you twice if you wanted some apple pie for dessert, with no response I might add. I never offer dessert more than three times, so if you hurry you can squeak in just under the wire."

"By all means!" As Travis took the plate of pie from Meghan, their fingers brushed lightly. He seemed transfixed as their eyes met, as much by the touch as by what he saw in her eyes, a look he didn't completely understand. But a look he definitely wanted to learn more about.

Chapter Nine

Travis sat in his pastor's study working on a sermon in between bouts of daydreaming and staring out the window. The warm spring day was calling to him, and he was finding it increasingly difficult to remain indoors. His thoughts kept turning to his favorite springtime activity – construction work. He had been back out to Meghan's construction site several more times to volunteer his carpentry skills. Each time, he received a warm welcome and was told that his assistance, although not necessary, was certainly appreciated. And each time, as he worked alongside Meghan, he discovered that he was becoming more and more drawn to this fascinating woman. It also surprised him to realize that every time he pictured a construction site these days, he pictured Meghan hard at work on her home.

Congratulating himself on finishing the rough draft of this week's sermon, Travis decided to reward himself with some time outside. He reached into his desk drawer and pulled out his keys, then locked his office and headed to his truck. He took the main road out of town to one of his favorite places to go hiking. After parking at the trailhead, he changed into his hiking boots, grabbed a water bottle, and started up the trail. Noticing several cars in the parking lot, he remarked to himself, "It appears I'm not the only one with a touch of cabin fever today.”

About three hundred yards up the trail, Travis began to encounter several small groups of teenage boys. He greeted each group as they passed, wondering why they weren't in school in the middle of the day. The boys didn't seem to be creating any trouble, so his thoughts didn't linger on them. His thoughts were soon interrupted by the sounds of laughter up ahead on the trail. As he rounded the next bend, he saw the source of the laughter. A group of teenage girls were laughing and singing as they made their way down the trail.

“Pastor Harmon!” yelled one of the girls, waving as she ran down the trail toward him.

“Well, hello Kaci,” Travis replied with surprise. “I didn't expect to see you out here in the middle of the day.”

“Our biology class had a field trip today.”

“That explains all the kids I've been passing on the trail,” Travis nodded in understanding.

“Yeah, we've been out here for a couple hours already, so we're getting ready to head back to the school.”

“Well, your teacher sure picked a great day for a field trip. I was having a hard time staying inside myself.”

Kaci chuckled as she said knowingly, “Looks like cabin fever won, huh?”

Travis laughed in reply. “Yeah, it looks that way.”

“I'd better catch up to the rest of the class. See you later, Pastor Harmon.”

“See you, Kaci.”

* * *

Hiking always seemed to clear his mind, yet today, especially after seeing Kaci on the trail, his mind was as restless as ever.

Keeping his mind settled was becoming increasingly difficult for Travis lately, and he wasn't exactly sure why. However, if he were entirely honest with himself, he knew that part of the cause was a certain auburn-haired construction worker who kept popping into his mind on a regular basis.

As Travis steered his pickup back toward town, he made a last-minute decision to make a short detour. Pulling into Meghan's construction site, Travis was immediately disappointed to find her Jeep was nowhere in sight. He parked his truck alongside what he recognized as Todd's pickup, and walked toward the back of the house where he heard voices. Just as he rounded the corner of the house, Todd spotted him.

"Hey, Travis," Todd greeted him as the two men shook hands. "You're sure an answer to prayer."

"Oh, really?" Travis replied with a questioning look.

"Yeah. We were trying to install this large picture window when John got the call that his wife was in labor and on her way to the hospital. Meghan is at a doctor's appointment, and Randy and I were just telling God how much easier it would be to install this window if we had an extra pair of hands. And here you are!"

"Ask, and you shall receive!" Travis replied with a chuckle. "I'd be happy to help."

In no time at all, the three men had the window installed. "Would you like me to stick around and give you a hand with those other windows?" Travis asked, noticing two smaller windows leaning against the side of the house.

"I'm sure you have better things to do," Todd answered.

"Actually, I'm rewarding myself with a little time outside. I finished the biggest portion of my sermon, and I was losing my battle with cabin fever, so I went for a short hike. I think I'm ahead of the curve a bit, and I'm really not ready to sit back down behind the desk, so you'd actually be doing me a favor by allowing me to help."

Todd slapped Travis on the back as he laughed. "Whatever it takes to justify getting outside! I know I couldn't sit behind a desk all day. Okay, never let it be said that I refused to help a friend. Grab a window and let's get these last two in before we call it a day."

Meghan rounded the corner just as Todd and Travis finished with the last window on the back side of the house. Travis turned around to find her staring at him with a grin on her face. "It seems, Pastor Harmon, that you are incapable of staying away from a construction site."

Travis hung his head in shame as he replied, "Yes, ma'am, that's true. I keep trying to reform my bad habits, but it appears that I'm fighting a losing battle."

"And why do you think that is?" Meghan was having a difficult time not laughing.

"I blame the construction industry," Travis stated seriously.

"Oh, really? I can hardly wait to hear your reasoning."

"Well," Travis began slowly as he looked up at Meghan, "it seems that construction workers are much easier on the eyes than they used to be. It can be a bit distracting at times."

Meghan nodded as she locked eyes with Travis. "I see what you mean. I can understand how that could be a problem."

"Yes, ma'am," Travis replied as he gazed deep into Meghan's eyes. "It does make it hard to stay away."

Watching the brief exchange from a few feet away, Todd decided it was a good time to rescue his sister. And his friend. Stepping up behind Meghan and putting his arm around her shoulders, Todd broke into their thoughts. "I, for one, am mighty glad Travis showed up when he did. John left right after you did because Leslie went into labor, and Randy and I were left standing around trying to figure out how the two of us were going to install that big window by ourselves."

Her eyes still on Travis, Meghan said quietly, "God does seem to work in mysterious ways."

"He does indeed," Travis agreed.

Finally breaking eye contact, Travis said with hesitation, "I hope you don't mind that I stopped by."

"Not at all," Meghan replied, her cheeks still feeling a bit warm. "You're welcome to stop by anytime. I just don't want you to feel obligated to help."

"I don't feel obligated, but I do like to help."

"So, you can take the boy out of construction, but you can't take construction out of the boy?"

"Something like that." Travis laughed, relieved that the previous tension had been diffused. "Although, it apparently isn't limited to just us boys."

It was Meghan's turn to laugh as she agreed, "Yeah, something like that."

"Are you free for dinner tonight?" Travis surprised himself by asking.

"Uh...." Meghan began.

"I'm sorry," Travis said. "I shouldn't have asked. It's pretty short notice."

"No, don't apologize. I was just trying to remember what Kaci's schedule is for tonight."

Being the perceptive brother that he was, Todd sensed that there might be something more than friendship brewing between Travis and his sister. "Isn't tonight the night Kaci said she was going to be working on a history project with Brittney?"

"You're right, it is. She's going home with Brittney after school."

Travis looked hopeful. "Does that mean you're free for dinner tonight?"

"Yes," Meghan replied. "I believe I am."

"Can I pick you up at seven?"

Meghan felt the heat creep up the back of her neck. She had not dated since before she and Danny were married. Lord knows she hadn't had any time to date since the divorce. Where was her mind going, she silently chastised herself. Why was she so sure this was a date? Suddenly realizing that she never answered Travis's question, she quickly replied, "Seven will be fine."

* * *

Travis had picked Meghan up just before seven, and they were now silently leaving the parking lot of her apartment complex. Not completely understanding why she felt so nervous, since she and Travis had actually spent quite a bit of time together these past few weeks, she hoped talking would ease her sudden case of nerves. "You never did say where we're going for dinner."

"You're right," Travis replied secretively. "I didn't." He glanced sideways at Meghan and grinned.

"So," Meghan began, relaxing a bit, feeling much more comfortable with the playful side of Travis's personality. "Is it a surprise, or will you just be driving around aimlessly because you don't have a clue where we're going?"

Travis couldn't help himself – he laughed out loud. "You are a delight to be around. You always manage to say something to make me laugh. That's one of the things I appreciate about you. And in answer to your question, Ms. Maxwell, no, I won't be driving around aimlessly. I happen to know exactly where we're going."

"Would you care to share some of that knowledge, oh great one?"

"I might, if you were to ask nicely."

Meghan grinned as she humbly asked, "Oh great bearer of much wisdom, might you please tell me where we will be dining tonight?"

"Most certainly, Ms. Maxwell. We will be dining at La Esperanza's."

"Oh, they have great Mexican food. I haven't eaten there in ages."

"Me neither. Dave took me there once not long after I arrived in Hope. That's the only time I've been there. And speaking of there," Travis said as they pulled into the parking lot, "here we are."

Travis went around to the passenger side of his pickup and opened the door for Meghan. Taking her hand, he helped her out of the truck, knowing that if she were in her Levis, she probably would be waiting at the restaurant door for him. He gently put his hand against the small of her back and led her into the restaurant.

After placing their orders, Travis and Meghan engaged in small talk, both seemingly a bit nervous. "You really look nice this evening, Meghan." Travis suddenly felt unsure of himself. "Not that you don't usually look nice. I just don't get to see you in a dress very often. You look nice in jeans too." *Oh, great,* Travis thought to himself, *that sounded intelligent.*

Meghan reached across the table and placed her hand over his. Looking into his hazel eyes, she said with more confidence than she felt, "Relax, Travis. You look pretty good yourself."

Travis appeared to relax a bit as a smile slowly crept across his face. "You know, we've spent quite a bit of time together recently and have shared several meals, so I don't know why I can't seem to string two intelligent sentences together tonight."

Realizing that her hand still covered his, and in no hurry to remove it, Meghan agreed. "I know what you mean. It just seems different tonight. Maybe it's because it's our first date." Meghan gasped and covered her mouth with her hand, realizing too late that she said the last words out loud, and not in her head. She ducked her head as she felt her cheeks begin to flame.

"Meghan," Travis tried to get her to look up. She was horribly embarrassed and refused to look at him.

"Meghan," he tried again. "Please look at me." Still no response. Travis reached across the table and gently lifted her chin, so they made eye contact.

Tears were pooling in her beautiful eyes, and Travis felt his heart squeeze. "I'm so embarrassed, Travis. I'm so sorry. I don't know why I said that. I shouldn't have assumed that just because we were having dinner, that this was a date."

"I'm the one who owes you an apology, Meghan. I should have made it clear to you that this was a dinner date. You shouldn't have been put in a position to have to assume. In my mind, I knew this was our first real date. I'm sorry. This is all pretty new to me. It's been a long time since I've asked a lady for a date."

Travis saw the uncertainty in her eyes and ached at the pain he had caused. He took Meghan's hands in his own, gently rubbing the back of her hand with his thumb. Slowly her features began to relax, and her normal color soon returned to her face.

"Can you ever forgive me, Meghan?" Travis pleaded.

"Yes," she replied with a weak smile. "How can I refuse to forgive a pastor?"

The tension further dissipated with the arrival of their meal, and before long conversation flowed easily between them.

* * *

"Would you like to come in for a few minutes?" Meghan asked as they arrived at the door to her apartment.

"Sure, I'd like that."

Kicking her shoes off as she came in the door, Meghan headed to the kitchen. "Would you like some iced tea, Travis?"

"That sounds great," Travis replied, following Meghan into the kitchen. As he reached into the cupboard and pulled out two glasses, he said, "Did I tell you I saw Kaci today?"

"No, you didn't," Meghan replied in surprise. "Where did you see her?"

"I went for a short hike late this morning and ran into a bunch of teenagers up on Cowiche Ridge. Kaci was among them. Apparently, her biology class had a field trip this morning."

"Oh, that's right. I had forgotten about that."

Travis filled both glasses with ice and started toward the living room. Meghan followed with the pitcher of tea and a plate of cookies. Travis poured the tea, grabbed a cookie, and settled onto one end of the sofa. With her iced tea in her hand, Meghan curled up on the opposite end of the sofa, tucking both her feet under her as she sat down. They sipped their tea in silence for a few moments, as Meghan looked at Travis in confusion.

Travis didn't quite understand the look on Meghan's face, but she was smiling so he hoped she wasn't still upset about their earlier misunderstanding. "What's putting that smile on your face?"

"Oh, I was just thinking," Meghan replied, not taking her eyes from Travis.

"Would you care to share your thoughts?"

"I was just thinking how different you are from Danny."

"Oh?" Travis questioned as he raised his eyebrow.

"Yeah. You just automatically followed me into the kitchen and began helping. Danny never would have done that. Danny would have sat in his chair and demanded that I bring him a beer. He never would have considered helping me."

Her smile faded a little as her thoughts went back to a more painful time in her life.

Seeing the subtle change in her face, Travis hoped to bring the smile back. "Well, you know me," he said smiling. "I just plunge in without asking most of the time. Sometimes it gets me into trouble."

Meghan laughed in agreement. "I'll just bet it does. I bet you probably got into your share of trouble as a boy, too, didn't you?"

Travis shook his head, "I'm not even going to go there. And don't you dare talk to my mother about it!"

"Now, how could I possibly do that? I've never even met your mother!"

"And that's probably a good thing. Mothers just love sharing all the most embarrassing stories with their son's dates."

"Trust me; it's not just limited to mothers! My dad was relentless when it came to embarrassing me in front of my dates! I remember one time in high school I was dressed for a semi-formal dance, and when my date picked me up at the house, Dad told him how I got bored at my thirteenth birthday party and sneaked away from the party. When they finally found me, I was happily moving a pile of dirt with the front-end loader, still wearing my party dress. Not exactly the impression I was hoping to make on my date!"

Travis roared in laughter. "I knew you were no typical woman, so I should have suspected that you weren't a typical girl either! I can just picture it! I'll bet your ponytail was flying in the breeze and a huge smile was gracing your face!"

"I'll have you know, Travis Harmon, I was wearing a hard hat! Dad never let me on any of the equipment without a hard hat."

The mental picture was Travis's undoing. He was laughing so hard he nearly upended the plate of cookies.

"Just you wait, Travis, someday I will meet your mother and I will convince her to tell me your most embarrassing story. Then we'll see how funny you think it is."

"Okay, okay, I give up," Travis replied, still trying to regain his composure.

"Sorry, it's too late. So, is your mother planning to visit Hope anytime in the near future?" Meghan asked innocently.

"I certainly hope not. At least not until you have forgotten this entire conversation."

Chapter Ten

Travis tossed and turned all night, unable to get any rest. Whenever he managed to get a few minutes' sleep, he was plagued by nightmares. Frustrated, exhausted, and drenched in sweat, he finally got out of bed and went to the kitchen for a glass of water.

Lord, I thought all these nightmares were behind me. Why now? I'm finally beginning to feel a certain measure of peace in my life. I haven't had nightmares for a couple months. Why now?

Sitting at the kitchen table, his head in his hands, his thoughts turned to Angela. "I miss you so much, Angela. It's been nearly three years, but sometimes the pain is still more than I can bear. Sometimes it still feels like my heart has been ripped out of my chest. I don't know what to do. I can't stand feeling half-alive. I know you would want me to move on with my life, but I don't know if I can. I wish you were here so I could talk to you. You always handled matters of the heart better than I did."

Too exhausted to think clearly, Travis let his head fall into his arms on the table. He awoke with a start a short time later, glancing at the clock on the microwave. He groaned when the bright blue numbers flashed 4:35 and the darkness outside confirmed that it was dawn. He lifted his head and ran his fingers through his tousled hair as he tried to work the kinks out of his stiff neck.

"Well, that was certainly a restful night," he said aloud. "Oh, great," he muttered as he plodded down the hallway. "Now I'm beginning to talk to myself."

Knowing it wouldn't do any good to go back to bed, Travis headed to the bathroom, hoping a nice long shower would make him feel better. Looking into the mirror as he ran his hand over the stubble on his face, he frowned at the haggard man staring back at him. He barely recognized the lifeless eyes peeking out from the dark shadows of his face. "Just great, Harmon, you really look like somebody who should be preaching a sermon this morning on resting in the arms of Jesus."

* * *

Finding his friend slumped in the chair behind his desk with his head in his hands, Dave lightly knocked on the open door to the pastor's study.

"Mind if I come in?" he asked, as Travis raised his head.

Travis sat up in the chair and tried to stretch his back as he replied, "You know you're always welcome, Dave."

Dave took a seat in the easy chair next to the desk, crossed one leg over the other, and silently watched Travis. When several minutes went by with neither of them speaking, Travis finally asked, "Is there something on your mind, or were you just looking for a place to sit for a while?"

"You disappeared pretty quickly after your sermon this morning."

"I had some things to take care of."

"Normally, greeting your congregation after church is one of those things you take care of."

"You and Rick were both in the lobby. I didn't think I needed to stick around."

His eyes never breaking contact with Travis's, Dave replied, "Needed to? No. But that's something you have always *wanted* to do."

"I had other things that needed my attention this morning, so I thought the elders could handle greeting the congregation."

With a slight smile tugging at the corners of his mouth, Dave shook his head. "Sorry, pal, not buying it."

Knowing how well his head elder could read him, Travis still hoped to pacify his curiosity. "Look, Dave, it's no big deal. I'm just tired and have a headache, so I thought the elders could handle it."

"Well, I can tell by looking at you that you're tired. But I think there's more to it than that."

"No," Travis replied unconvincingly, "just tired."

Dave uncrossed his legs and leaned forward in the chair, compassion evident on his face and in his voice. "Look, Travis, we've been down this road before. The topic of today's sermon is one of your favorites, but I have to tell you that I didn't even recognize my friend giving the sermon this morning. There was no passion. That's not like you."

"Okay, I have to admit that I'm a little off my game today. But it was just one sermon."

"Travis, you and I both know that there is no such thing as 'just one sermon' to you. You give a piece of yourself with every sermon you preach. That's what makes you so special. Your sermons aren't just empty words to you. They're part of who you are."

Not answering, Travis simply tipped his head back in the chair and closed his eyes.

"Talk to me, Travis. Something's bothering you and I don't

want to have to drag it out of you again."

Travis stood up and walked around his desk to the window, closing the door on his way. For several long minutes, he stared out the window, saying nothing. After a while, his shoulders sagged as he let out an anguished sigh. Still staring out the window, he nearly whispered, "I don't think I can preach anymore."

Dave walked across the room to his friend and put his arm around his shoulders. "What's going on, Travis? You haven't been yourself for the past several days. I've been giving you some space, hoping you would either come talk to me or be able to work it out on your own. But I'm not going to sit by and watch you drown in your problems because you won't ask for help."

Travis turned to face his friend and leaned against the windowsill. "I just don't know what to do anymore, Dave. I feel like I'm being pulled in two different directions, and neither of them feels right. I can't eat. I can't sleep. I'm having a hard time concentrating, and obviously, it's beginning to affect my work. What do I do?"

It pained Dave to see the torture on his friend's face. The only thing that pained him more was the possibility of Travis leaving the ministry. He wasn't about to let that happen, not if he could do anything to prevent it.

"You've been spending a lot of time with Meghan Maxwell lately, helping on her home construction, eating some meals together, getting to know her family."

"So? What does that have to do with anything?"

"I don't know. You tell me."

"Dave, I'm tired and I have a headache. I don't really feel up to guessing games. What are you getting at?"

Dave leaned against the desk and folded his arms across his chest. "Are you developing feelings for Meghan, something more than just friendship?"

"Of course not," Travis replied, not even convincing himself.

Dave raised his eyebrows and didn't say a word.

"Well, maybe… possibly… I don't know. You know how much I love construction, Dave. She can use the help building her house, and I can use the time outside working with my hands."

"Are you sure that's all it is?"

"I'm not sure of anything anymore. What does any of this have to do with me not being able to eat or sleep?"

"You mentioned feeling like you were being pulled in two different directions and neither of them felt right."

"Yeah. So?"

"So… could it be that you really are developing feelings for Meghan, and you have conflicting emotions about it because it makes you feel disloyal to Angela's memory?"

After several minutes of silence, Travis said softly "I have nightmares, Dave. About Angela's death. I had them for a long time right after she died, then they went away for a while. I hadn't had any for a couple months, but now they're back again. I can't stand it. It feels like reliving her death over and over again. I feel like I'm trapped in a replaying movie with a bad ending, and there's no way out." Travis looked up, and Dave could see the unshed tears lingering just behind his eyelids. "I didn't get much sleep last night. Every time I fell asleep, I would have the same horrible nightmares. I could have prevented her death. She was running an errand for me when she was killed. She wouldn't have been at that intersection if it weren't for me. Seven months pregnant, and I have her running errands for me. What kind of husband was I?"

Dave had never felt so helpless in his life, seeing the turmoil his friend was going through and not quite sure how to help. "Travis, you weren't responsible for your wife's death. A drunk driver killed her. You didn't."

"I know you're right. But it doesn't make it feel any better."

"Maybe it's time for you to move past it. I'm not saying to forget about Angela and the baby, but maybe it's time to move on with your life."

"That's just it. I don't know that I can. Don't you think I want to move on? I hate feeling like part of me is dead. But I can't escape the fact that a part of me died with Angela and my son that night. And nothing will ever change that."

"Angela wouldn't want you to be trapped by their memory. She would want you to move on." Seeing the defeated look on his friend's face was almost Dave's undoing. "Take some time, Travis. Take a week off. Go somewhere to think, to regroup, and to do some soul-searching. The best way to honor Angela's memory is to take a part of her with you when you move on with your life."

Dave reached out and wrapped Travis in a hug. His eyes wet with tears, he offered, "Call me if you need anything. And don't forget to take God along with you when you do your soul-searching."

* * *

As he knelt on the ground, pounding in a tent stake, Travis almost smiled as he thought about his impromptu camping trip. Maybe Dave was right. Maybe he did need to get away for a few days and try to regroup. This camping spot at the foot of Crystal Mountain had always been a favorite retreat of his. He had a lot of good memories of camping here with his family as a young boy, and as newlyweds, he and Angela spent a lot of time on Crystal Mountain. They logged more hours than he could count on both the ski slopes and the snowmobile trails. Winter was

Angela's favorite time of the year, and even though it didn't compete with spring in Travis's heart, he took to winter sports with a vengeance. But it was certainly hard to beat mid-spring weather in the mountains where everything was beginning to come to life again.

A rebirth, Travis thought to himself, *that's what makes springtime so special.* Seeing things blossom to life again, resilient after being beaten down by a hard winter, helps put things back into proper perspective. It's a reminder of who's in control.

Standing back, Travis surveyed his campsite with satisfaction. "Yes, I believe this is just the place to clear the cobwebs out of my head."

* * *

Travis stood up along the bank of the river and wiped his face with the towel draped over his neck. He had been out here for five days and still felt unsettled. There was no doubt that he had enjoyed his time in the mountains, away from the constant demands of everyday life, but he was really hoping to have some answers by now. He normally slept soundly whenever he was in the mountains, but his sleep had been sporadic at best for the past several days.

Lord, why do I still feel so torn? I always try to follow Your leading, but for the life of me, I don't have a clue what You expect of me. I'm not sure I can continue preaching when I feel like my life is in a shambles right now. How am I supposed to counsel and direct others when I can't even get my own life together?

A rustle in the brush behind him drew Travis out of his thoughts. A young spotted fawn, followed closely by its mother, emerged from the brush about twenty yards away from him and walked down to the river, seemingly unaware of the presence of a human. The fawn drank from the river, while its mother kept a protective lookout for any potential danger. She turned and stared at Travis for several long seconds, but turned back to her offspring, apparently satisfied that he posed no threat.

What a comforting feeling that must be, knowing that someone is always looking out for you, Travis thought as he pondered the fawn's oblivious behavior.

I am here for you. I am watching over you and will protect you.

The sudden thought took Travis by surprise. He was ashamed that he had forgotten, too wrapped up in his own troubles, that his Heavenly Father was constantly watching over him.

I'm sorry, Lord. Please forgive me.

Glad that he had arranged for Dave to give this weekend's sermon, Travis decided to break camp and head back to town a couple of days early. He was disappointed that he still felt pulled in two different directions, and was frustrated that he didn't quite understand his jumbled feelings. The only thing he felt settled about was that he couldn't leave the ministry. He knew in his heart that God had called him to the ministry, and even though his emotions were a mess, he planned to follow God's call.

Chapter Eleven

Meghan parked her Jeep in front of the office of Byers Construction, still not sure how she was going to sound nonchalant in questioning her youngest brother. Todd looked up from his desk and smiled as she walked in.

"Hey, sis, what brings you into the inner sanctum?"

"Hey, Todd. Can't a girl come say hello to her favorite brother without having a special reason?"

"Not the particular girl standing in front of me," he replied with a playful grin.

"Okay, you're right. I am here for a specific purpose."

"Now that's the ever-efficient, goal-oriented sister I know and love."

"Yeah, yeah, always ready to give me a hard time. But how many times over the years has my meticulous planning come in handy, Mr. Byers?"

"You know I wouldn't change a thing about you, kiddo. I love you just the way God made you, faults and all."

"Me? Faults? I have no idea what you're talking about. Besides, little brother, I wouldn't pull out the 'faults' card unless you're prepared to defend your reasoning for chasing off every single woman in the county who happens to smile in your

"""

direction."

Todd threw up his hands in defeat. "Okay, I surrender. Let's not go there again. I thought we agreed that you wouldn't meddle in my love life."

"We did agree. And I can't possibly meddle in something that's nonexistent."

Todd groaned but, as always, still had a smile for his sister. He couldn't get mad, or stay mad at her if he tried. "So, what's the real reason you stopped by? Other than to give me a hard time, of course."

"Of course. Actually, I wanted to check on my Sheetrock order. Any idea when it's going to be in? I'd like to get started on it this week if I can."

"Well, it looks like you'll get your wish. I just got off the phone with Jeff, and he said his driver will have it here sometime this afternoon."

"Okay, great, that's good news. Well, I've got plenty to do, and I'm sure you have some more papers to shuffle around on that desk of yours, so I'd better get out of here."

"Someone's got to do the paperwork. A business won't just run itself, you know."

Meghan leaned over and gave her brother a kiss on the cheek. "I know it doesn't, Todd. And you do a great job running the business. Dad would be proud of how much the company has grown under your leadership."

"Thanks, Meg. That means a lot coming from you."

Todd watched Meghan walk to the door, and then hesitate as she reached for the door knob. She turned, trying to act casual, "By the way, have you seen Travis around lately?"

"Now that you mention it, I haven't seen him for several days. You mean he hasn't stopped by the construction site at all? You can tell that's one guy who has construction in his blood. He just thrives on getting in there with his hands and working hard. You couldn't ask for a better volunteer. He does quality work."

"Yeah, he's been a big help. I wouldn't be as far along in the construction process as I am if it weren't for his help."

"How long has it been since he's stopped by?"

"Over a week," Meghan said, trying to sound unconcerned. "I'm sure he's been busy at the church."

"You're probably right. Why don't you give him a call?"

"Actually, I have called and left messages on his cell phone a couple times. He told me he wanted to know when I'd be ready to start hanging Sheetrock. But I haven't had any luck getting hold of him."

"I'm sure you're right and he's been busy. Don't worry, he'll call you back."

Meghan felt a warm blush work its way up the back of her neck. "I'm not worried. I have no reason to worry about him. It's just that he wanted to know when I'd be hanging Sheetrock."

As Meghan started out the door, Todd said, "Hey, Meg, I'll let you know if I hear from him." His sister nodded as she closed the door behind her. "Well, it's about time," Todd said to the closed door. "I never thought she'd ever let anyone into her heart again after what she went through with Danny."

*　*　*

Standing in the middle of what would eventually become their front yard, Meghan smiled with satisfaction at her future home. The construction had been going faster than she anticipated, due in large part to the willing hands of her local pastor. Her smile faded ever so slightly as she thought of the absent Travis. It has been fun working alongside him during the construction. They work well together as a team, sharing an easy camaraderie. She finds herself incredibly drawn to the playful side of his personality. He's so different from the controlling nature of her ex-husband. She and Danny were never able to work on any kind of project together without it turning into a war.

Walking toward the house, anxious to put her hands to work, Meghan sighed heavily as she realized how much she missed having Travis around. Stopping in her tracks just inside the front entryway, the truth of that realization slammed into her heart like a freight train.

It's true, she thought to herself. *I really do miss him. How did that happen? We've only known each other for a few months, but he has managed to subtly inch his way into my life. And my heart. Wow. Is it possible, God, that there really is life after divorce?*

With a renewed optimism in her battered heart, and a fulfilling project in the works, Meghan began whistling as she tackled the work that needed to be done prior to starting the Sheetrock this afternoon. She became so engrossed in what she was doing that she didn't hear a vehicle pull up out front until a door slammed.

That sounded like the door to a pickup, she thought as she worked her way around interior framing toward the front of the house. An instant smile lit up her face at the possibility that Travis had stopped by.

Her trademark smile quickly gave way to a teeth-clinching grimace as anger immediately clouded her face. "What are you doing here?"

"Now, babe, is that any way to talk to your husband?"

"Ex-husband, Danny. Don't ever forget that. Ex-husband."

"I've missed you, babe. Three years is a long time."

"Not nearly long enough. How did you know where to find me?"

"It's a small town, Meg. I still have friends here. It wasn't difficult." Danny began walking around the outside of the house, peering into the windows, nodding his approval.

"You always did quality work, babe. Looks like we're going to have a pretty nice setup here. Good piece of property."

"There is no 'we,' Danny," Meghan stated matter-of-factly as she stood with her hands in the back pockets of her Levis. "The only 'we' in my life is me and Kaci. You are no longer a part of our lives."

"That's where you're wrong, babe. I will always be part of your life. We have a daughter together, remember. Besides, I'm moving back to Hope, and I figure we can pick up where we left off. Our new home will give us a fresh start. It will be different this time."

"No, Danny, there will be no picking up where we left off. In case you didn't quite get the message during the divorce proceedings, let me be perfectly clear. There is no 'us.' There will never be an 'us.' This will never be your home. You will never live here. You will never be a part of my life again. Ever."

"I've changed, babe. Just give me a chance and I'll prove it to you."

"You exhausted all your second chances before the divorce. I gave you more chances than you ever deserved. I won't make that mistake again, Danny. No way. You nearly destroyed me. And you came close to destroying our daughter. Never again, Danny. Never again. Now get off my property. Now."

Instead of retreating, Danny stepped closer to Meghan, grabbing her upper arms in a viselike hold. "You have to give me another chance," he pleaded. "You and Kaci are all I have left."

"No, Danny, it's over. If I thought there was anything left, or any chance to salvage our marriage, I never would have filed for divorce. Now I want you to get off my property."

Tightening his grip, he insisted, "I'm not leaving until you agree to give me another chance."

Meghan recognized the building rage in his eyes, and her mind plummeted to a very dark time in their marriage. "Let go of me, Danny. You're hurting me!"

"Tell me you'll take me back."

Meghan's throat began to tighten as panic started to set in. Angry that he could still turn her world upside down, she tried unsuccessfully to pull away from him. "Let me go!" she screamed, struggling harder as her anger took hold.

"Get your hands off her! Now! I don't plan to tell you a second time."

Meghan fought a natural urge to run to her brother, but the look in her eyes told him everything he needed to know. She was an independent woman who preferred to fight her own battles, but she was sure glad he had shown up when he did.

Todd walked up to his sister and put his arm around her shoulder, as Danny slowly backed away. He looked Danny square in the eye, shaking his head. "I strongly suggest that you get off this property right now. And you better not let me catch you here again."

"I'm going, tough guy," Danny said defiantly as he turned to leave. "But this isn't over, Meghan."

"Oh, and Danny," Todd called out, "if you ever touch my sister again, you will find out just exactly how tough I am."

Todd pulled his sister into a protective hug as they watched Danny spin his tires, kicking up dirt until he hit the pavement.

"Well, little brother," Meghan said as she looked up at Todd with relief on her face. "I'm not sure why you showed up out of the blue when you did, but I'm sure glad you're here."

Todd gave his sister's ponytail a playful tug. "Smart money would have been on you, sis," he said with a smile. "You would think Danny would have learned by now that you will never roll over and play dead. But, for his sake, he better not think he's going to start coming around here giving you any trouble. There is no doubt that you are a force to be reckoned with, but if he messes with you, he will quickly find out that protective brothers will make his worst nightmare seem like a day in the park."

Meghan laughed out loud as Todd flexed his biceps, then asked, "So why did you stop by? You had no way of knowing that Danny was here."

"Jeff called, and apparently your Sheetrock order was short. He wants to deliver the complete order all at once, so it will be here in the morning instead of this afternoon. I told him that would be okay."

"Yeah, that's fine. I still have a few things to do before I'm ready for it anyway. I didn't anticipate the little visit from Danny, so my schedule was thrown off."

Todd chuckled. "I don't know about you, Meg. Only you could receive an intimidating visit from your ex-husband and come away with your biggest concern being your schedule was thrown off. You are so much like Dad."

"I wouldn't talk, little brother. I wasn't the only one who inherited Dad's penchant for planning!"

"Yeah, yeah. Since you have managed to fritter away the better part of the morning, why don't you let me buy you some lunch."

"That's a pretty weak attempt to change the subject, but I never pass up an offer for you to buy lunch. Luigi's, I assume?"

"Is there any other place?"

Chapter Twelve

After having been out of touch with civilization for several days, Travis unlocked the door to his office at the church, thinking how much he, like most everyone these days, had become dependent upon technology. He had no doubt the inbox on his email would be overflowing, and he noticed earlier that he had several voice messages waiting for his attention on his cell phone. Being in the mountains for several days with no cell phone service definitely had its advantages, but he was never comfortable being out of touch with his congregation. The emails could wait, but he needed to check his voicemail.

Pen and paper in hand, he began making notes about people to call and details to handle when he encountered the first of three voice messages from Meghan. The inevitable smile began to creep across his face as he listened to her voice. Fighting the urge to replay the message simply to hear the sound of her voice again, he jotted down her name and number so he could listen to the remaining messages. Finding nothing urgent that required his immediate attention, Travis picked up the phone to call Meghan, just as his head elder appeared in the doorway.

"I see you're smiling," Dave noted. "I hope that means you left some of your troubles in the mountains, even though you're back a couple of days early. Hey, you're not trying to take away my sermon for this weekend, are you?"

"No, Dave." Travis laughed. "This weekend's sermon is all yours. I was just ready to come back."

Dave settled into his favorite chair opposite Travis's desk, crossed one leg over the other, and smiled at his friend. "Are you sure? I know how protective you can be over your sermons."

"Yes, I'm sure. Besides, it's not my sermon. I gave it to you, so that makes it your sermon. If you blow it, it's all on you!"

"Oh, don't you worry, Travis, I have no intention of blowing it!"

Travis laughed out loud, enjoying the close friendship he shared with his head elder. "I hope you know, Dave, just how much I appreciate you. I don't know what I'd do without you."

"Well, obviously, you'd be up the proverbial creek without a paddle!"

"I'm serious, Dave," Travis replied. "I couldn't do what I do without you. You're indispensable to me and to this church."

"No, Travis, I'm not indispensable. None of us are. We're all in this crazy world together, and hopefully we heed Paul's advice in Galatians 6:2, 'Bear one another's burdens, and so fulfill the law of Christ.' That's all I'm doing. Just like you. You, my friend, are a shining example of Paul's advice. Your biggest problem is not letting anyone share your burdens. It's a two-way street, you know. Besides, by not letting others share your burdens, you are depriving others of the blessings they could be receiving."

"Ouch! You don't hold back, do you?"

Dave smiled. "I try not to."

"Point taken. I assume you came here for something other than pointing out my obvious character flaws?"

"I just happened to notice your pickup in the parking lot a few minutes ago and I thought 'Gee, Travis has been gone for nearly a week, and I don't know anyone else with any character flaws to point out, so I must rush right over there and do that!'"

Travis roared in laughter, "Yeah, I missed you too, buddy!"

Dave stood and started toward the door. "No, I just stopped in to say 'hi' and see how you're doing. Oh, and to make sure you weren't trying to steal my sermon back! But now that you've reassured me about the sermon, and you have a smile on your face, I guess my work here is done. Talk to you later."

"Thanks for everything, Dave," Travis called to his retreating head elder. Dave raised his hand in acknowledgment and was gone, leaving Travis alone with his thoughts.

And his thoughts immediately turned to Meghan. He picked up his cell phone for the second time and started to punch in her number.

* * *

Todd dropped Meghan off at her property after lunch, saying he needed to get back to the office. Meghan was making a half-hearted attempt to focus on the task at hand, but the run-in with Danny had taken the wind out of her sails. She still had a few small details to take care of before the Sheetrock arrived in the morning, so she needed to just get them done. It wasn't much, but she had to wire in a couple outlets before the inspector showed up, and they couldn't start the Sheetrock until he signed off on that portion of the electrical work.

Oh well, she thought to herself, *I've already had my distraction for the day, so it's time to get to work*. Just as she grabbed her tool belt, her cell phone rang. Pulling it out of her back pocket, she smiled as the caller ID read Travis Harmon.

"Hey, stranger," Meghan answered. "I was beginning to think you had either fallen off the planet or were avoiding me. I decided I didn't really care much for either scenario."

"Ah, so you did miss me," Travis replied with obvious pleasure.

"Well, you did say you wanted to know when I'd be hanging Sheetrock, and I've been trying to call you for several days."

Travis's heart dropped a little when it appeared the Sheetrock project was the only reason she had called. Trying not to let the disappointment show through in his voice, he asked, "Did I miss the Sheetrock? I really was hoping to help you with that because I know it's not a one-person job."

Meghan chuckled as she replied, "No, my dear, you didn't miss it. Delivery was actually delayed because of a short order, so Jeff is delivering it in the morning. It should arrive about the same time the inspector shows up to sign off on the electrical. Assuming I ever get it finished. I had a bit of a bump in my plans earlier today when Danny showed up unexpectedly."

"Your ex-husband Danny?" Travis was not surprised to discover his protective instincts had kicked in immediately.

"Yes, the one and only. I was trying to finish up the last of the electrical outlets when he showed up."

"What did he want? How did he know where to find you?"

"As he was quick to remind me, it's a small town. He has some wild notion that we will be getting back together."

"Oh?"

"Yeah, that's typical for him. Every time he's between girlfriends, between jobs, out of money, or any combination of the above, he thinks I'm his meal ticket."

"I assume he left when you set him straight?"

"Eventually, after Todd showed up and convinced him that pushing me around was not in his best interests," Meghan chuckled weakly.

"What do you mean he was pushing you around? Did he hurt

you?"

"No, he didn't hurt me. He had grabbed me and wouldn't let go. That's when Todd showed up and put the fear of little brothers into him."

"I'm coming over! You're at the house now, aren't you?"

"Travis," Meghan replied, "you don't have to come over. He's long gone, and I don't expect him to be back."

"Well, just in case he returns, I'll be there," Travis stated with conviction. "He's not going to push you around, physically, mentally, or emotionally. I won't allow it. Besides, I can help you finish those pesky outlets so you're ready for the inspector in the morning."

"Okay, if you insist," Meghan agreed, then added as an afterthought, "It will be nice to see you."

"It will be nice to see you, too, Meghan," Travis replied with a smile. "I'll be over in a few minutes."

* * *

Almost before Meghan had time to grab her tools and get started on the project at hand, she heard a truck pull up. Buckling her tool belt as she walked to the front of the house, she grinned as Travis climbed out of his pickup.

"Were you parked around the corner?" She laughed. "That didn't take you long!"

"No, not exactly," the grinning pastor replied. "But I was already in the truck and pulling out of the church parking lot by the time we got off the phone."

"Having construction withdrawals, are you?"

"Well, it has been over a week, you know. How long can I be expected to stay away from a construction site?"

"Not long, is my guess," Meghan said with a chuckle.

"It was nice to get away for a few days, though. Sometimes a person needs to do that to clear their head and refocus. I think I was overdue."

"Is everything okay?" asked Meghan, suddenly concerned.

"Maybe not everything. But I think it helped. I still have some things to sort out." Anxious to change the subject, Travis asked, "So, where are those pesky outlets that need to be wired? It shouldn't take long."

"They're in the dining room." Meghan watched Travis as he headed in the direction of the dining room, wondering why he changed the subject so abruptly.

"If you want to nail in the boxes where you want them," Travis suggested, "I can start running the wire."

"Sounds good. I've already drilled the holes in the two-by-fours, so you should be able to run the wire to the outlet boxes pretty quickly."

Without the need for a lot of conversation, they got right to work. As expected, in no time at all they had the wiring completed. Meghan removed her tool belt and began gathering up the scattered tools as Travis rolled up the unused electrical wire. Used to doing things on her own, Meghan started to move a table saw out of the way so she could set up an area for working on Sheetrock the next day.

"Let me get that," Travis insisted. "You really don't need to be moving heavy things on your own."

Meghan chuckled as she moved out of the way. "How do you think I did things before you came along?"

"I'm sure you found a way to get things done. But as long as I'm standing here with nothing to do, there is no reason for you to be doing the heavy work."

"You do realize that I'm not a helpless damsel in distress, don't you?"

Travis looked her directly in the eyes before replying. "Yes, I do realize you are not a helpless damsel in distress. And I understand that you aren't a typical woman. I believe we have covered that before. But I also believe in teamwork and working smarter, not harder. Besides, I wouldn't want you to think that chivalry was dead."

"That's good to know," Meghan replied with a laugh.

"Where are you planning to start hanging Sheetrock in the morning? I can help you get things set up so we can get started as soon as the truck arrives."

"My, you certainly are an eager beaver! From what Todd told me, it sounds like the Sheetrock will be here around eight o'clock, and the inspector should be here at eight as well. Hopefully, we will be able to get started by nine. I thought we would start in the living room. What do you think?"

"That sounds like a good plan," Travis agreed as he removed a sheet of plywood from the sawhorses. Working instinctively as a team, Meghan grabbed the sawhorses and set them up in the middle of the living room, just as Travis was ready to lay the plywood back down.

As they gathered the tools that would be needed in the morning, Meghan wondered how she might be able to find out what issues Travis was trying to sort through. "It sounds like you took a few days off. Did you go do anything fun and exciting?"

"I went camping in the mountains for a few days. I enjoy the mountains. It's peaceful and relaxing. Normally it's a good place for me to regroup and recharge."

"Normally? Meaning that wasn't the case this week?"

"Not entirely. It was successful to a point, but not the complete success I was hoping for. Maybe I was overly optimistic."

"Is there anything I can do to help? Maybe you're having a

tough time recharging because you're burning the candle at both ends. I mean, think about it. You're very busy at the church doing all your pastoring stuff. That's a full-time job. Plus, you give Bible study classes three evenings a week, you're involved in several outreach programs, you still have to find time to write your sermons, and you've been spending a lot of time helping me here at the house. Face it, Travis, you have a lot on your plate!"

"Says the woman who is raising a daughter single-handedly, working in the family construction business, working a second job in the evenings, building her own home, and fighting off her ex-husband in her spare time! I hope you know you're not one to talk about someone having a full plate. Besides, working on your house is relaxing for me."

"Okay, you're right. So, we both apparently have a lot going on in our lives. But doesn't the Bible say something about how we're supposed to share each other's burdens?"

"Wow. Déjà vu. You're the second person who has told me that today."

"Well, maybe God's trying to tell you something."

"Probably," Travis admitted reluctantly.

"Hey," Meghan said as she reached over and put her hand on his arm, "I'm not trying to interfere. I just want to let you know that I'm willing to help. If there's something you need, or some way I can help, even if you just need someone to talk to, I'm here."

"Thanks, Meghan. I appreciate that. Maybe at some point. But right now, I think it's something I've got to work out on my own."

In an effort to lighten the mood, Meghan said nonchalantly, "Okay, if you insist. I just hope you know that adding Superman to your résumé is only going to make your life busier."

"Probably," Travis admitted with a smile. "Would you like to go to dinner tonight?"

"I would love to," Meghan replied, "but I can't."

"Oh. I'm really bad about short notice, huh?" Travis said with obvious disappointment.

"No, that's not it! I don't mind spur-of-the-moment things. It's just that this is Kaci's last week of school, and she's going to be working part of her summer break at church camp. I promised that tonight we would go over the list of things she thinks she needs for camp and see how much of the list is actual needs rather than things she simply wants."

"Well, if you don't think Kaci would mind, I could bring over pizza and help you go through her list. I have to warn you, though, I would probably tend to side with Kaci on questionable needs."

"Of course, you would! That doesn't surprise me a bit. I'm sure Kaci wouldn't mind if you came over. She likes you. But you don't need to bring pizza. She's making spaghetti for dinner. She makes really great spaghetti, so you will need to bring a healthy appetite."

"I think I can manage that," Travis laughed. "What time should I come over?"

"Probably around six."

"Great. That gives me enough time to get home and take a shower." As he got into his pickup, Travis asked, "Do you need me to bring anything for dinner or dessert?"

"We wouldn't object if you happened to bring some ice cream."

"Ice cream, it is. Any particular flavor?"

"As long as you asked, our favorite is chocolate caramel swirl."

"You got it! See you later."

* * *

Kaci opened the door just as Travis approached. "Hi, Pastor Harmon."

"Hi, Kaci."

"Mom said you were coming over to help us eat spaghetti. That's good because I always make so much we end up eating it for a week!"

Travis laughed, "You give me a call anytime you have that problem. I'm a problem solver, you know."

"I'll remember that," Kaci replied with a smile. "After we eat, Mom said she would go over the list of things I need for camp. Maybe you could help me out on that. I'm sure you would have a pretty good idea what I need, and Mom may think some of the things I put on the list are questionable."

"I think better on a full stomach," Travis said with a grin. "But I'm sure we'll be able to come up with a reasonably accurate list."

Hearing the exchange in the living room, Meghan walked around the corner smiling. "You two aren't plotting against me now, are you?"

Wearing faces of pure innocence, Travis and Kaci said in unison, "No way!"

Looking from one to the other, Meghan shook her head in disbelief and started toward the dining room. "Dinner is ready," she said over her shoulder. "I hope you don't plan to let that ice cream melt all over the carpet, Travis!"

"And waste perfectly good ice cream? Not a chance!" he replied in mock horror.

Travis put the ice cream in the freezer. Then he pulled out chairs for both the ladies before seating himself at the table. After asking a blessing on the food, they dished up their plates and dug into the hearty meal, eating in silence for a few minutes.

Breaking the silence, Travis asked, "You made this spaghetti,

Kaci? This is incredible! I believe it's probably the best spaghetti I've ever eaten."

Beaming with pride, and blushing ever so slightly, Kaci replied, "Mom taught me how to make it. It was one of Grandpa's specialties. I remember eating it a lot at Grandpa's house."

"Did you make the garlic bread too?"

"I did. When we have spaghetti, I make the spaghetti and the garlic bread, and Mom fixes the salad. That way I can give her a break and she doesn't have to do all the cooking."

"I really appreciate the help, too, kiddo. It's nice to have a break from cooking occasionally."

A casual and comfortable conversation filled the dining room as the three took their time and enjoyed dinner. After his second full plate of spaghetti, Travis pushed his plate away and stated, "I can't believe I'm going to say this, but I don't think I could eat another bite!"

Mother and daughter looked at each other, sharing an identical thought. Kaci shrugged her shoulders and stated simply, "I guess that means only two bowls for ice cream. What a shame."

"Oh, hey, wait a minute! I want ice cream too! Any chance I can convince you two lovely ladies to hold off on the ice cream until after we go over the camp list? I'm sure I will be able to make room for it by then! Please?"

"I don't know, Mom. What do you think? Can we wait a while before ice cream? That's asking an awful lot."

Showing his playful boyish side that Meghan enjoyed so much, Travis pleaded, "Oh, come on. Please? After all, I brought the ice cream."

"Well," Meghan conceded, "it's true. You did bring the ice cream. I guess it wouldn't really be fair for you not to get some. I suppose we can wait. But only because you brought the ice cream, and because we like you."

The three laughed as they settled in on the sofa, ready to pore over the list for camp. Travis was expecting a hand-scribbled list, so he was surprised when Kaci pulled out a folder containing several computer-generated lists, one of which appeared to be compelling arguments for some of her "questionable" items.

"Wow." Travis marveled softly, quickly glancing at the sheets of paper. "This is very organized. Did you put this together, or is this what they gave you at school?"

Blushing slightly, Kaci replied, "I put it together. I like having all my ducks in a row, especially when I know I'll be presenting a case to Mom, and she might not agree with everything."

"Smart thinking," Travis agreed. "You would make a good businesswoman someday. I've already recognized some of those organizational traits in your mom. You certainly can't slip anything past her, huh?"

"No. That's why I need to make sure I'm prepared," Kaci said with a smile.

As the three began going over the list, item by item, Travis asked, "What are you going to be doing at camp, Kaci? That might come into play on some of these 'questionable' items."

Her eyes lit up as she replied with obvious excitement, "I will be teaching archery classes to the younger kids. That's going to be so much fun! I love watching them when they hit the target for the very first time."

"Archery, huh? Why doesn't that surprise me? No basket weaving for any daughter of Meghan's," he chuckled.

"Well, actually, I really like basket weaving too. See that basket on the top shelf of the entertainment center? I made that at camp a couple years ago."

Walking over to inspect the handiwork, Travis was obviously impressed. "I stand corrected. That is a very nice basket. It appears that you are a well-rounded young lady. How long have you been doing archery?"

"I started when I was five years old, with a little pink bow and arrow set. Now I use a compound bow, and I like that a lot. That's what I use for competitions. But I'll be using a standard recurve for teaching the classes because that's what the younger kids will be using."

"You do archery competitions?"

Knowing her daughter didn't like to brag about her accomplishments, Meghan interjected, "She is quite good. She has a shelf full of archery trophies in her room."

"You Maxwell women never cease to amaze me. I have no doubt I will continue discovering little gems about both of you as I get to know you even better. It will be an interesting journey. By the way, wasn't I promised some ice cream earlier?"

Meghan laughed. "Apparently, nothing can be slipped past you, either! I think we've finished the camp list, so I know what I need to get this week. I guess it's now time for ice cream. Three bowls, I assume?"

Chuckling again when Kaci and Travis replied in unison with a hearty 'Absolutely!', Meghan headed toward the kitchen with her little entourage close on her heels.

Chapter Thirteen

Meghan dropped her daughter off at school then hurried over to the property. She wanted to make sure she was there before either the Sheetrock or the electrical inspector showed up. It was going to be a busy day, and she was anxious to get started. Each phase of the construction put their dream one step closer to reality, and she was beginning to envision being in their new home before the holidays.

Very doable, she thought, *as long as a certain local pastor continues to lend a hand.*

That thought had barely formed in her mind when she saw that Travis had beaten her to the construction site. The now familiar butterflies in her stomach quickly made an appearance at the sight of his pickup. Not seeing him at a glance, Meghan parked her Jeep and made her way to the front door of the house.

"I can't believe you beat me here," Meghan said in amazement when she located Travis in the living room, already setting things up.

"Good morning to you, too, sleepyhead. Did you sleep in this morning?"

"Sleep in? That's a laugh! It's not even seven-thirty yet! I would have been here earlier, but I needed to drop Kaci off at school this morning."

"Likely story," Travis teased. "I'd be willing to bet you hit the snooze button on your alarm at least twice."

"Well, that shows how much you know, hotshot. I don't even bother to set an alarm. I always wake up before I need to get out of bed anyway."

Travis laughed just as they heard a truck pull up out front. "It looks like your Sheetrock guy is here."

"Yes! I can't wait to get started. Todd said he might be able to stop by later today to give us a hand."

Putting his arm around Meghan's shoulder as he shook his head, Travis gently guided her outside. "I don't believe I've ever seen a woman quite so excited to see a truckload of Sheetrock before. You truly are a unique little redhead."

"Just remember, a little bit of redheaded Irish temper has been known to show up occasionally, so you'd better be on your toes. I don't tolerate slackers on the jobsite."

Snapping to attention and giving a rather impressive mock salute, Travis replied, "Yes, ma'am! No slacking on the jobsite. I'll try to remember that, ma'am." He then gave a quick little jerk on her auburn ponytail as she walked off shaking her head.

"Good morning, Jeff. I'm glad to see you were able to get here bright and early this morning. We've got a long day ahead of us."

"Mornin', Meghan," Jeff replied as he climbed down from the truck. "You're just like that ornery brother of yours, so I knew you'd be here early. Sorry I didn't get over here yesterday afternoon, but I prefer to deliver a complete load, if possible. Dealing with partial loads can be a nightmare sometimes."

"That's a fact. Jeff, have you met Travis Harmon yet? He's the pastor over at Hope Community Church and a closet construction man. He's been helping me out on the house."

"Haven't had the pleasure yet," he replied, shaking hands with Travis. "Todd mentioned you had a pretty talented volunteer working over here. That certainly makes things go quicker."

"Hi, Jeff, it's nice to meet you," Travis told the aging truck driver.

As the two men exchanged greetings, a white SUV with a City of Hope emblem on the side pulled onto the property. "That's the electrical inspector," Meghan noted. "Travis, would you mind showing Jeff where to unload the Sheetrock while I work with the inspector?"

"No problem," he replied. "Go take care of business and Jeff and I will get the Sheetrock squared away."

"Thanks, Travis." Walking toward the SUV, Meghan greeted the inspector by name. "Good morning, Tom."

"Good morning, Meghan," he replied, reaching into the SUV and bringing out a wrapped parcel. "As soon as Debbie heard I would be seeing you this morning, she insisted on sending over a fresh loaf of banana bread for you."

"She is such a sweet gal. You better hang onto her, Tom."

"You know it! After thirty-two years with her, no one else would want me anyway," he replied, chuckling.

"That's not true, and you know it. Dad always said you and Debbie were a match made in heaven. How is that new grandson of yours doing?"

"He's a little pistol, that's for sure! You know, what they say about being a grandparent is true. There's nothing better. You can spoil the little rug rats all you want then send them home to their mama and daddy. It's a pretty sweet deal."

"I'm sure of that. I know Dad did his best to spoil Kaci every chance he got!"

"Your dad sure loved that kid. Talked about her all the time. There never was a prouder grandpa than George. Boy, I miss that man."

"Me too, Tom. Me too. You and Dad worked together a long time and were friends even longer. You were like a brother to him." Seeing her dad's best friend tear up a bit made Meghan change the subject quickly. "I'm sure you have better things to do than stand around here reminiscing with me. So why don't we go check out the electrical work and you can tell me if it's up to Dad's high standards."

"I'm sure it is, Meghan. You were trained by one of the best." Tom put his arm around the young woman he had known for her entire life, and they headed into the house so he could put the official stamp of approval on her quality electrical work.

* * *

Travis added another sheet of Sheetrock to the growing pile in the living room, then looked up just as Meghan entered the room. "How did the electrical inspection go?"

"No problem at all," replied Meghan as she surveyed the stack of Sheetrock. "It looks like you and Jeff have been busy. Is he still here?"

"He's out back unloading the last of the Sheetrock."

"If you had waited, I could have helped carry some of that in."

"Oh, don't worry, you will have lots of opportunities to wrestle with Sheetrock today," Travis replied with a smile.

Jeff entered through the back of the house and found them in the living room. "I just finished unloading the Sheetrock, Meghan. Did you need me for anything else before I head back to the shop?"

"I don't think so, Jeff. Thanks for all your help. I really appreciate it."

"Anytime. I assume Tom signed off on your electrical?"

"Yes, he did. But not until after checking everything and making sure it was correct. He may be a friend of the family, but he takes his inspection duties seriously."

"I know he does," Jeff nodded in agreement. "You can bet if Tom says something isn't up to snuff, it darn well isn't up to snuff. And he won't sign off on it no matter who it is. Well, I better get going. I have a couple more loads to deliver this morning." Jeff placed his hand on Meghan's shoulder and admonished, "Now don't you go working yourself to death out here today. You remember to take breaks. Do you have your water jug here?"

Meghan chuckled as she replied, "Yes, it's still out in the Jeep. Don't worry about me, I'll pace myself."

"Sure, you will," replied Jeff, as he turned to Travis. "You make sure she doesn't overdo it today. She tends to get wrapped up in her work and forgets she needs food and water."

"I promise I will keep a close eye on her," Travis assured.

Jeff patted Travis on the back, winking. "I'm sure you will, Travis. I'm sure you will." His laughter followed him back outside.

Travis turned to find Meghan blushing ever so slightly, and he smiled. "Well, boss, we're burning daylight, so I guess we better get to work."

A little flustered, Meghan replied, "Uh, yeah, we need to get started."

* * *

An outsider watching the scene inside the house would have assumed it was a construction team that had been working together for many years. Meghan and Travis worked together like a well-oiled machine. They had good instincts, which allowed for steady progress. They had mutually decided to concentrate on getting Sheetrock on the walls first, saving the ceiling for later in hopes that Todd would show up and provide an extra set of hands. Both workers were so engrossed in their work that the steady noise of the drills screwing Sheetrock into place prevented them from hearing a vehicle pull up out front. Suddenly Travis put down his drill and looked at Meghan with a confused expression on his face. She stopped and returned the look.

"Do you smell pizza?" Travis asked.

"Uh-huh."

Just then a suppressed chuckle escaped from Todd's mouth. "Boy, you two don't hear a thing when you're working, do you? I've been standing here holding this pizza for at least five minutes."

"Well, don't just stand there, little brother, bring it on in!" Meghan said as she cleared a spot on the makeshift table. "It can't be lunchtime already, is it?"

"Yep. It's about twelve-thirty, and I don't know about you two, but I'm hungry! I knew you wouldn't be paying attention to the time. Jeff told me I'd probably have to rescue you from yourself."

Travis and Meghan dropped their tool belts as Todd opened the pizza box and produced a small stack of paper plates. Once they were settled on the floor, it was quiet for a few minutes while they enjoyed the pizza. Todd looked around, surveying the progress. "You've got a lot done already. I'm impressed. I'm glad to see you didn't start on the ceiling. I don't like Meghan trying to do ceiling work."

Meghan smiled at her protective little brother in appreciation. "We were hoping you might be able to lend an extra pair of strong arms."

"I'm all yours for the afternoon. Oh, before I forget it, Zach

Carter called this morning and wanted to know how you're coming on that last set of blueprints."

"I'll be able to finish them tonight. Do you want me to call him back, or will you?"

"I'll call him as soon as we finish with lunch. He will be pleasantly surprised. He was thinking you were probably still a week out."

"I wanted to get them done as soon as possible," Meghan explained. "I want to get started on the Enget job because that's going to take a while."

Travis nudged Meghan with his shoulder. "Is there anything you don't do?"

Without missing a beat, Meghan replied, "I don't do bull riding."

The two men roared in laughter at her deadpan reply. By way of explanation, Todd said, "She does design work and blueprints in her spare time."

"Spare time?" Travis asked, looking at Meghan. "When exactly do you have any spare time?"

"Didn't we just recently have this conversation? And it seems to me we decided that neither of us should be talking about having full plates."

"Speaking of having a full plate, I see that yours is empty," Todd said as he put another slice of pizza on her plate. "Eat up, sis. You have a lot of work to do before you can call it a day. I plan to work you hard this afternoon, so you need your nourishment."

"Don't you worry about me, little brother. I can hold my own on the jobsite."

"That's true," Travis said. "She informed me this morning that she doesn't tolerate slackers on the jobsite."

"She's true to her word, too. She once kicked a cousin of ours off the job because he wasn't working up to her satisfaction. Poor guy had to come back a week later, begging for a second chance."

Travis looked at Meghan with admiration. "Did you give him his job back?"

She simply nodded. By way of explanation, Todd added, "He learned she meant business. He turned out to be one of our best workers. He heads up one of our crews now, and they can work circles around the best in the construction industry. Speaking of which, let's go, people. We've got work to do."

Travis reached a hand down to help Meghan up, as he tossed his paper plate into the trash can. "You heard him, little lady. Apparently, slave driver runs in the family!"

Todd just chuckled as he grabbed his tools and hard hat. Meghan rolled the scaffolding into place so the guys could get started on the ceiling, then went out to her Jeep to get another box of drywall screws. By the time she returned, they nearly had the first piece of Sheetrock up on the ceiling. She smiled, thinking how well the three of them got along, and hoping that camaraderie would continue well into the future.

* * *

Meghan stepped down from the front door opening thinking how nice it would be once the wraparound porch was built. She stood, stretching her back from the long day, and staring off into space. Todd and Travis were gathering the last of the tools after being satisfied with the accomplishments of the day. She sat down in the door opening and looked across the street. There appeared to be a pickup parked among the trees in the vacant lot.

That's odd, she thought, *I don't remember seeing that before.* She was sure that property had not been recently sold, so she couldn't think of a reasonable explanation for a vehicle being parked there.

"Hey, sis," said Todd as he stepped around her. "You look exhausted."

"Yeah, it's definitely been a long day," she agreed. Her gaze still lingered on the vacant lot.

"Just staring off into space?" asked Travis. "Or has something caught your attention? You seemed to be pretty intent on something."

"I'm not sure. It's probably nothing."

"What?" asked her brother, instantly defensive as his gaze followed hers. "It's never nothing with you."

"Do you know if Scotty sold his lot across the street? It's been in his family forever, so I can't imagine he sold it."

"No, I would have heard if he had even been thinking of selling it. We play softball together. Why are you asking?"

"It's probably nothing, but there's a pickup parked in the trees over there," she replied as she pointed in the direction of the truck.

Looking in the direction she indicated, Todd said, "Travis, let's take a walk across the street. It's probably just some teenagers hanging out where they shouldn't be, but let's check it out to be sure. You stay here Meghan. We'll be right back."

The two men had only taken a handful of steps when there was the sudden roar of an engine and a dark-colored Dodge pickup emerged from the trees. Todd took off on a dead run, with Travis close behind, as the pickup tires kicked up dirt and rocks in an effort to gain some traction. Before they reached the edge of the property, the truck was quickly disappearing down the road.

"I'm still relatively new to the area, but there appeared to only be one guy in the truck, so I don't think it was teenagers just hanging out where they didn't belong," stated Travis.

Still staring in the direction the truck headed, Todd replied,

"I don't think so either. That pickup looked a bit familiar to me, but I just can't recall why."

Meghan was on her feet when the men got back up to the house. She slowly shook her head and said, "That's just great. Just what I need."

Todd had always been able to read his sister better than anyone else. They had an undeniable connection that was difficult to explain. "What is it, sis? Do you know anything about that truck?"

"I'm not one hundred percent positive, and it left in a big hurry, but I'm pretty sure that was Danny's truck."

Both men tensed up immediately, and Meghan noticed the prominent veins on her brother's neck make a rapid appearance. That was always a surefire sign that he was fighting to keep his anger in check. Travis moved beside Meghan, put his arm around her shoulder, and pulled her close.

"I thought you made it pretty clear to him that he was supposed to stay away from you," said Travis as he saw the concern in Meghan's eyes.

Todd jumped in with a reply, "Oh, trust me, I made it very clear to him that he better stay off this property and stay away from my sister. If he didn't get the message the first time, I can certainly deliver a reminder!"

"Don't get all worked up, Todd," advised Meghan. "We don't even know for sure if it was him. And he didn't come onto my property. There isn't anything we can do about it."

"Oh, you can be sure there is something I can do about it! I'll ask Scotty to put up a No Trespassing sign on his property, then it would become a legal issue for him to be hiding in the trees over there. That would at least give us a reason to call the authorities."

"But there would be nothing to prevent him from parking along the street," Travis pointed out.

"That's not Danny's style," Todd replied. "He's a weasel and a coward. He would hide in the trees, trying to intimidate her, but wouldn't sit out in plain sight. If he knows what's good for him, he will stay as far away from here as possible. I'll run him out of town if I have to!"

"Maybe it wasn't even him," Meghan reasoned in an attempt to diffuse her brother's anger.

"Since we have no way of knowing one way or another, I want you to keep your eyes open. Don't let your guard down when you're out here working. It's easy to get buried in your work and not hear someone come up behind you. I discovered that firsthand today when I showed up with the pizza. I want you to be careful."

"I know, Todd. I'll be careful. But I'm not going to shrivel up and hide in a corner just because my ex-husband is back in town. He's never going to have that kind of control over me again."

Still holding her close, Travis suggested, "You let me know when you're going to be over here working and I'll try to be here with you as much as I can."

"I'll do the same," said Todd. "I'll see if I can free up one of the guys to come help you out if it looks like you'll be here alone."

Stepping away from Travis in an act of defiance, Meghan planted her hands on her hips and stated in a no-nonsense tone, "I will not have the two of you disrupting your schedules to come babysit me! I am a grown woman, and I am quite capable of taking care of myself. You both have jobs and responsibilities to attend to, and neither of you has the time to come running over here every time I get a notion to get some work done. I will not be posting my work schedule for review, and I will not be asking for anyone's permission to work on my own house. Do I make myself perfectly clear?"

Travis had the decency to look properly chastised. Todd, on

the other hand, just shook his head and smiled. "I knew it wouldn't take long for that redheaded Irish spitfire to show up. Sis, I've known you my entire life, so I am the last person you need to convince that you can take care of yourself. I have been on the receiving end of your independence more times than I can count. But I'm here to tell you one very undeniable fact. You are my sister, and that fact is never going to change. I promised Dad that I would always look out for you, and I would always protect you from harm. Unfortunately, that sometimes means I have to protect you from yourself.

"Yes, it's true you are quite capable of taking care of yourself. You are the most stubborn, bullheaded, independent woman I have ever known. But I will swear on a stack of Bibles that if I ever think you're in danger, or if anyone ever tries to hurt you, there is nothing in heaven or on earth that will stop me from making things right. If that means I have to juggle my schedule occasionally, then so be it. That's a small price to pay to keep my promise to Dad. And you know how I feel about promises, so there's no point in you wasting your breath arguing. So, do *I* make myself perfectly clear?"

Her shoulders slumped ever so slightly in a weak sign of defeat, but she knew there was no arguing with her brother when he dug in his heels. "Okay, you can do whatever you think you need to do. But I still have no plans to cower in my apartment and put my life on hold just because Danny is back in town."

"I wouldn't expect you to, sis. I just want you to be careful."

Travis tentatively reached over and touched her shoulder. "I want you to be careful too," he said softly. "I don't want anything to happen to you." Their eyes locked for the briefest of moments. Travis swallowed the lump in his throat. "Would it be okay if I stop by to visit tonight?"

"Well…" Meghan hesitated. "I'm going to be busy finishing

up Zach's blueprints, but the company would be nice as long as you don't mind just hanging out. Kaci will be studying for finals over at Brittney's house."

"How about if I bring over something to cook for dinner? That way you can work on the blueprints while I take care of dinner and you won't have to worry about what to eat. Maybe I'll even work on this week's sermon while I'm there."

"That sounds great," she replied.

Seeing his sister's eyes light up in a way he hadn't seen in a very long time, Todd smiled as he said, "And that's where I came in. I'm going to swing by the shop before I head home. Travis, she's a stubborn one, but try to keep her out of trouble. See you guys later." He chuckled as he gave a quick tug on his sister's ponytail on his way to the pickup.

* * *

Travis showed up at Meghan's apartment with a bag of groceries in each hand and a wide grin stretching across his tanned face as he rang the doorbell with his elbow. He didn't have to wait long before Meghan answered the door with a smile. He loved her casual look of Levis, a short-sleeved button-up shirt and tank top, and bare feet. Her still-wet hair, pulled back in her trademark ponytail, gave indication that she had managed to squeeze in a quick shower before he arrived. He had done the same, and still managed to hit the grocery store within an hour. His bachelor lifestyle meant he frequently shopped when he needed something specific, and he definitely had something specific in mind for tonight's dinner.

"Two bags of groceries?" Meghan asked, chuckling softly.

"Well, Ms. Maxwell," he replied, "if you would allow me to come in, I would be happy to show you what's in the bags.

Besides, they are getting heavy!"

"Oh, sorry," she replied, stepping aside quickly.

She followed Travis into the kitchen and watched as he emptied the contents of the bags onto the counter. A package of very nice rib steaks, a small bag of fresh green beans, a bag of baker potatoes, a pound of butter, a container of parmesan cheese, assorted seasonings, and a package of Texas toast lined the countertop. He added to the pile an assortment of vegetables to make a salad, a half-gallon of chocolate caramel swirl ice cream, and a small jar of chocolate sauce.

All she could manage was a whispered, "Wow."

He grinned like a silly schoolboy as he started putting the perishables into the refrigerator. He then planted his hands firmly on her shoulders and steered her toward the living room. "Don't you have some blueprints you should be working on? I have a feast to prepare, and I don't need you underfoot."

"Okay, okay," she laughed. "I'm going." She settled in at her desk in the corner of the living room and fired up her laptop. Travis wasted no time getting busy in the kitchen and before long she heard him whistling a worship song as he cut up vegetables. She sighed contentedly as she thought, *I could certainly get used to having him around.*

Meghan soon found herself immersed in her blueprint project and had nearly forgotten anyone else was in the apartment. Without a lot of distractions, she completed the task much quicker than she imagined. As she pushed back her chair and stretched her back, she had a satisfying sense of accomplishment. A very subtle aroma of garlic and freshly barbecued steaks wafted its way through the apartment, urging her out of work mode and back into real life.

Oh, that's right, she thought, *Travis is cooking dinner*. The thought instantly made her smile. That seemed to be happening a lot these days.

The patio door opened just as she made her way into the kitchen. "Would you like to eat inside, or out on the patio?" Travis asked.

"It's a beautiful evening, why don't we eat outside. Let me grab some plates and utensils."

"Actually, I anticipated your response and have already set everything up on the patio," Travis replied happily.

"Hmmmm, it seems you are beginning to know me quite well."

"It's pretty easy to see that you prefer being outside doing pretty much anything, rather than being stuck inside. That's something we have in common," Travis stated as he pulled out a chair for Meghan at the patio table.

"Wow!" Meghan marveled. "This is quite a spread. And everything smells great!"

"I'm anxious to see if my steaks are even close to being as good as yours. I remember Todd saying that you make the best steaks around, and they were certainly very good, but I think mine would give yours a run for their money."

After a brief prayer of thanks, a comfortable silence settled in as they enjoyed their meal. "Were you able to finish the blueprints you were working on?" Travis asked.

"Yes, I did. I was amazed how well everything fell into place. I'll be able to deliver them to Zach first thing in the morning."

"I'm glad. You've had a long day, and I was hoping you wouldn't be working well into the evening."

"Me too," Meghan said. "Thanks for all your help today. I couldn't have done it without you and Todd. And the fabulous dinner is like icing on the cake. You're a very good cook. I think you can safely report back to Todd that your steaks are every bit as good as mine."

"You can be sure I plan to tell him what you said. Oh, make sure you save room for dessert. Remember, I brought ice cream. Your favorite."

"I can't eat another bite. Can I take a rain check on the ice cream?"

"Sure. That just means I'll have to come back over another night so we can have dessert." Travis then added softly, "I'm okay with that."

Meghan was surprised to realize that she still blushed whenever he said something like that. Without comment, she started gathering food to take inside. Travis instinctively joined in to help. With the leftovers refrigerated and the dishes in the dishwasher, the two went back outside and settled in the patio swing. Gently pushing the swing into motion, she said with a contented sigh, "The moon is beautiful tonight."

"Ummm," Travis replied as he put his arm around Meghan's shoulder and pulled her close. "The moon isn't the only beauty out tonight."

Their eyes locked briefly as she relaxed against his shoulder. *Yes,* she thought, *I can most definitely get used to having him around.*

* * *

Travis lay in bed with his arms stretched behind his neck, watching the clock tick away the minutes and hours. Sleep eluded him, and even though he was physically tired, he felt emotionally rested and relaxed. He realized what a strange feeling that was. It had been at least three years since he felt even moderately at peace emotionally. It was no longer a secret to his tortured heart that maybe, just maybe, there was a reason for his newfound peace. A cute little auburn-haired construction worker was never far from his mind, and had now taken over his heart as well. Maybe it was time. Maybe he could finally move on. He would never forget about Angela and the son he never got to hold, but maybe he had grieved long enough.

"Could it be, God?" Travis wondered aloud. "Is it really time for me to be happy again?"

Staring up at the ceiling with a contented smile on his face, Travis replayed the events of the day. He truly enjoyed spending time with Meghan. It didn't seem to matter if they were hard at work on her house, or if they were enjoying a nice meal and pleasant conversation together. He simply felt at home whenever they were together. She was so easy to talk to, and their personalities just seemed to click right from the beginning. They loved joking around with each other, and she never seemed to mind his teasing nature. In fact, he got the impression that she liked it.

It did bother him a bit that Meghan didn't attend church regularly. He could understand the reasons behind her sporadic attendance, but not once had he ever questioned her faith in God. She had an unshakable faith that was evident to everyone around her. She was one of those unique individuals who quietly lived a Christlike life without fanfare and without the need of validation from others. She knew what she believed, and lived a life in line with her beliefs. He admired that about her. Still, he would certainly like it if she began attending church on a regular basis. Besides the obvious boost that Christian fellowship can provide, it would give her a break from her grueling schedule.

Maybe I should suggest that to her, he thought.

In her own time, my son, in her own time. I know her heart. Don't push.

As he slowly drifted off to sleep, Travis smiled at this new gentle reminder from God.

Chapter Fourteen

The pleasant days of late spring were rapidly slipping into early summer as mother and daughter stood in front of their future home. Progress had been hectic the past couple weeks as Meghan divided her time between home construction and being a single parent. Kaci had been busy finishing final projects and taking final exams at school, trying hard to remain focused while simultaneously getting geared up for summer camp. Meghan looked at her daughter out of the corner of her eye, marveling at how quickly she was growing up.

It's hard to believe I only have a couple more years with her at home before she heads off to college. She didn't realize her sigh had been audible.

Kaci put her arm around her mom's shoulder and laughed. "It's okay, Mom, the house will survive without you for one weekend."

"What?" Meghan asked, obviously confused.

"I heard that heavy sigh. This house is your baby. You work over here every day. But it's okay. Your baby can be left alone for a couple days."

"Actually, kiddo," Meghan replied with obvious love in her voice. "That's not the baby I was thinking about."

"Oh?"

"I was just thinking about how quickly my little girl has turned into an amazing teenager. In a couple years you'll be going off to college. I guess I just wish you weren't growing up so quickly. I wish I could have finished our home a couple years ago so we would have more time in it together."

"Mom, you got this way when I went off to camp last summer too. If I didn't know better, I would think you kind of like having me around."

"Oh, maybe just a little bit," she said smiling. Turning back to look at the house, Meghan remarked, "You won't recognize the house by the end of the summer."

"Sure, I will," Kaci replied knowingly. "We have talked about this house for so long that I know every nook and cranny about it, even though it's not completed. Believe me, no matter what phase of the construction it will be in by the time I get back from camp, I will most definitely recognize it. How could I not? It's our dream, remember."

"How did I ever get such an incredible daughter?"

"You're just lucky, I guess," Kaci replied with a grin. "Well, are you ready to cut the apron strings for a couple days and hit the road? We're supposed to be at MiVoden before dinner and it's about a five-hour drive."

"Sure. Before we head out of town, are you sure you remembered everything?"

"Yes, Mother," Kaci answered with mock annoyance. "We made lists. We cross-checked the lists. We both double-checked everything as we were packing. The lists had lists. If we forgot anything, it can't be very important. Remember, I'm your daughter, and I'm Grandpa's granddaughter. We have list making and organization down to a science!"

"Well, then, child of mine, let's get this show on the road!"

* * *

The last few winding miles to camp always seemed to take as long as the several hours before on the interstate. In reality, it was probably the anxiousness of ending the long drive, combined with the anticipation of the many activities available at the camp. The scenery was certainly a draw as well. Camp MiVoden sat on the edge of a beautiful lake high in the mountains of Northern Idaho.

As Meghan pulled the Jeep into a parking space in front of the camp office, the hustle and bustle of summer camp was evident everywhere. Young teenagers, trying to show their independence, wasted no time exiting family vehicles and connecting up with their friends. The much younger kids were more than happy to keep mom and dad within eyesight.

The camp not only had a wide variety of classes and activities for preteens and teens but also catered to the younger kids by having family camp. That allowed the under-ten crowd to have the summer camp experience in a family setting, knowing mom and dad were nearby. It also gave the parents an opportunity to volunteer their expertise by teaching various classes, cooking meals, or serving in nursing or pastoral roles. Since Meghan was only going to be at MiVoden until Monday morning, her role would be limited to teaching a drawing class Sunday afternoon, while Kaci was teaching archery.

Meghan started walking toward the camp office to complete their check-in procedure and turned to find that Kaci had already connected with some friends. She shook her head and smiled at her daughter's self-confidence. "Kaci, do you need to check in, or can I do that for you?"

"I think you can do it, if you don't mind," Kaci replied hopefully. Seeing a young friend approaching from behind her mom, Kaci let out a squeal. "Jayme! Oh, my gosh! I can't believe how tall you have gotten!" And just that quickly, Meghan lost her daughter to the world of preteens and teens.

The check-in process went quickly. Meghan confirmed the time she would be teaching the art class Sunday and then got Kaci's archery schedule and their cabin assignment. She knew exactly where their cabin was, and was pleased to see one of her best friends would be the other adult chaperone in their cabin. It would be a fun and relaxing weekend. Just what she needed to be able to regroup from the stressful week.

"What say we go get settled in before dinner," Meghan suggested as she walked up to Kaci and her group of friends. "We are in Bear Cabin."

"Yay!" replied Kaci enthusiastically. "I love the location of Bear Cabin. The sound of the river is so relaxing." Kaci linked arms with her mom as they walked back to the Jeep to head to their cabin. "It's going to be a great summer. I wish you could stay longer, Mom."

"Me, too. But the whole working-for-a-living thing tends to interfere with fun sometimes."

Kaci looked at her mom with understanding then said, "Have I told you recently that you're the best mom ever?"

Meghan pretended to be deep in thought. "Gee, I don't know. I think it's been a while," she laughed. "You're a pretty good kid, too, you know."

* * *

Meghan watched her daughter eating dinner with a boisterous group of teenagers. Although she wasn't quite sure how much actual eating was going on. They appeared to be doing more talking than eating. You would think most of the teenagers had not seen each other for months. In reality, many of them attend the same school so had just been together last week.

Ah, to be young again, she thought. She was once again struck by how fortunate she was that her child had such a great group of Christian friends.

Someone nudged her shoulder and pulled her out of her thoughts. "Kaci sure is a great kid, Meghan." Meghan turned to the friend sitting beside her and apologized for letting her thoughts wander.

"No need to apologize," Shannon replied. "You're a wonderful mom. You give her the freedom to be herself and to enjoy being a kid. They grow up so fast. It's hard not to simply watch them and marvel, isn't it? At least you're only a 'helicopter mom,' hovering just close enough to protect her but far enough away not to smother her. Those 'stealth bomber' parents can be quite a challenge!" The two women laughed as the other parents sitting at the table joined in knowingly.

Someone at the front of the room tapped on a microphone, and conversations began to die down. People looked toward the sound and smiled, seeing one of the church's favorite music teachers standing at the podium.

"Welcome to Camp MiVoden, everyone! I hate to be the one to break up all the fun and exciting conversations I've been hearing, but I just wanted to let you know that the worship service will be beginning over in the chapel in twenty minutes. Tonight's service will be pretty informal. Mostly praise songs and fantastic music. We have several people with guitars, including yours truly. I'll try not to drown out the good music!" Everyone laughed at the inside joke, knowing that Steve was an accomplished musician.

"Pastor Tyler will have a short sermon and then we'll all gather out at the flagpole for the flag-lowering ceremony. So, we'll see you all over at the chapel in a few minutes. Be sure to bring your singing voices because we want everyone to know we are here worshipping our Lord and Savior!"

* * *

The worship service had been so uplifting that it reminded Meghan how much she truly missed attending church.

I've got to make a point of getting back to church, she thought. *I really need the time to break away from the daily responsibilities and replenish my soul, so to speak. Life gets so busy that it's difficult to find time for everything. I know I've never sacrificed my devotional time, but maybe it's time to get back to the fellowship.*

She was glad that Kaci had chosen to sit with her during worship. They were surrounded by friends, both young and not so young, and it was a good feeling. A very good feeling. They were blessed, and that fact was not lost on the single mother. She was part of a good Christian fellowship, and she needed to start becoming a more active participant.

A group of teenage boys were shooting baskets near the flagpole, while some of the younger kids were playing on the swings and monkey bars. Kaci and some of her friends were laughing and giggling down by the lake, while the assortment of parents mingled throughout the crowds, on the verge of reminding everyone they should start heading back to the cabins before curfew.

The flag-lowering ceremony, followed by the evening prayer, always brought the day to a close on a positive note. But, then, it was really hard to find anything negative in this environment. A large group of Christians of all ages, positive activities for everyone to engage in, uplifting music and prayer, and the most beautiful surroundings a person could imagine. Camp

MiVoden was definitely a little bit of heaven on earth. It was exactly what Meghan needed at this point in her life. Even if only for a couple days.

* * *

Kaci found her mom sitting on a bench in front of the cabin, with her legs stretched out and propped up on the porch railing. A very light breeze softly rustled the thin pages of her Bible as she did her morning devotions. Kaci walked up behind her mom, bent over, and put her arms around her neck.

"You look right at home, Mom. I can very easily see you doing this at home," she said smiling. "That's why you wanted a wraparound porch, isn't it?"

"Well," Meghan replied, patting the bench seat beside her, inviting her daughter to have a seat. "It is definitely one thing I would be doing on the porch. I have always loved wraparound porches. It reminds me of the home I grew up in. There is just something about sitting out on the porch in a porch swing that makes it feel like home. Dad and I used to sit out on the porch for hours. Just talking about our days. Talking about whatever happened to come to mind. Or not talking at all. Just enjoying each other's company." Meghan put her arm around her daughter's shoulder and pulled her close. "Your grandpa sure loved you. You are so much like him. He would be very proud of you. It's too bad you probably don't remember him."

"But I do remember him, Mom. You have talked about him my entire life. Even though I only saw him when I was very little, believe me, I know my grandpa. He is very much a part of my life and a part of who I am. Besides, from all the stories Uncle Todd has told me, I see Grandpa in you every day. And that is so awesome! He would be very proud of you, too, Mom. I hope you realize that."

"Thanks, kiddo. That means a lot to me. What do you say we go get some breakfast? I'm absolutely famished!"

"Sounds good to me. I'll take your Bible back inside then we can head over. What are you going to do this morning? I have my first archery class at ten."

"It sounds like I'm going to be on KP. My dear friend volunteered me to help with breakfast cleanup."

"Let me guess," Kaci laughed. "Mrs. Gilbert?"

"Yep. I asked if she was doing dishes too, and she offered some excuse about having nursing duties in the medical building. I think she just doesn't want to wash dishes."

"Sure," Kaci replied sarcastically. "I'm sure that's exactly what it is!"

They entered the cafeteria and quickly went through the food line. Spotting her friends seated at a nearby table, Meghan suggested, "Why don't we go sit with Shannon and Jack."

"Okay, Mom, as long as you agree to play nice," Kaci said, laughing.

"Don't I always?" she replied, feigning innocence.

Joining their longtime friends at the table, Meghan greeted them with a mischievous grin. "Good morning, Jack. Do you know what your wife did to me?"

"It's hard to tell," he replied. "I gave up years ago trying to keep up with her antics!"

"She volunteered me for kitchen duty after breakfast, then claimed she couldn't help because she had to go play nurse. Can you believe that?"

"I can absolutely believe that! She signed me up for washing dishes after breakfast too!"

"She is quite the recruiter!" Meghan said as they all broke into friendly laughter.

After a hearty breakfast, the cafeteria began emptying out as people found their way to their various activities and responsibilities. The day flew by quickly, with people hustling around all over camp. By the time the Maxwell girls met up in the late afternoon, Meghan had completed teaching her drawing class and Kaci had taught three separate archery classes. With a little more than an hour remaining before dinner, they decided to take a kayak out on the lake for a while. It was a perfect way to unwind before dinner.

Kaci had been outside most of the day with her archery classes, but Meghan had been cooped up inside all day. She was really looking forward to some time in the sun. By the end of the day, they were both exhausted physically, yet refreshed emotionally and spiritually.

Tomorrow morning Meghan would begin the long drive home. She was anxious to get back to her normal routine, but didn't look forward to saying good-bye to her daughter for the summer. She rationalized that this summer should be easier because all her spare time would be spent on the house, so she would be busy. But it was never easy leaving her daughter behind at camp. The fact that she had been doing it every summer for several years didn't make it any easier.

* * *

Her bags were packed into the Jeep, and they had eaten breakfast, so Meghan was saying good-bye to her daughter in the parking lot. Kaci hugged her mom tightly and said, "I'm sure you're going to get a lot done on the house this summer, but remember that I get to help pick out the colors for the outside of the house."

"Don't worry; I'm sure I won't get that far. Although, I do want to get the exterior completely finished and painted before winter. We can finish the inside when the weather turns bad, but the outside needs to be done."

"Okay. I don't want to rush you off, Mom, but I have another class in about 15 minutes."

"I need to get on the road anyway. It's a long drive home." She gave her daughter another hug then said, "Have fun this summer. Remember to call me occasionally. And be sure to call me if you need something. Are you sure you have enough money?"

"Mom, I'm fine. You worry too much."

"A hazard of the trade, I'm afraid," she replied. "I love you, kiddo."

"I love you, too, Mom. Drive safe, and send me a text message when you get home."

"I will." Then Meghan got in her Jeep and headed out of the parking lot. Tears began to form in her eyes as she drove down the road, thinking that two months was a very long time.

A couple hours into the drive home, Meghan's cell phone rang. Expecting it to be Kaci, she was surprised to see Travis's name on the caller ID. She picked up the call on her Bluetooth, and there was a smile in her voice. "Hey, stranger. I didn't expect to hear from you today."

"Hi, Meghan. Am I interrupting anything?"

"Not at all. I'm just driving down the road, headed home."

"That's good to hear. How did things go at MiVoden?"

"Just great. I think I needed the time away worse than I thought. It was nice to be able to forget about everything for a couple days. And I had forgotten how much I enjoyed the worship services with all the praise songs. It was very uplifting. It made me miss going to church."

Travis didn't miss the wistful tone in her voice, and it made his heart happy. Not the fact that she felt bad; but the fact that maybe she was considering coming back to church. "Maybe it's time. Maybe going to Camp MiVoden this weekend was God's way of giving you a little nudge. You know that I would love to see you back at church."

"I know," she replied softly. "I've gone back a couple times, but maybe it's time to get back into the habit of going on a regular basis. I didn't realize how much I had missed the fellowship. It's just that life has gotten so busy. I know that's not an excuse, but it's the reality."

"I understand, Meghan. Maybe when life gets so busy, that's exactly when you need to take time out for worship."

"Ah, words of wisdom from my friendly neighborhood pastor. Thanks, Travis. You're probably right."

"What time will you be home today?"

"Depending on how many stops I make, I should be home by three. But at this point, I only plan to stop for gas."

"You need to eat."

"I'll be stopping for gas in about twenty miles or so. I'll just grab something at the mini-mart when I get gas."

"Will you be up to going out for dinner tonight?"

"That sounds good, Travis. But I really doubt that I'll want to go anywhere when I get home."

Not willing to give up easily, Travis suggested, "How about if I bring some pizza and salad over around five? That would give you a little time to relax and recover from whatever mini-mart fare you force-feed yourself, so you will be ready for something real to eat."

"Thanks, Travis. That would be nice."

"Okay, I'll see you around five."

"It will be nice to see you. I've missed you," Meghan admitted quietly.

"I've missed you too." Travis disconnected the call thinking how incredibly true that statement was. Somehow, over the past few months, Meghan had taken up permanent residence in his heart. And he could honestly admit to himself that he didn't mind that fact a bit.

Chapter Fifteen

Time has a way of slipping away almost unnoticed when life becomes busy. That was certainly the case in Meghan's life. With Kaci away at camp for a couple months, Meghan had buried herself in her work. She somehow found a way to divide her time between the family construction business, working on her house, and doing design work. She didn't see as much of Travis as she would have liked, but he seemed to show up at the house whenever she found she needed an extra set of hands. She tended to work later at the house than she had been used to doing so she could take advantage of the longer days summer provided. Unfortunately, that also meant she didn't always pay close attention to eating on a regular schedule, and that sometimes created problems for her.

Meghan sat cross-legged on the floor of her future dining room, trying to convince herself that the peanut butter and jelly sandwich she was eating was part of the four basic food groups.

Well, at least it has some protein, she thought to herself. *And maybe the apple offsets the sugar in the jelly.* Any way she tried to rationalize it, she still had to admit that she needed to make more of an effort to eat better. She seemed to do better when Kaci was around. Left to her own devices, she nearly always just grabbed whatever was handy, not giving much thought to nutritional value.

With the early afternoon sun shining through the glass of the French doors, she realized how tempting it would be to give in to exhaustion and take a quick nap curled up in the corner. Just as that thought began to take on a life of its own, Meghan heard a truck door slam. Before she could pull herself up off the floor, the front door opened, and she heard a voice.

"Anybody home?" Travis's voice spurred her into action. In an effort to jump up quickly, she tripped over the tool belt lying on the floor beside her and instantly found herself sprawled across the floor in a most unladylike fashion.

Travis was instantly at her side, offering her a hand, and chuckling the entire time. "Are you okay?" he asked as he pulled her up.

"It appears my pride is the only casualty," she replied with a blushing smile. "And a nice little scrape on the heel of my hand."

"Why weren't you wearing your gloves?" Travis inquired with raised eyebrows.

"I've found it's more difficult to eat a peanut butter and jelly sandwich wearing gloves than it is if you take them off."

Shaking his head in disapproval, Travis said, "I suppose that's true, but you couldn't find anything better than a peanut butter and jelly sandwich to eat for lunch?"

"Funny you should ask," she explained. "I was just sitting here trying to convince myself that it had some nutritional value and, at the same time, telling myself that I need to do a better job packing a lunch."

"Well, at least it's good to see you eating some lunch, rather than simply working straight through the day. You tend to do that a lot, I've noticed."

"I know," Meghan admitted. "I lose track of time when I'm

working."

Looking around the dining area and seeing the tremendous amount of progress, Travis silently chastised himself for not getting over here to help her more often. But, like most people, his days were pretty busy this time of year as well.

"I see you have all the texturing done. It looks good!"

"I still have the bedrooms to do upstairs, but it's all done down here. I wanted to finish this first because Jason is going to come over this week to install all the kitchen cabinets and the built-in china hutch."

"What kind of flooring are you putting in the dining room?"

"It's stacked over there in the corner if you want to look at it. I'm going to continue the tile from the kitchen and bring it on into the dining room. I really like the looks of that tile."

"This is a good choice," Travis agreed. "It's a very classic-looking tile, but with a modern feel to it. I think it will look very nice in both rooms. You have a good eye for flooring."

"I'm glad you like it. Kaci helped me pick it out. It was pretty easy. Once I knew I wanted tile flooring, we were both instantly drawn to this one. I'm still debating on the flooring for the living room, though. I can't seem to decide between carpet and hardwood floors. I like the warmth and feel of carpeting, but I like the look of hardwood flooring much better. Maybe you could give me some input. You have built houses, so I assume you've had the carpet versus hardwood floors debate at some point."

"For me, some of it comes down to a personal preference. I've even put ceramic tile throughout an entire house before, and I was very happy with how that turned out. I personally don't put much carpeting in houses that I've built. It looks good, and it's definitely warmer to walk on, but it's nearly impossible to clean. Once you've seen the grime on the underside of carpet and carpet pads that you've ripped up, you realize how much dirt remains trapped in those fibers. I've always been partial to hardwood flooring. The newer hardwood laminates that are available are great. They are very durable and give a warm look to the rooms. Of course, that's just my opinion."

"Your opinion is what I wanted. That actually helps me quite a bit. I was leaning toward hardwood laminates. In fact, I have a bunch of samples in the living room," Meghan said, walking toward that room.

Within minutes, they had flooring samples spread out across the subfloor and were on their hands and knees perusing the options available. Travis pulled out a few that he was instantly drawn to, while Meghan did the same. In no time at all they had their choices narrowed down to three.

"The weathered ash is the one you want," a voice surprised them from behind.

"You know, Todd," Meghan said, "you are beginning to make a habit of sneaking up behind us!"

Todd just laughed as he bent over and picked up the sample he was referring to. "Maybe you need a hearing aid, sis."

"And maybe you need to make your presence known before sneaking up on people."

"It wouldn't matter if I laid on the horn outside. You two get so wrapped up in what you're doing that you wouldn't hear me anyway." Todd gave Travis a good-natured slap on the back as he walked into the dining room. Eying the half-eaten sandwich on a paper plate in the corner, he said, "You've been eating healthy again, I see."

"I've already given myself a good talking to about it, so I don't need to hear it from you too. It was the easiest thing to grab this morning."

"You need to pack your lunch the night before then," Todd admonished.

"You should talk, little brother. How many times have I seen you eating a bag of chips for lunch?"

Knowing it was best to change the subject quickly, Todd asked, "What do you need help on this afternoon?"

"It seems to be feast or famine around here. I've been over here for several days by myself, then both of you show up at the same time. Not that I'm complaining! I will take all the help I can get, whenever I can get it!"

"I'm available all afternoon, too," Travis added.

"Well," Meghan replied, thinking. "How can we best make use of three people? I still have the texturing to do in the bedrooms upstairs, but I can do that by myself if I need to. Should we work outside on the exterior siding while we have more hands available? What do you guys think?"

"That would be my vote," Todd offered. "I've been cooped up inside all morning. Working outside for a while would be a nice change."

"Sounds good to me," Travis quickly agreed. "I can always help you with the texturing later, Meghan. It wouldn't take long with the two of us working. But installing siding would definitely go faster with three people."

"Okay, let's do that," she said as the three of them headed out the French doors onto the side porch.

"By the way, Meghan," Travis commented. "I noticed when I came in that you finally got the wraparound porch built. It looks great. I like the decking you used."

"Thanks," she replied, smiling. "Todd and a couple of the guys came over a few days ago and we got that done. It definitely makes it easier to get in and out of the house."

Todd and Travis rolled the scaffolding into place, while Meghan filled the tool belts with the necessary supplies. "By the way, sis, I'm going to shake a crew loose tomorrow to come over and work on the siding. Depending on how much the three of us get done today, on top of what has already been done, maybe the crew will be able to finish it tomorrow."

"You're not pulling a crew off another job, are you? I don't want you doing that."

"No. There was a glitch in a materials order for the job they were scheduled on for tomorrow. So, I figured I might as well put them to work over here."

"If you can use an extra pair of hands, I can help tomorrow too. I will be able to finish writing my sermon tonight, so I like to reward myself with some outside time," Travis suggested hopefully.

"Yeah, buddy," Todd responded. "I've already figured you out. You haven't been over here in a while, so you are having construction withdrawals!"

"I'm that transparent, huh?"

"Oh, yeah!"

Meghan laughed at the friendly banter as she buckled her tool belt. She once again found herself hoping the friendship they shared would continue for a very long time to come. And for the first time, it was important to her that Todd liked Travis. Suddenly she realized that her brother's opinion of Travis mattered to her a great deal.

* * *

When Meghan pulled her Jeep onto the property, there were already two pickups with the Byers Construction logo parked near the house.

Todd certainly doesn't waste any time, she thought as she grabbed her water jug and headed toward the sound of hammering. Noticing the flurry of activity, she glanced at her watch thinking she was much later than she had planned. Scaffolding was set up on the side of the house, as well as the back of the house, and several men were already hard at work. She stared into the still-rising sun, searching for her brother. Before she spotted him, another pickup pulled up out front. Travis climbed out of his truck, grabbed his hard hat, and headed toward her.

"Boy, I see Byers Construction doesn't even give the rooster a chance to wake the neighbors!" Travis said as he shook his head.

"I know what you mean," Meghan replied. "I just got here, and I discover what appear to be two crews already working! I'm going to have to talk to that brother of mine. If he pulled two crews off other jobs, I'm not going to be very happy."

Giving a quick tug on the ponytail hanging below her hard hat, Travis warned, "Now don't get too excited until you find out the whole story. You know he already told you one crew was available because of a materials glitch. I'm sure there is a logical explanation for a second crew if that indeed is the case."

Meghan located her brother just as he was climbing down from the scaffolding at the back of the house, and strode toward him like a woman on a mission. Todd recognized that look of determination and wondered what could have set her off so early in the morning. He wisely decided to tread lightly until he found out what had her so worked up.

"Hey, sis, glad to see you could join us." Well, okay, so maybe that wasn't exactly treading lightly.

Planting herself directly in front of him, with her hands firmly on her hips, Meghan looked him in the eye and said, "You better tell me, little brother, that you have not pulled two crews off other jobs."

"Not even a good morning before you start second-guessing my scheduling abilities?" Todd replied with a smile. "That surprises me, sis."

"Well, Todd," she said as she looked beyond him. "I count six men out here. You know I don't want you pulling guys off other jobs."

"Settle down, Meg, and I can explain what's going on. I told you yesterday I was going to have a crew over here today."

"Unless something has changed that I'm unaware of, the crews at Byers Construction consist of four men, not six."

In an attempt to keep his sister from getting worked up unnecessarily, Todd bravely put his hands on her shoulders as he explained. "That is true. And I have a four-man crew here. The extra two guys are waiting for a load of lumber that has been delayed a couple hours. Rather than sit around the shop playing cards for two hours, they offered to come help on the siding. Believe it or not, sis, all the guys at the shop like you and want to help out. Although there are times when I wonder why. You need to relax and not jump to conclusions so quickly. I've been running this business and scheduling crews for ten years. I think I know what I'm doing."

"I know you do, Todd," she said apologetically as she lowered her head a bit. "I'm sorry. It's just that…"

Todd reached down and gently pulled her chin back up, so she was looking him in the eye. "I know. It's just that this is your project. Your dream. And you like to know what's going on. Actually, you like to be in charge," he said chuckling as he glanced over at Travis. "I understand that, Meghan. And I respect that. You accept nothing less than the best from everyone and everything. And you give nothing but your best. You have very high standards, which is why you have the respect of everyone in the company. That's also why this house will be a quality home." Todd then reached over and put his arm around Meghan's shoulder. "But you need to lighten up, girl! Let people help you. As much as you may hate to admit it, you're not a one-woman show. Nor should you be. Now why don't you go say hi to the guys and grab a donut? Josh made sure no one took a maple bar until you got one."

"Thanks, Todd," Meghan replied as she walked toward the guys, smiling.

Todd stood next to Travis as they watched Meghan chatting with the men. "I hope you know, buddy, you're going to have your hands full with that one!"

"Oh?" Travis asked in surprise.

Todd just smiled. "I'm not blind, my friend. I see the way you look at her. Just remember. She's a very special woman. She deserves someone special who will treat her the way she should be treated. From what I have seen, you just might fit the bill. But don't say I didn't warn you. I promise that if you get involved with my sister, you will most definitely have your hands full!" With that, Todd wandered off, leaving Travis standing alone, thinking this was shaping up to be a very interesting day.

* * *

By the end of a very long day, all the exterior siding had been installed and some of the trim was in place. Meghan and Travis had even managed to finish texturing the bedrooms and had hung all three of the bedroom doors. During their brief lunch break, Meghan instructed the workers to contact their wives and invite them all to Luigi's for pizza, pasta, and salad for dinner. It was the least she could do for the men and their families. They were all hard workers, and she wanted to repay them in some small way. Only one wife had a prior commitment, but everyone else would be there.

Everyone pitched in to get things picked up and make sure there weren't any tools left lying around.

"Good job, guys," Todd said as he gave one last visual sweep of the work area. "Go home and get cleaned up. We'll see you all at Luigi's at seven. Don't forget your wives! I've been looking at your ugly mugs all day. I expect the scenery at dinner to be much better."

They all laughed as they headed to the trucks, removing hard hats and tool belts as they went. Todd made a point to shake the hand of each one of his workers at the end of the day, and today was no different. He was a good boss, and they were good workers. But they were much more than simply hardworking employees. He considered each of them a friend as well.

Travis was leaning against his pickup, watching the scene in front of him. The more time he spent around Meghan, Todd, and their friends, the more he appreciated the fact they were such a tight-knit group. He had no doubt each one of them would be there for anyone in the group if they ever needed something. That was a heart-warming thought.

As Todd approached, Travis reached out to shake his hand. "You have a great crew, Todd. It's unusual to see a construction crew get along as well as they do."

"They're a great bunch of guys," Todd agreed. "They all know to leave their egos at the curb when they get onto a jobsite. I won't tolerate fighting and bickering, and they understand that. You fit right in with the guys. If you ever decide to quit your day job, let me know."

Travis laughed. "Thanks for the offer, Todd, but I think my boss wants me right where I am."

"No doubt."

"Thanks for your help today, Travis," Meghan interjected. "It was certainly a productive day, inside and outside. You will be joining us at Luigi's, right?"

"Just try to keep me away, little lady," Travis said with a grin.

"I seem to have worked up an appetite today. Well, I'm going to head home and get cleaned up before dinner. Why don't I stop by and pick you up about six forty-five and we can ride together. There's no sense in each of us driving separate vehicles."

"Okay," she responded. "That makes sense."

Meghan gave her brother a quick hug. "Thanks for everything, Todd. You're a pretty good brother."

"Just pretty good? Really? That's the best you can do?" Todd asked, trying desperately to come up with a believable pout. "I think I should be insulted."

"Yeah, yeah," Meghan replied as she gave her brother a playful slap on the arm. "Okay, you're a pretty great brother. How's that?"

Todd puffed out his chest, nodded his head, and stated matter-of-factly, "Much better. Much better indeed! Now go home and get cleaned up, sis. You smell like a construction worker!" One last tug on her ponytail, and he walked off to his truck whistling.

Chapter Sixteen

Travis had spent the better part of the day in his office at the church getting caught up on things that needed his attention. Dave just left after having a meeting to discuss a new youth outreach program. One more meeting with the music director and he would be finished for the day. Since she wasn't due for another thirty minutes or so, Travis decided to take the opportunity to give Meghan a quick call.

After the fourth ring, Meghan answered just as Travis was about to hang up. "Hey, Travis. What's up?"

"Did I catch you at a bad time?"

"No, not at all," Meghan replied. "I just had my hands full, so it took me a minute to get my cell phone out of my pocket. Are you at the church?"

"Yes. As much as I would love to be outside, occasionally I have to remind myself that I have work to do inside. But I'm hoping to have some relaxing time outside this weekend."

"You mean doing something other than working on construction?" Meghan asked, laughing.

"Maybe. It depends on whether or not you like to fish."

"Whether or not I like to fish will determine if you get to relax this weekend?"

"Hopefully," Travis replied, trying to sound nonchalant.

"Well, it just so happens that I love to fish."

"Okay. So far, so good. You got the correct answer for question number one. The next question might be a little more difficult."

Meghan laughed at his silly game but thoroughly enjoyed it.

"Question number two. Do you like to hike?"

"Is this a game of twenty questions about my likes and dislikes?" Meghan asked.

"No, I promise to stop long before I get to twenty. I knew you liked baseball, but I didn't know if you liked to fish or not."

"How did you know I like baseball? I don't remember ever discussing that."

"That was one of the things I noticed that first night when Rick Sanders and I came over to your apartment to visit you and Kaci. You have a nice assortment of impressive baseball memorabilia, so I assumed you must like baseball."

"You get ten points for having a good memory, then."

"Thank you. I try to be observant. Now, for the third and final question, would you like to go fishing with me this weekend at Paradise Lake?"

"I was planning to work on the house this weekend, but I think a break might do me some good."

"Is that a yes?" Travis asked hopefully.

"Yes. I would love to go fishing with you this weekend. It's been a long time since I've taken much 'me' time. I'm long overdue, and fishing would be a lot of fun. I've heard the fish are really biting right now at Paradise, so I hope you can keep up with me. I'm usually quite successful when I fish."

Travis laughed as he replied, "That doesn't surprise me one bit. But I'm pretty sure I can give you a run for your money."

"We'll see about that," Meghan replied confidently. "The

loser has to clean all the fish."

"Well, then, Miss Meghan, you better sharpen up your knife before this weekend!"

"Oh, my knife will be sharp. But I don't expect to have to take it out of the sheath."

The phone call ended with laughter as they both looked forward to a fun weekend.

* * *

The early morning drive up the pass toward Paradise Lake was quiet as both Travis and Meghan greeted the morning in their own way. Country music was playing softly in the background from a CD Travis had popped in before arriving at Meghan's apartment. He had an assortment of CDs available just in case she didn't care for Country, but he had heard her softly humming along to most of the songs, which brought a smile to his face.

Just as a Garth Brooks song ended, Travis pulled his pickup into one of the few remaining parking spaces in the lot near the boat dock. Paradise Lake was a short hike along a well-traveled trail through the trees that lined the lake. Travis jumped out of the truck and hurried around to open Meghan's door before she had a chance to do so on her own. He was well aware of her independence, so he tried to stay one step ahead of her when it came to the common courtesies his mother had instilled in him from a young age.

Travis reached into the truck and grabbed Meghan's jacket. "You're going to need this until it warms up a bit," he said as he held out the jacket for her.

"Thank you," she replied as she zipped the jacket and pulled the collar up around her neck. "It will warm up quickly enough once the sun gets a little higher." She grabbed her tackle box and fishing pole from the back of the truck and waited, while Travis locked up the pickup and retrieved his fishing gear.

"It looks like the fish are biting," Travis mentioned as he pointed toward the lake. "That kid has one on, and the guy beside him is taking one off his hook. Should be a good morning of fishing. I hope you're ready to clean some fish."

"You just head on down the trail, mister. And we'll see who's cleaning fish later."

Travis winked at Meghan, then led the way toward the lake.

By midmorning, the fishing was beginning to die down as the sun beat down on the lake. Meghan had already caught her limit, and Travis was one shy of his limit. He was not about to give up until he caught his last fish. Since Meghan was done fishing for the day, she had her pole and tackle box sitting beside her as she relaxed in the sun on a blanket. Travis still had his line in the water but was obviously not too concerned about it. He appeared to be resting with his eyes closed as he leaned against a tree stump.

"Fishing is relaxing to you, isn't it, Travis?"

"Uh-huh," he replied lazily, his eyes still closed behind his dark sunglasses.

"Did you do any fishing when you went camping for a few days recently?"

"A little," he replied as he opened one eye long enough to peek at the end of his pole.

"But you said that trip wasn't as rejuvenating as you had hoped. Do you have any idea why?"

Travis sat up, pretending to concentrate on his fishing pole. "I had a lot on my mind. I was trying to work through some stuff. That's why I went camping. It normally helps me sort things out and clear my head."

"But it didn't that time?"

"Not entirely. It's complicated."

"What was bothering you so much that a week in the mountains wasn't enough to clear your head?"

Travis looked at Meghan intently, knowing she couldn't see his eyes because of his dark sunglasses. He knew in his heart that if anyone else was asking him those questions, he would probably get irritated. But Meghan was different. She wasn't asking because she was nosey or even out of curiosity. She was asking because she genuinely cared and wanted to understand.

Since he didn't answer right away and appeared to be simply staring at her, Meghan instantly regretted asking him such a personal question. "I'm sorry, Travis. I guess that was a pretty personal question. You don't have to answer if you don't want to. It's none of my business; I was just trying to understand."

Travis's heart melted as he stared into her hazel eyes and saw the compassion that came so naturally to her. It was one of many things that drew him to her. He smiled slightly as he patted the ground beside him. "Come sit over here. It's not like you're fishing anyway."

Meghan made sure her stringer of fish was secure, got up and stretched her back, then sat beside Travis so they were leaning against the same tree. Travis put his arm around her shoulder and pulled her close. They sat for several minutes staring out at the lake, not talking. "There's a lot you don't know about me, Meghan." When she didn't respond, he continued. "It's not that I've been purposely keeping things from you. I just don't like sharing a lot of the intimate details of my life with people. I guess you could say I'm not an open book," he said as he smiled down at her. She returned his smile, but kept quiet in the hopes he would continue opening up to her.

Even though he seemed relaxed sitting next to her, Meghan could tell that it wasn't easy for Travis to talk about himself. "You asked what was weighing so heavily on my heart that a week in the mountains didn't resolve the issues. Let me ask you a question, Meghan. You've been coming back to church now on a semi-regular basis, so you've had the opportunity to hear me preach. When I'm preaching, do my messages reach you? Do you feel like you are getting anything out of my sermons?"

"Are you kidding me?" she asked incredulously.

Travis took off his sunglasses and looked her directly in the eye. "No, Meghan, I'm dead serious. I need to know if my messages are reaching you."

Meghan pulled away from him slightly so she could turn to face him more directly. "Travis, I wasn't being flippant when I asked if you were kidding. I seriously thought you must have been joking. Having grown up in the church, I have listened to preachers my entire life. Some good, some not so good, and some great. Then there's you. You are in a class by yourself, Travis. I don't say that lightly. You really are special. When you are preaching, it's not like you are preaching to a congregation. You are talking to each person in the room individually. It's as if there is no one else in the sanctuary. And every single person in the room feels exactly the same way. That's a gift, Travis. Not many people can do that. I'm surprised you didn't know that."

"Oh. It's good to know that I'm reaching people."

"You are, Travis. Believe me, you are."

Travis leaned back against the tree and pulled Meghan close again. They sat in silence for several minutes, as Travis gathered his thoughts. Meghan respected his silence and waited until he was ready to continue. She admitted to herself that she was quite content being held in his arms and relaxed easily against him.

Travis finally felt ready to share his thoughts with Meghan. Up until now, his friend and head elder was the only person he had ever trusted with his most personal inner turmoil. "The reason I needed to know if my sermons were reaching you, reaching anyone really, was because I've been struggling with some personal issues and had reached the conclusion that maybe I wasn't cut out for preaching."

Meghan tried to simply listen, but that idea struck her as being so wrong that she had to ask for clarification. Looking up at him, she asked, "I don't know what personal issues you were dealing with, but why would it cause you to think you weren't cut out for preaching? Spreading the gospel is who you are. It's what you do."

"I was beginning to think if I couldn't even get my own life together, how could I possibly counsel other people."

"But, Travis, you are the most put-together person I know."

Travis chuckled as he replied, "Looks can be deceiving, Meghan." Taking a deep breath, he decided it was time to explain. "As I said earlier, there's a lot about me you don't know. I've been married before." Travis looked over at Meghan and seeing no perceptible reaction, he continued. "Her name was Angela. She was a pretty incredible woman. We fit together so well. It was like she made me complete."

Travis stopped, seeming to be struggling to gather his thoughts. Hoping he would continue, Meghan commented, "You keep saying 'was.' Did something happen to Angela?"

Looking out at the lake, Travis continued. "We had been married a couple years. I had just finished building our home. Our ministry was growing, and life seemed to be going great. Angela was very active in our ministry. We were working on a special project for the new outreach program for the teens in our church. It was Angela's brainchild. She always had some of the best ideas on how to reach troubled youth. She connected with them in a way that was remarkable. Anyway, I was working at the church one day and knew she would be coming over soon. I called and asked her to run an errand." Travis's voice began wavering, and

Meghan reached over and took his hand in hers. "An errand for me." After pausing briefly, Travis pushed on. "She never made it to the church, Meghan. She was hit by a drunk driver who ran a red light just a few blocks from the church. She died at the scene of the accident."

"Oh, Travis." Meghan sighed sympathetically. "I'm so very sorry."

Meghan could see tears roll down his cheeks behind his sunglasses. She reached up to wipe away a tear, as her own tears were beginning to well up. She softly stroked his cheek as he worked to regain his composure. Somehow she sensed there was more to the story.

"Angela wasn't the only casualty. She was pregnant. Our unborn son also died at the scene."

Meghan quickly covered her mouth as an audible gasp escaped. "Oh, no! How terrible!" By now the tears were flowing down her face and she made no effort to stop them. Travis muffled a couple anguished sobs then pulled Meghan back into his arms. They leaned back against the tree in silence and simply held each other tightly. Travis wanted to give her time to process what she had just learned, and he needed time to gain control of his emotions before continuing.

"Needless to say, I was devastated. That happened three years ago. Sometimes it seems like I'm doing okay. Other times I think I'm just going through the motions. There are days when I think the pain might eventually go away. Then I see or hear something that triggers a memory, and I'm right back in the middle of the worst day of my life. I had nightmares for a long time after the accident. I blamed myself. I tried to convince myself that if she weren't running an errand for me, she might not have been in the middle of that intersection at the wrong time. But I know I had no control over that. Even if she had not been running my errand, her timing might still have put her there at the wrong time. People say that it gets better with time. I'm not sure I believe that. It's been three years and at times it feels like it was just yesterday. The nightmares went away for a while, so I thought maybe things were going to get better. They suddenly returned a few months ago, and I guess I couldn't deal with it. It made me start second-guessing everything."

"Do you have any idea why the nightmares returned?"

"I'm not really sure. Dave has an idea, but I don't know if he's on the right track or not. Anyway, since I was having so much trouble dealing with things, it made me question whether or not I really was fit for the ministry. That's when I decided to take a few days and head to the mountains. It usually helps me clear my head."

"It's no wonder it was only partially successful," Meghan said in understanding. "That's a lot to process."

"You're right, it was. Even though I wasn't completely successful in sorting things out, the one thing I came away from the mountains knowing was that I couldn't leave the ministry. In fact, I felt that God reinforced my calling during my soul-searching. With all my faults and insecurities, apparently God still thinks I can do the job." Travis shook his head in amazement.

Meghan smiled as she noticed a small grin appear on Travis's face. "You know, Travis, God doesn't expect you to be perfect. Maybe you shouldn't expect it either."

"I suppose."

"Travis?" Meghan hesitated. "Do you mind if I ask you a personal question?"

"No. Go ahead."

"You don't have to answer it if you think it's too personal. Just say so."

"Okay."

"What was your son's name?"

Travis hesitated for a long time before answering. "We were going to name him Levi Joshua Harmon."

"Levi Joshua," Meghan repeated, nodding her head. "Two strong biblical names."

"Angela picked Levi because it means 'joined in harmony.' She thought that described our life and our ministry together. I picked Joshua because it means 'God is salvation.' It didn't hurt that it's also my middle name," he added smiling.

"Travis Joshua Harmon. Did you ever go by TJ?"

"I was called TJ a lot growing up. Especially in high school. Apparently initials are cool for jocks."

"You were a jock in high school? That doesn't surprise me a bit!"

"Mostly baseball," he replied with a grin, as he stood up. "I guess that's something we have in common."

"I knew I liked you for a reason," she replied as Travis took her hand to help her up. "Does anyone still call you TJ?"

"My dad does occasionally. Mom never liked it. She was happy when I decided to go into ministry and went back to using Travis. She said, 'TJ isn't a proper name for a minister.'"

"I think I'm going to like your mom. She sounds like a wise woman." Pulling her stringer of fish out of the water, Meghan teased, "I wonder what your mom would have to say about you being out-fished by a girl?"

Travis laughed as he replied, "She wouldn't be surprised at all. She used to out-fish Dad all the time!"

"I'm definitely going to like your mom!"

As Meghan bent to pick up her tackle box, Travis reached for her hand and turned her toward him. He took her sunglasses off and placed them on her head, then pushed his sunglasses onto his head as well, his eyes never leaving hers. He pulled her into his arms, simply gazing into her beautiful hazel eyes. He leaned down, and their lips touched lightly as they shared a gentle kiss. Meghan looked up at Travis and smiled. She then put her hand on the back of his neck and guided him into another tender kiss. With a barely audible sigh, she rested her head against his chest as Travis held her tightly.

After a couple of minutes where time seemed to disappear into nothingness, Travis reluctantly released his hold on Meghan and slipped his sunglasses back down to shield his eyes against the bright sun. After giving her hand a squeeze, he picked up his tackle box and they began to gather their fishing gear and the stringers of fish before hiking back to the truck.

Meghan slid over next to Travis when she got into the truck. He put his arm around her and pulled her even closer as they shared another kiss. As Travis began backing out of the parking space, Meghan nonchalantly said, "I bet your dad got pretty good at cleaning fish."

"Message received, my dear. Yes, it looks like I'm stuck cleaning the fish!" Travis rolled down the windows and cranked up the Country music as their laughter filled the cab of the truck.

Chapter Seventeen

Meghan pushed her chair away from the desk, satisfied with the accomplishments of the day. She had managed to finish two design projects she had been working on simultaneously for over a week. It always gave her a sense of accomplishment knowing that she finished ahead of schedule and her clients would be pleased. It was times like this, when she had several things on her plate, that she appreciated the work ethic her dad had instilled in her from a very young age. She headed toward the kitchen to refill her glass of iced tea when her phone rang. Seeing Becky's name on the caller ID brought a smile to her face. Because of the work on the house, she had not had much time to visit with her best friend.

"Hey, Becky, how are you doing?"

"Hey, stranger," her friend replied. "I'm doing great. How about you?"

"Between the house, the construction company, and my design work, I've been busier than I care to be!"

"That, my dear friend, is exactly the reason for my call. It seems like it's been forever since we've gotten together for some girl time. You don't call. You don't write. You don't stop by the office to buy me lunch. I'm beginning to feel neglected."

The two women laughed together at their old joke. Meghan and Becky had been best friends since grade school, and now their daughters were best friends. If Meghan were being completely honest with herself, she would have to admit that she had not been very good lately about holding up her end of their friendship. She made a mental note to do what she could to change that. She never would have survived her divorce if it hadn't been for Becky, and she owed it to her to be a more involved friend.

"Well," Meghan suggested, "we can't have you feeling neglected now, can we? What does your schedule look like this week? Do you think you have time to squeeze in a lunch with an old friend?"

"Absolutely! We could even make it a long lunch if you want to. You need to fill me in on what's been going on in your life. Rumor has it that you've been spending a lot of time with a certain pastor. I understand you even went fishing with him this past weekend."

"Wow! Word sure travels fast! I didn't think anyone even knew we went fishing."

"You can thank your little brother for that! I ran into Todd at the grocery store yesterday, and he mentioned it. I got the impression that he was glad you were taking some time for yourself. And he seemed to be okay with you spending time with Pastor Harmon."

"I should have known it was Todd. I think he was the only person I had mentioned it to. So, what day do you want to do lunch?"

"How about tomorrow? Will you be able to have a semi-leisurely lunch tomorrow?"

"Sure, tomorrow sounds great. Why don't we meet at Luigi's around noon? That way we can go in with the intent of eating a healthy salad for lunch, knowing full well that we are going to end up eating pizza!"

"Ah!" Becky laughed. "You know us so well!"

"Yep. Well, I have known us for a few years, you know! See you tomorrow, Beck."

* * *

Meghan spent the morning working at the house, then made sure she left in plenty of time to meet Becky at Luigi's by noon. She was looking forward to catching up with her friend. It seemed that no matter what was going on in their lives, or how long it had been since they saw each other, whenever they got together, they simply picked up right where they left off. It was a comforting and secure feeling to have a friend like that. Becky was waiting for her just inside the door. They ordered their salads, then grinned as they looked at each other and settled on which pizza to share.

They had barely found their way to a table when Becky started her round of questions. "So, you've been busy working on the house and with all your other obligations, but you still manage to find time to spend with the new pastor? Tell me, Meghan, what's up?"

Meghan laughed as she took a seat. "Boy, you don't waste any time, do you?"

"Nope."

"Okay. What do you want to know? It sounds like you're just dying for a scoop of some kind!"

"Tell me everything!"

"You really are a nut, Becky! Okay. Where do I start? First of all, yes, I've been spending a fair amount of time with Travis. That's Pastor Harmon. Besides being a pastor, he's also a carpenter by trade. And a pretty darn good one. He has built several custom homes, so he definitely knows his way around the construction site. He loves working with his hands, and he likes doing construction as a way to relax and unwind. So, he has offered to help out on the house when he has time. He was there helping the day you dropped Kaci off when I was going to barbecue."

"I remember seeing him there working with Todd."

"Right. So anyway, whenever he has some free time, he just stops by to see if there's anything he can do to help. He's been a tremendous help. There's no way the house would be as far along as it is if it weren't for him. And, of course, Todd and the guys help whenever they can as well."

"Todd is a good brother. He's a great guy. We should fix him up with my sister! They would be perfect together!"

Meghan put her hand up immediately. "You leave me out of any matchmaking scheme you have in mind that involves Todd! He has already made it very clear that he doesn't want me meddling in his love life. You're on your own with that one!"

Becky laughed and said, "I'll just file that away in my memory bank for now. Right now, we're concentrating on you!"

"Yeah, right," Meghan replied. "Moving on. Anyway, Travis has been helping me out on the house, so we've been working together occasionally. We seem to get along really well when we're working, and we work well together as a team. He's very talented, and he has a lot of good ideas."

Waving her fork in a dismissive gesture, Becky said, "Okay, I get it. He's a great construction worker. But I'm not interested in Travis the builder. I'm interested in Travis the man. Well, *I'm* not interested in him. I'm interested in him for *you*! Tell me about Travis the man."

"Ugh! You're not going to give me a break, are you?"

"Not even a little one. After all, what are friends for?"

"Okay. Well, he's a great guy. He's funny. I love his sense of humor. He's caring and compassionate. He's understanding. He loves kids. He really connected with Kaci right off the bat. Other than Todd and Rick Sanders, I've never seen her connect with a man like she does with Travis. We seem to have a lot of things in common. He loves the outdoors. He likes to camp and fish, and he loves baseball. And he has such a heart for Christ. You should hear him preach, Becky. He's incredible. It's not even like he's preaching a sermon. It's as if he's just talking to you. No one else. Just you. And he wants everyone to know Christ like he knows Him. I don't know how to explain it, but he is so passionate about the gospel. When he told me he had considered giving up the ministry, it just broke my heart."

"Wait a minute. He's still the pastor at Hope Community Church, right? When was he thinking of quitting?"

"Just recently. He has been struggling with some personal issues and began to feel like he shouldn't be preaching. He's still trying to work some things out, but after taking a few days off and doing some soul-searching, he decided that the ministry is where he's supposed to be. He just has some things to figure out."

"What kind of things?"

"I'm not sure. When we went fishing, we talked about some of the things that have been bothering him, but there are some things he doesn't seem to be ready to talk about yet. He did tell me about his wife though."

"His wife? I thought he wasn't married."

"He's not married. His wife was killed in a car accident three years ago. She was pregnant at the time, and their unborn son was also killed."

"Wow. That's got to be difficult."

"Yeah, he's still having trouble dealing with it at times. It's obvious that he really loved her. It just broke my heart when he told me about losing his wife and unborn son at the same time. I don't know how someone gets over a loss like that. It has to be devastating."

The two women ate in silence for several minutes. Meghan returned to the salad bar in an effort to avoid the inevitable pizza binge. Becky started on the pizza, making no apologies. When Meghan returned to the table, Becky started in on round two of the inquisition. She simply stared quizzically at Meghan for several minutes. Eventually, Meghan could feel her friend's eyes boring into her heart and soul.

"What?" Meghan asked. "Do I have salad dressing on my face and you're trying to decide whether or not to tell me about it?"

"Would I do that?" Becky questioned with the innocence of a child caught with his hands in the cookie jar.

"Of course, you would," Meghan replied with laughter. "You have a history of that type of behavior. I remember a particular incident in elementary school when you allowed me to walk all the way down the hallway with a piece of toilet paper stuck to the bottom of my shoe!"

"What can I say? It was funny!"

Meghan just shook her head and reached for a slice of pizza.

"I was just sitting here," Becky began, "wondering exactly what is wrong with your pastor friend."

"What do you mean? There's nothing wrong with him."

"Exactly my point! You two seem to get along well. He's obviously a hard worker if he goes out and volunteers to help build your house in his spare time when he wants to relax. You say he has a great sense of humor. He likes fishing and baseball. He likes kids. And even though he's not drop-dead model gorgeous, he's definitely ruggedly handsome. I can't see a single flaw about the man. So, what are you waiting for? Marry that man!"

Meghan laughed out loud. "You are a crazy woman. You do know that, right?"

"No, seriously, Meg, what are you waiting for? You're not getting any younger, you know."

"Hey, you make it sound like I'll be getting the dreaded AARP fliers in the mail any day now!"

"Well, you don't want to wait until that happens! But seriously, Meg, I just want to see you happy. And your eyes just light up whenever you talk about him, so I can tell that he makes you happy. What's holding you back?"

Meghan was quiet as she pondered her friend's cut-to-the-chase question. "I don't know, Becky. He seems to have some emotional baggage. He admits that he has some issues he's trying to sort through and deal with."

Becky pointed her fork at her friend in a no-nonsense manner. "You listen to me, Meghan Maxwell. You cannot be dismissing this great guy just because he has a little baggage. We all have baggage. You have a nutcase alcoholic ex-husband. You want me to explain to you the size of bag you need to carry that around?"

"Okay, you might have a valid point."

"You know I do. And you know I'm right. So, again, what are you waiting for? Are you interested in Travis? Does he make your heart go pitter-patter? Can you envision a future with him?"

"You seem to be skipping right over a very crucial fact, Becky. Whether or not I can envision a future with him doesn't mean he can envision a future with me. Maybe he doesn't even like me all that much."

"Oh, I think he likes you, my friend. According to Todd, the way Travis looks at you indicates he most definitely has an interest in you!"

"Oh, great," Meghan groaned. "Now my wonderful little

brother is spreading rumors about me."

"Don't be so hard on Todd. You have always known that he has your back no matter what. And it sounds like he really likes Travis. That's a big deal. He's pretty protective over you. Especially after what Danny put you through. I can't imagine he's going to allow anyone to get very close to you unless he's comfortable with the guy and approves of him. He approves of Travis. And he wants to see you happy. We all do, Meghan. You deserve to be happy. And I personally think Travis is the guy who is going to make that happen."

"Well, then," Meghan began sarcastically, "it's apparently all settled. You say Todd likes Travis. You like Travis. I like Travis. Everybody likes Travis. So obviously we're going to end up married and live happily ever after. Again, you're a crazy woman."

"Did you hear what you just said, Meg?"

"What? I said you're a crazy woman."

"Before that. You said you like Travis. That's the first time you've admitted that." Becky smiled like she had just solved a centuries-old mystery. "You like him, Meg. He makes you happy. And that makes me happy. So, there you have it. It took over an hour, but I finally coaxed a confession out of you. I guess my work here is done!"

As the two friends stood up to leave the restaurant, Meghan looked at Becky with a grin and asked, "Why do I put up with you?"

Becky grabbed her hand like a schoolgirl and replied, "Because I am amazing, and you love me!"

Meghan simply shook her head and agreed, "True enough, Beck. True enough!"

Chapter Eighteen

Work on the house seemed to be progressing at an astonishing rate once all the exterior siding had been installed. With the wrap-around porch and deck finished, the only things remaining on the outside were some final trim pieces and the rain gutters. With an immense feeling of satisfaction and gratitude for her many helpers, Meghan walked into the dining room through the open French doors from the back deck. The interior of her dream home was beginning to take shape as well, now that the kitchen cabinetry was finished, and all the countertops were being put into place. Jason and his crew were working on the kitchen and bathrooms simultaneously. It was easy to see rapid progress, and the house was quickly beginning to look like a home.

Meghan rounded the corner into the living room, smiling and nodding her approval. "Girard, your artistry never ceases to amaze me!"

The middle-aged Swedish stonemason stood, wiped his hands on a rag, then reached out to shake hands with Meghan. He smiled broadly, as he joined her in the middle of the room. "Thank you, Miss Meghan. I do okay, but sometimes I wonder if I will ever have the talent Dad has."

"You two make a wonderful team," Meghan reassured him.

"The fireplace is going to be incredible! By the way, where is your dad? I didn't see him when I came in."

"He's out back. He came across a stone he deemed 'not perfect,' so, of course, it had to go back to the pile!"

"And back to the pile it shall go, by golly! Along with any other rock that is not perfect," said the senior stonemason as he walked up behind them. Giving Meghan a fatherly hug, he winked as he said, "Ya know, ye have to watch these young'uns or they would be putting just any old rock into your fireplace."

The three friends laughed together, knowing full well that the father had the utmost respect for his son's talent. "How are you doing this morning, Mr. Johansson?" Meghan asked.

"Now, Miss Meghan, I've known ye since ye were a wee lass. I've been telling ye your whole life to call me Anders. By golly, one of these days ye just might remember that, ya betcha!"

Meghan just smiled as she replied, "You can blame my dad for that. He taught me to respect my elders."

"Indeed, he did, Miss Meghan. Your daddy was a good man. Rest his soul. He was the first friend I made when I moved to Hope. He sent a lot of work my way, that's a fact."

"What you and Girard do with stones is nothing short of artistry. Dad was so proud of the fireplace you built at the construction office. He always said it was the largest, most beautiful piece of art he had ever seen."

"By golly, that was one of my best pieces. Wanted nothing but the best for your daddy. That's why I want nothing but the best for you, too, Miss Meghan. Every stone in your fireplace must be perfect or it doesn't belong. That's a fact."

"Well, it's absolutely beautiful. I better let you two get back to work. Girard, don't let your dad work too hard, okay?"

Anders Johansson waved a dismissive hand in her direction as he headed back to work. "I'm not too old to do an honest day's work yet, ya betcha. Ye don't be worrying about me."

Girard winked at Meghan and replied, "Don't worry, Miss Meghan, I'll try to keep him from overdoing it."

* * *

Over the next several days, various projects around the house began to wrap up, thanks in no small part to the help of Todd and Travis. One or the other, and oftentimes both, would show up whenever their schedules allowed and pitch in with whatever needed to be done. Two of the three bedrooms upstairs had been painted and the carpeting installed. Meghan had opted to go with carpeting in the bedrooms because she simply liked the warmth and feel of it. The rest of the house would either have tile or wood flooring. The only bedroom that remained unfinished was Kaci's room. She wanted to choose the paint and carpeting colors herself, and would be doing that once she returned from camp. The main bath and master bath upstairs were also finished, as was the bath down on the main floor. It was certainly nice to have functional bathrooms while work continued on the house.

Other than Kaci's bedroom, the only rooms still left unpainted were the living and family rooms. Kaci wanted to choose the color for the family room, but Meghan had already purchased paint for the living room since the two had agreed to go with a soft French gray. Meghan was busy spreading a drop cloth over the fireplace and taping off the edges in preparation for painting when she heard a vehicle pull up outside. Since Travis had mentioned that he would be stopping by this afternoon, and Meghan was up on a ladder taping the drop cloth, she didn't give it a second thought when she heard the front door open. As she turned to climb down from the ladder, she found Danny standing a few feet away.

171

Danny smiled when she let out a soft involuntary gasp. "Not who you were expecting, huh?"

Meghan stepped off the ladder, feeling much safer on solid ground. "What are you doing here, Danny? I thought Todd and I made it very clear that you are not welcome around here."

Ignoring her completely, Danny slowly walked toward the dining room, glancing around the room before looking out onto the deck and into the back of the property. He returned to the living room where Meghan stood rooted in the same spot near the fireplace. "No helpers today, huh? That's unusual."

Meghan stared harshly at Danny and asked, "How would you know what's unusual? Have you been spying on me?"

Danny didn't reply. Instead, he walked past Meghan and looked out the living room window. She was not surprised to smell alcohol as he passed her. Standing with his back to her, he stated in a wistful tone, "This is a nice piece of property, Meg. I can see why you like it."

"That was you parked in the trees across the street, wasn't it, Danny? What are you doing here? What do you want?"

Still staring out the window, he replied, "I told you. I want a second chance. We can have a good life together here."

"And I told you that's never going to happen. You don't get another chance, Danny. I would have thought you could figure that out when I divorced you. We're through, Danny. We've been through for a long time. The only way you remain a part of my life at all is because you are Kaci's father. That's it. You need to understand that. It's not going to change, so you need to accept it."

"I can't accept it, Meg," Danny stated matter-of-factly as he walked toward Meghan. "I still love you."

Meghan could feel his eyes boring into her soul with his unwavering stare. "You need to leave, Danny. Right now," she said with more bravery than she felt. But he continued walking toward her with his eyes locked on hers. Meghan took a couple steps back, wishing with all her might that she had not been working alone today.

Danny suddenly reached out and grabbed her by her upper arms in a vice-like grip. "Let me go!" Meghan said loudly as she struggled against his hold. The more she struggled, the tighter his grip became. Her eyes began to dart around the room quickly like a caged animal, hoping to find anything she might be able to use as a weapon if necessary. Realizing the only thing within her reach was the ladder she had been standing on a few moments ago, she snagged one of the legs of the ladder with her foot in hopes it would fall into them and force him to release his hold on her. The ladder crashed against Danny's shoulder, taking him by surprise.

Meghan took advantage of the distraction and pulled free of his grasp, but Danny caught her by the wrist just as she tried to turn away. He held tight as she twisted to free herself. With his free hand, Danny attempted to push the ladder off them. Meghan gave a final desperate pull just as Danny shoved the ladder toward her, causing her to trip. There was a sickening thud as Meghan fell, hitting her head on the stone hearth.

"No!" Danny screamed in horror. He quickly tossed the ladder aside and knelt down beside Meghan. She wasn't moving. He turned her head to discover a gash on the side of her forehead and a rapidly growing pool of blood. In a panic, he stood and ran out the front door, got in his pickup, and sped toward the road, leaving a cloud of dirt and rocks in his wake.

* * *

As Travis approached Meghan's property, the hair on the back of his neck instantly stood at high alert when he spotted a dark-colored pickup speeding away. He screeched to a stop in front of the house, climbing out of his truck almost before it came to a complete stop. Running toward the front door, Travis yelled, "Meghan?"

His heart nearly stopped when he spotted the overturned ladder near the fireplace, and Meghan lying motionless nearby. He knelt beside her, softly calling her name as tears ran down his face. She was still breathing, but was out cold. Travis quickly called 911 to get help on the way then punched in Todd's number on his cell phone.

Todd answered his phone on the first ring when he noticed Travis's name on the caller ID. "Hey, buddy, how are you doing?"

"Todd, you need to get over here to Meghan's house right away. She's been hurt!"

Already running to his truck, Todd asked his friend, "What happened?"

"I don't know. There was a truck speeding away from her house just before I got here. She's on the floor in the living room, next to the fireplace. She's out cold and has a huge gash on the side of her forehead. It's bleeding pretty badly, Todd. I called 911 and they are on the way."

"I'll be there in less than two minutes!"

"I hear sirens, so they've got to be close."

Travis had just disconnected his call with Todd when the fire department's rescue unit pulled onto the property, with Todd right behind them. Todd rushed into the house as the EMTs grabbed their bags. He knelt beside his unconscious sister, seeing that Travis had already made an unsuccessful attempt to stop the bleeding. "Sis, can you hear me?"

Todd and Travis both reluctantly moved aside to allow the EMTs to do their job. Before long, Meghan had a white bandage wrapped around her head and was being lifted onto a stretcher. As his sister was being loaded into the rescue unit, he looked over at Travis. "Why don't you ride with Meghan, Travis. I'll follow in my truck."

"Thanks, Todd," Travis replied with obvious relief. "I really appreciate that."

Todd put his hand on his friend's shoulder and said encouragingly, "She'll be okay. She's a tough lady."

Overcome with emotion, Travis simply nodded as he climbed into the rescue rig and immediately bowed his head in prayer.

As he stared at the closing doors, Todd said, "Thank you, God. You found the right man for her." Then he ran to his pickup and fell in behind the rescue unit as it started down the road with its sirens blaring.

* * *

The two men sat impatiently in the waiting room of the hospital, trying to distract themselves by piecing together what might have happened.

"Did you see that pickup leave Meghan's property?" Todd asked Travis.

"No, I didn't actually see it pull off her property, but I wasn't far away. When I saw it speeding down the road, the cloud of dust hadn't settled yet, and it was obviously from Meghan's place." Travis hesitated before adding, "It was a dark-colored pickup, Todd."

"It was? Could you tell if it was the same truck that was parked in the trees across the street a while back?"

"No, I couldn't tell. We didn't get a very good look at that truck, and this one was also speeding away, so I have no way of knowing if it was the same truck. I wish I had gotten to Meghan's fifteen minutes earlier."

"I know. I should have been there, too. But you know how she is about any of us changing our schedules to make sure she's not working alone over there."

Both men stood, as Dr. Patterson walked up to Todd and shook his hand. "Hi, Todd."

"Hi, Doc. Have you met Travis Harmon?"

"Oh, sure," he replied as he shook hands with Travis. "The pastor and I are getting to be good friends."

Travis didn't waste any time. "How is Meghan? Is she going to be okay?"

The elderly doctor put his hand on Travis's shoulder and answered, "She's going to be fine, son." The relief the men shared was audible. "She's awake now, but she's pretty groggy. I ran some tests and stitched up the gash. She has a mild concussion and she's going to have a horrible headache for a few days, but she'll be fine. I'm going to keep her overnight for observation. Anytime you have a head injury like that, you need to keep an eye on it for a few days. She needs to rest, and I'd rather she wasn't home alone for the next several days since I know Kaci is at camp. Would it be possible for her to stay with you, Todd, for three or four days after I release her? I could have Sue stop by to check on her during the day while you're at work."

"Of course, Doc," Todd replied. "In fact, if necessary, I could work from home for a few days."

"I could stop by and check in on her too, Todd," Travis offered. "And I'm sure I won't have any trouble getting some of the ladies from church to swing by. Can we see her now, Ken?"

"Just for a few minutes. She still isn't very coherent, and I want her to rest. I thought it was odd that she kept saying 'Danny.' I didn't know he was back in town."

Travis and Todd looked at each other in understanding then

Todd said, "So it was him."

"It looks like it," Travis agreed.

Dr. Patterson looked confused. "Am I missing something?"

"We think Danny is responsible for Meghan getting hurt," Todd explained. "Travis saw a dark-colored pickup speed away from her house just as he was arriving to help her with some painting this afternoon. A while back, there was a dark-colored pickup parked in the trees across the road from her place when we were there working. When Travis and I walked over to check it out, whoever it was took off in a hurry."

"So, you think the dark-colored pickup both times was Danny?" the doctor asked.

"After we saw the truck parked in the trees, Meghan said that it looked like Danny's truck," Travis explained.

"Meghan will be able to tell us what happened," Todd stated.

"I don't want you two asking her a lot of questions right now," the doctor instructed. "She needs to rest. That can wait until tomorrow."

"Okay," Todd agreed reluctantly. "Can we go in to see her now?"

"Sure, follow me." Dr. Patterson led them to Meghan's room, reminding them to make their visit brief and not to ask her questions.

Meghan's eyes were closed, and she appeared to be sleeping when the men walked into her room. Todd walked over and placed his hand on her arm, being careful not to disturb the IV. "Hey, sis, can you hear me?"

She mumbled something unintelligible, as Travis stepped over to the opposite side of her bed. He reached over and tenderly pushed the hair out of her eyes, then slowly ran his fingers down the side of her face. "I'm sorry I didn't get there earlier, Meg. If I had been there, this wouldn't have happened."

Todd could see tears forming in his friend's eyes and knew without a doubt that this man loved his sister. He simply did not realize it yet. They only stayed for a few minutes, but Travis held her hand the entire time. Finally, Todd walked around the bed, put his arm around Travis's shoulder, and said, "We should go, buddy. She needs to rest. We'll come back in the morning and see when Doc is going to release her."

Travis reluctantly released her hand, then bent over and placed a gentle kiss on her forehead. "Get some rest, my dear. I'll see you in the morning."

The two men were quiet during the walk to the parking lot, each lost in their own thoughts. An overprotective little brother who made a silent vow to make sure she was never alone again while working on the house. And a widowed pastor who was suddenly aware that God had brought love into his life a second time.

Chapter Nineteen

When Todd pulled into the hospital parking lot just after seven-thirty the next morning, he was not surprised to see Travis just getting out of his pickup a few spaces away. He sent up a quick prayer that not only had Travis figured out how much he cares for Meghan, but that his sister would also recognize her feelings for Travis.

"Hey, Travis," Todd called out as he approached his friend from behind. "How are you doing this morning? I hope you got some sleep last night."

"To tell you the truth, Todd, I didn't get a lot of sleep. I spent the better part of the night in prayer and soul-searching."

Todd reached out and put his arm around Travis's shoulder just as they arrived at the main entrance of the hospital. "It's a nice morning. Why don't we sit over here and talk for a few minutes before we go in."

They found a bench a few yards from the door, and Todd gave Travis a chance to sit before he began speaking again. "First off, I want you to know that you don't need to worry about Meghan. She's always been a fighter, and she's a lot tougher than she looks. I know that from firsthand experience," he said with a smile. "It will take a lot more than a bump on the head to slow her down!"

"I've already figured out that she's tougher than she looks," Travis replied with a chuckle.

"She can hold her own, that's for sure. But she can also be her own worst enemy at times because she tends to think she's indestructible. So, between the two of us, we are going to have to make sure she takes it easy for the next few days. No working on the house. And she's not going to like that, but I don't think she'll argue too much as long as you and I put on a united front. We need to protect her from herself for a while."

"I agree completely, Todd. I've learned that she can be just a little bit stubborn at times."

"Just a little bit, huh? Travis, that girl takes stubborn to a whole new level! And that brings up another point we need to discuss. Danny. We need to find out from her exactly what happened. If Danny was involved in any way, I'm going to insist that she get a restraining order against him. And I'd like you to back me up on that if you can. She's not going to want to do it. But we know for sure that he's already been over there harassing her once, and we had to run him off. And I'm pretty sure that was him parked across the street in the bushes. If he was responsible for Meghan getting hurt yesterday, in my book that's three strikes and he's out!"

"You're right. Do you really think she won't want to get a restraining order? It sounds like he's been a problem to her for quite a while."

"She won't want to because of Kaci. Danny is Kaci's dad, and she would think Kaci would feel bad if there was a restraining order against her dad. I know for a fact Kaci wouldn't feel that way. I talked to her last night and told her what happened to her mom. Meghan won't like that either, but Kaci isn't a little kid. She has a right to know. When I told Kaci what happened, the first thing she asked was if her mom was okay. The second thing she wanted to know was if her dad did it. Kaci's a pretty sharp kid. Not much gets past her."

"What did you tell her? We still don't know exactly what happened, and won't know until we talk to Meghan."

"That's what I told her. I said I would let her know after talking to her mom."

"Well, one thing I know for sure, if Danny was involved, restraining order or no restraining order, I'm not letting her work at the house by herself anymore."

"I'm way ahead of you, buddy." Todd nodded in agreement. "I had decided that when we left here yesterday. There's one more minor issue I want to bring up before we head in to see Meghan."

"What's that?" Travis asked.

"Like my niece, not much gets past me either. I've been watching you around Meghan for the past few months, and I've come to the conclusion that you are in love with my sister. I was just wondering when you were going to reach the same conclusion."

A slow smile began working its way across Travis's face. "Boy, you cut right to the chase don't you, Todd?"

"Yep. I don't see any sense in beating around the bushes. Can I assume from that goofy smile you're wearing that somewhere along the line you figured it out?"

"I've known for a little while that I had feelings for her. But when I saw her lying motionless on the floor and a pool of blood at her head…" His voice trailed off as he tried to get his emotions under control. Travis looked Todd directly in the eyes before continuing. "When I saw her lying there and thought I might have lost her, I knew in my heart that I couldn't let that happen. I knew that if God's plan was for her to be okay, I needed to be honest about my feelings. That's why I spent most of the night in prayer and soul-searching."

"I was wondering how long it was going to take you to figure it out," Todd teased.

"How long have you known?"

"Me? I'm pretty perceptive about those things," Todd laughed. "I knew from the first time I saw you two together that you had more than a passing interest in my sister. But the day when Meghan spotted that pickup in the trees across the road, when your protective instincts kicked in immediately, that's when I knew you were in love with her."

"Since you seem to think you're so perceptive about those things, what about Meghan? Do you think she's interested in me?"

Todd stood and smiled. "Travis, that girl's crazy about you. And, yes, she loves you too. She just doesn't know it yet! Now why don't we go see how she's doing? I'm sure she's chomping at the bit to get out of here."

* * *

Meghan was sitting up in the hospital bed when her brother poked his head in the door. He looked behind him and said, "The party's in here. And the guest of honor is actually awake this time."

Travis followed Todd into the room and was pleased to see Meghan eagerly return his smile.

"Hey, guys," Meghan greeted, obviously still not herself. "I didn't expect to see you this morning."

Todd gave Travis a playful slap on the shoulder and said, "I'm surprised I didn't find this guy camped outside your door when I got here. But he did beat me here this morning, if only by a couple minutes."

Travis walked around the bed and immediately reached for

Meghan's hand. "How are you feeling this morning?"

"I have a headache," Meghan replied, chuckling as she touched the bandage on her head. "But I guess that's obvious, huh?"

"Yeah, we figured that would be the case. Dr. Patterson said you would probably have a horrible headache for a few days."

Todd sat in the chair beside the bed, looking intently at his sister. "Doc wants you to take it easy for a few days, so you're going to be staying at my place."

"That's not necessary, Todd. I'm fine. I just have a headache."

"I don't think you heard me, sis. I said you will be staying at my place for a few days. It's not open for debate. That was Doc's suggestion, and Travis and I both agree completely. In fact, I will probably work from home so I know you will be following Doc's orders. And, you don't just have a headache. You have a headache, and a concussion, and a gash on the side of your head that required twelve stitches to close. So, for the next week, you will be doing exactly what Travis and I tell you to do."

Meghan looked from her brother to Travis, hoping for an ally. Travis nodded his head in agreement and said, "He's right, Meg. You don't want to mess around with a head injury. You need to take it seriously and follow Dr. Patterson's instructions."

Disappointed in not finding an ally, she pulled her hand away, which made her wince. Letting out a sigh, she resigned. "Okay, you guys win." Travis smiled when she reached back out for his hand.

True to his character, Todd immediately wanted to address the elephant in the room. "What happened at the house yesterday, Meghan? And I want you to be honest with us. Don't tell us you fell off the ladder because neither of us will buy that story. Travis saw a dark-colored pickup speeding away from your house. Was it Danny?"

Meghan knew it was pointless to try and hide the truth from her brother. He could see through it every time. "Yes, it was Danny," she whispered.

Todd's face hardened instantly, and Meghan could feel Travis's grip on her hand tighten. "Tell us what happened."

"It was an accident, Todd. Just an accident. He didn't mean to hurt me."

"But he did hurt you," Travis interjected. "What happened?"

"I was getting ready to paint the living room, so I was up on the ladder, taping the drop cloth around the fireplace. I knew you were going to come over to help with the painting, Travis, so I didn't climb down from the ladder when I heard the front door open. I assumed it was you. When I looked around, there was Danny. I climbed down and asked what he was doing there. He told me the same old story, that he wanted another chance. He looked around and made some comment about it being unusual that I was at the house by myself. I asked if he had been spying on me and if that was him in the trees earlier. He didn't answer me. Anyway, I told him he needed to leave, and he grabbed me. I tipped over the ladder, hoping it would make him let go of me. When the ladder hit him in the shoulder, I was able to break free. But he caught me by the wrist. I pulled to get away, and he shoved the ladder. I tripped on the ladder and must have hit my head on the fireplace. I don't know what happened after that."

"What happened after that, sis, is that Travis arrived within a few minutes and called 911 and me. What happened was that you ended up in the Emergency Room because of Danny. What happened is that you have a concussion because of Danny. What's going to happen next is that we're going to get a restraining order against him because he can't seem to understand the meaning of 'stay away from you.'"

Travis could see that Todd was getting riled, so he decided to step in to give Todd a chance to regroup. "Meghan, this was the third time we know of that he has been over there harassing you. And we don't know how many times he has been hiding in the trees watching you. That's unacceptable. You can't be expected to live in fear of him showing up unannounced."

"I'm not afraid of Danny," Meghan replied, not even believing it herself. "And he only came onto the property twice."

"Let's not be splitting hairs, Meg. Had he been drinking when he surprised you at the house yesterday?"

Meghan didn't reply.

"Meghan? Answer me. Had he been drinking?"

"I think so. I was pretty sure I could smell alcohol."

Before Todd could reply, Travis stated, "He won't have another chance to surprise you. And he won't have another opportunity to hurt you. You won't be working at the house alone again."

"And we will be getting a restraining order to keep him away," Todd added.

Meghan became instantly defensive. "Neither of you have the right to tell me what to do!"

Travis tenderly stroked her shoulder and replied, "Meghan, Todd and I aren't trying to tell you what to do. We just want you to be safe. And until Danny realizes that it's over between you two, it's simply not safe for him to be around you. Especially when he's been drinking."

Meghan slumped back in the bed and admitted, "I know you're right. It's just that, how do I explain to Kaci that I have put a restraining order against her dad?"

"Kaci is a smart girl, sis. She will understand. I talked to her last night and told her what happened. After being assured that you would be okay, her first question was if her dad had anything to do with you getting hurt. I told her we didn't know what happened, but we'd let her know when we found out. You probably need to give her a call today after you get released so she knows for sure you're okay."

"I wish you wouldn't have called her, Todd, but I knew you would. Thanks."

"Knock, knock," said Dr. Patterson as he entered the room. "I see you have some early bird visitors this morning. How are you feeling, Meghan?"

"Other than a headache, I feel okay, Dr. Patterson."

"Well, let me give you a once-over, and if everything checks out, I don't see any reason you can't go home today."

Dr. Patterson checked her vital signs, checked her eyes, and removed the bandage covering the stitches, chatting with her the entire time. "Now you're going to feel like you've been kicked in the head by a mule for a few days, so I want you to take it easy. You will be staying with Todd for three or four days so people can keep an eye on you."

"Oh," replied Meghan, looking at her brother.

Dr. Patterson laughed when he saw the look on her face. "I see you were hoping Todd made that part up. He didn't. It was my idea. In fact, it's doctor's orders." Seeing the dejected look on Meghan's face softened his heart a bit. "Look at it this way, Meghan. It's better than being stuck here in the hospital, which is exactly where you would be if you didn't have a place to stay where you weren't alone. It won't be so bad. Your brother is a funny guy. I'm sure he will be able to keep you entertained. You should feel better in a couple days, but I don't want you doing any work on your house for the next week. Do you understand me?"

"Yes, I understand. I don't like it, but I understand."

"I don't expect you to like it. I just want you to do it. It's for your own good, Meghan."

"I know."

Dr. Patterson patted her on the shoulder and said, "I'm going to have the nurse come in to put a fresh bandage on your head. Keep that wound covered for a few days. I'll start working on the release orders so we can get you out of here."

That news put a smile on her face.

The two men shook hands with the doctor and thanked him for his care and compassion. Dr. Patterson had been Todd and Meghan's family doctor for years, so they felt very comfortable with him. Even though Travis had only known the good doctor for a few months, he had the utmost respect for him and knew him to be a godly man. That was all Travis needed to know.

"Well, sis, we're going to go down to the coffee shop and get some juice and a muffin, so you have a chance to get dressed. Then we'll be back to drag you kicking and screaming to my place."

"A muffin?" Meghan asked hopefully.

"Yeah," replied Todd teasingly. "I think I'll get one of those big spiced apple muffins. You know, the ones that have all that tasty maple frosting drizzled over the top. I know they're fresh because I could smell them when we came in."

Travis could see the love between brother and sister, even when Todd teased her mercilessly. "Don't worry, Meghan. I'll bring you a muffin. Maybe a chocolate muffin, filled with chocolate chips." Without thinking, Travis leaned over and placed a soft kiss on Meghan's forehead as naturally as if he had been doing it for years.

Todd simply smiled and gave his sister a playful wink as they left the room.

Chapter Twenty

Travis took Meghan by her apartment so she could pick up a few things she would need while staying with her brother. Todd headed directly to his place so he could fix up the spare bedroom and hopefully make his sister feel at home during her reluctant stay. Before long, Travis and Meghan pulled up in front of Todd's house. Meghan simply sat, staring straight ahead. Travis gently reached over and pulled her close. He knew this wasn't going to be easy for her. Even though she loved her brother completely, and knew he would do everything and anything he could for her, it was difficult to give up even a small bit of her independence.

"It will go quickly, Meg," Travis reassured her. "I promise."

"I don't know, Travis. I'm not used to just sitting around doing nothing."

"Well, maybe it's time to take a little 'me' time for a change," Travis replied with a grin.

About that time, the front door opened, and Todd yelled as he started down the sidewalk, "Are you two going to come in, or just sit out there and talk about it?"

Travis was already out of his truck and walking around to open the door for Meghan. He called over his shoulder, "If it was left up to your stubborn sister, we would still be sitting here talking about it."

"I have no doubt about that. If it was left up to her, she wouldn't be here at all. I think I should feel insulted." Todd winked at his sister as he reached into the truck and retrieved her bag.

As the three walked into the house, Todd said, "I have the spare bedroom fixed up for you, sis. I know it's not your own place, but at least it's not the hospital."

"Thanks, Todd," Meghan replied. She reached over and gave him a hug as he sat her bag down inside the bedroom. "I hope you don't think I don't appreciate it because I do. It's just that…"

"I know, Meg. I'll try to make it as painless as possible for you."

Meg looked around the bedroom that would be her home for the next few days. It was obvious Todd had been busy trying to make her feel at home. The room was spotless. There was a vase of fresh flowers on the bedside table, along with a small plate of chocolate chip cookies. Meghan looked over at Todd and smiled.

He grinned sheepishly as he said, "They're only store-bought cookies, so they won't be as good as yours."

"Have I told you recently that I think you're a pretty good brother?"

"Why don't you hold that thought? You might not feel that way at the end of the week."

Travis chuckled at their lighthearted banter. Meghan continued looking around the room, her eyes settling on a framed picture on the nightstand. She walked over, picked up the picture, and held it close to her heart. Travis stepped up beside her when he noticed she appeared close to tears. He reached over and tenderly pulled the picture away from her chest so he could see it. In the picture was a young Meghan, wearing a baseball cap and the biggest grin he had ever seen. She was holding a bat over one shoulder and leaning against a middle-aged man, also wearing a baseball cap, who had his arm around her shoulder and was sporting an equally big grin.

Travis looked from the picture to Meghan, then over to Todd, then back at the picture. The family resemblance was unmistakeable. "Is that your dad, Meghan?"

Todd had walked up beside her and put his arm around his sister's shoulder when she simply nodded. "I'm pretty sure that's her favorite picture of her and Dad."

"It is," Meghan whispered. "I love that picture." Her smile returned as she continued staring at the picture. "Dad coached one of our Little League teams. There were still a few old-timers around who didn't think girls should be allowed to play Little League baseball, even though the rules had been changed a few years earlier. That picture was taken after one of our playoff games. It was a great game."

"What my sister failed to mention is that she proved a thing or two to the skeptics in that game. Her team won the playoff game because of her two home runs."

"Well," she replied modestly, "it wasn't just my two home runs. We played really well that day."

"I don't think she stopped grinning for a week!" Todd said with obvious pride.

Travis sat the picture back down on the nightstand. "I can see why that's a favorite picture. It's a great picture. And it's obvious you and your dad were very happy."

"We had a lot of fun together, that's for sure!"

Todd steered them back to the living room as he said, "I need to run into the office for about an hour. I have a few things I need to take care of, but I won't be gone long. We need to establish a few ground rules before I leave."

Both men chuckled when they noticed Meghan's

stubbornness set in immediately. Travis tried to soften the blow a bit. "Maybe 'ground rules' isn't the best terminology. What your brother means is that we talked with Dr. Patterson, and he pretty much told us the conditions that were required for the next several days. So, we're simply following doctor's orders."

"You need to rest, sis," Todd explained. "And you can't be alone, especially for the first couple days after a head injury. So, Travis will stay with you while I run over to the office. I'm going to work from home for the next few days so you aren't alone. I have no doubt Becky and some of your friends from church will be stopping by to check up on you as well. So, you aren't going to be bored."

"I want to stop by the house and check on a couple things," Meghan protested.

"Meghan," Todd said a little too sternly, "Dr. Patterson said under no circumstances were you to be working at the house for at least a week. And I intend to make sure you follow doctor's orders."

"I didn't say I was going to work on anything. I just said I need to check on some things."

Travis interjected before Meghan had a chance to dig in her heels too deeply. "In a day or two, if you want, I can run you over to the house so you can make sure it's still there. You can check on anything you feel you need to check on, but you will not be doing any work. Not until next week."

"Even then, you will be taking it slow," Todd added. "And under no circumstances will you be working at the house alone. I will give you a day or two to rest first, but then we will be going down to get the restraining order against Danny. Enough is enough, sis."

Meghan slumped down into the recliner and agreed. "Fine."

"I'll be back in an hour or so," Todd said as he started toward the door. He reached out and patted Travis on the back. "It's going to be a long week, my friend."

Echoing the assurances he gave Meghan a short while earlier, Travis simply smiled and said, "It will go quickly. I promise."

* * *

Three days later, Travis pulled his pickup onto Meghan's property and stopped in front of the house. It had only been a few days, but to Meghan, it had seemed like a lifetime. They got out of the truck and Meghan walked away from the house, toward the road. She then turned and looked at the house, deep in thought. Travis walked up beside her and put his arm around her waist, pulling her close. She rested her head on his shoulder for a few quiet moments before looking back at the house.

Seemingly thinking out loud, rather than talking to anyone in particular, Meghan wondered, "Why does everything have to be so hard? Why is it that some people seem to always be fighting the odds, while others appear to skate through life without a care in the world? I have worked hard my whole life, and have always tried to do the right thing, and still, nothing comes easy. I'm not perfect, and I don't claim to be, but why can't I get a break occasionally? I don't get it."

She turned to look up at Travis. "You know, Travis, I used to be such an optimist. I used to think that I could do anything I wanted to do if I worked hard enough. Just like this house. I was convinced that if I wanted it bad enough, and worked hard enough, God would find a way to make it happen. Doesn't He understand how hard I've worked? Doesn't He understand I just want a normal life? Why are there always roadblocks? Sometimes I just get so tired."

Seeing the defeated look on her face, Travis's heart melted as he pulled her into a tight hug. He held her for a few moments before pointing toward the house. "When you first looked at this piece of property, Meghan, you didn't see a parcel of land with weeds up to your knees. You saw a dream. You had a vision of what it could become. You saw its potential.

"That's the way God looks at each one of us. He doesn't see our flaws and our weaknesses. He sees our potential. In a manner of speaking, just like this piece of dirt, we are all diamonds in the rough. On the surface, we may not look like much. But with some hard work and a little bit of polishing, we can shine like the brightest diamond. God knows our potential. He looks beyond the obvious, beyond the experiences that have taken a toll on our optimism. He looks at our character, our soul. And he looks through the loving eyes of a parent. Just like you want to bring out the best in this piece of ground, God wants to bring out the best in you. He has great plans for you, Meghan. Great plans, indeed. So don't you think otherwise."

Meghan looked at Travis hopefully. "Do you really think so, Travis? Do you really think God cares about me? Do you honestly think He wants me to be happy and have a normal life?"

"I have no doubt at all. Life isn't always easy, Meghan. You have had your share of trials, just like I've had my share. But I believe with all my heart that God wants each one of us to be happy. The trials we experience are necessary for us to become who God wants us to be. They are necessary so we learn to trust God, and to rely on Him. You are exactly where God wants you to be right now. And so am I."

Travis pulled Meghan close while he stared into her eyes, then bent down and gave her a tender kiss. As he pulled away, he smiled and said, "Oh, yeah, I am exactly where God wants me to be right now. Now, little lady, why don't we go check out your house so you can stop stressing about it." Travis took Meghan's hand, and they silently walked toward the house.

Meghan hesitated slightly when they stepped onto the front porch. "It's okay," Travis said as he took the key from her hand and put it in the lock. He unlocked the door then stood back, allowing Meghan to enter the house first. As soon as she walked into the living room, her eyes instantly went to the fireplace. She turned to look at Travis with a surprised and slightly relieved expression. There was no overturned ladder, no drop cloth taped to the fireplace and, more importantly, no signs of blood anywhere. In fact, the room was spotless. And freshly painted.

Travis grinned when she turned to him. He simply shrugged and stated matter-of-factly, "Todd and I had to have something to do while you were lounging around in the hospital. Besides, neither of us wanted you to walk back into this room the way it was left."

She quietly walked over and wrapped her arms around Travis, then reached up and kissed him gently. "You know, you continue to amaze me. Where have you been all my life?"

"Waiting for God's perfect timing," he replied with a smile.

Meghan reached for his hand and together they walked through the house, room by room, as she made mental notes of what still needed to be done. Occasionally Travis offered some input, but mostly he simply allowed her to do what she felt she needed to do. She did a lot of her thinking out loud, and Travis marveled at her abilities, her insight, and her work ethic. He knew that he and Todd would have their hands full trying to keep her from overdoing it. But he also knew they would find a way to protect her, at all costs. Even from herself.

Travis saw Meghan flinch as they heard the front door open. He started down the hallway ahead of Meghan, but had not gotten far before Todd called out. The two men had discussed ahead of time that they would be sure to announce themselves if they ever walked into the house when Meghan was there. They were sensitive to the fact that she would be understandably gun shy for a while.

"Well, sis," Todd began, smiling. "I see it didn't take you long to convince Travis to bring you over to the house."

Travis laughed in response. "You should have heard her yesterday! I have no doubt she would have walked over here if she thought she could have escaped our watchful eyes."

"Did you accomplish what you came over for?" Todd asked, looking at his sister, knowing full well her mind was still on the house.

"I think so," she replied. "Thanks for cleaning up the living room. That was my biggest concern. I'm glad you tidied things up and cleaned up the mess, but you didn't have to do the painting too."

"We were bored and had to do something while you were lounging around the hospital."

Meghan looked from her brother, over to Travis, then back at Todd. "Did you two compare notes or something? That's exactly what Travis said!"

The two men laughed, as Travis confirmed, "She's right, you know. That's almost word for word exactly what I said not twenty minutes ago."

Meghan's eyes were still scanning the inside of the house. "Do you think I can come over tomorrow and work for a little while?"

"No way!" Todd responded adamantly.

"Absolutely not!" Travis added quickly. "Dr. Patterson said no working on the house until at least next week. And Todd and I plan to make sure you follow doctor's orders."

"I was just going to –"

"No!" Todd cut her off. He softened his tone as he continued.

"Listen, sis, I know you better than anyone. I understand that you want to be over here working on the house. I also know that you want to get moved in before winter. And I know that you are working in your head, even if you are supposedly resting at my place. But it's only for a few more days. It's important that you do what Dr. Patterson said. You know that. I will personally make sure you are able to move in before winter. Everything is coming together. Don't worry so much. Now, on another note, are you finished here for now?"

"I guess. There's not much you will let me do anyway."

"You're right. Are you up to going over to the police department? We need to get that restraining order filed. The sooner, the better."

"Do you really think that's necessary, Todd?"

"Yes, I do. We've already discussed this, Meg. It has to be done. Danny has to understand that he needs to stay away from you."

Travis hated seeing the defeated look on Meghan's face. He pulled her close and said, "I'll go with you, too. It shouldn't take long. But Todd's right. It's not safe for Danny to be around you."

"Okay," she agreed reluctantly. "Let's get it over with."

* * *

The next few days dragged by slowly, with Meghan becoming increasingly antsy every day. She was looking forward to getting back to the house, even if it was going to be for light duty. Little did she know Todd and Travis had been subtly delaying her return, hoping to put it off a few more days until after Kaci returned from summer camp. Todd had gone to the office for a few hours, and Travis was making some lunch in the kitchen. Meghan walked up behind Travis just as he was putting sandwiches and fruit on a tray.

She reached around him and plucked a fresh strawberry from the bowl. "Travis, I want to go back to my apartment this afternoon."

"I could stop by and pick something up for you if you'd like."

"No," she replied. "I mean I want to go home. Dr. Patterson said I needed to stay with Todd for three or four days. It's been almost a week. I want to go home and sleep in my own bed. I don't need a babysitter."

"Have you talked to Todd about that?"

"No," she replied as she looked away.

Travis grinned as he stepped around so she could see him. "You're hoping I will say yes before you mention it to Todd, right?"

She smiled. "Maybe."

"Mention what to me?" Todd asked as he stepped into the kitchen.

"I didn't know you were coming home for lunch," Meghan stated innocently.

"Obviously," Todd replied with a grin. "What have you been plotting behind my back?"

Meghan looked at Travis, silently pleading for an ally.

"She was just saying that she has been here longer than the doctor required, and she wants to go home. Oh, and something about not needing a babysitter."

Todd plopped a grape into his mouth and grabbed a tuna sandwich from the tray. He leaned back against the counter as he chewed slowly, seeming to be in no real hurry to consider his sister's request. "So, you don't think you need a babysitter, huh?"

Meghan tried to sound forceful, but fell short in her attempt. "No, I don't. I'm not a little kid, Todd."

"Be honest with me, sis. If you were alone at your apartment, and had no one around to make sure you were taking it easy, what would you be doing right now?"

Meghan considered trying to bluff her way around his question, but knew her brother well enough to know that would never work. So, she decided to use her backup plan – humor. "That just shows how much you know, Mr. Smarty-Pants. I wouldn't even be at my apartment. I would be at the house. Working. Probably painting, in fact. Maybe even up on a ladder."

Travis laughed out loud, as Todd just about choked on his sandwich. "Well, Todd, you did ask her to be honest!"

"I sure did! Well, you apparently are still able to think quickly, so there must not be any permanent damage to that thick skull of yours!"

"Yeah, yeah," she retorted. "I love you too, little brother."

"Since you were honest with me, I suppose I should be honest with you. I've been purposely dragging my feet on allowing you to go home. For the exact reason you just pointed out. When do you have to pick up Kaci from Camp MiVoden?"

"On Thursday."

"Okay. That's still three days away. I will agree to let you go back to your place this afternoon on two conditions. First, you will not go over to the house today. Second, for the next two days, you will only be at the house when one of us is with you. And that will be for no longer than four hours on either day. Can you live with that?"

"Do I have a choice?" she asked, already knowing the answer.

"Nope. Those are the conditions. And by the way, in case you have any idea of twisting that to mean you can work at the house alone *after* the two days are up, don't go there. You will not be working at the house by yourself. Period. Do you agree to those conditions?"

"Grudgingly, but yes."

"Okay, little bird, fly! Be free! But eat some lunch first."

Travis couldn't help but chuckle as Meghan began dancing around the kitchen, imitating a bird in flight.

Suddenly she stopped, in midflight. "I just thought of something. It's a long drive to MiVoden and back. Do you think I should ask Dr. Patterson if it's okay for me to drive that far? I feel fine."

Travis reached for a sandwich from the tray and put it into her hands, knowing that she probably would forget to eat otherwise. As he expected, she began eating, but her mind was already going a hundred miles an hour. "Todd and I already talked about that. I will have my sermon done by then so I will go with you. We can either take my pickup or your Jeep, whichever you prefer. Either way, I plan to drive so you can relax."

"Let's take my Jeep. Can you take me back to my apartment now?"

"Todd, your sister is hopeless," Travis laughed, shaking his head.

"I know," he agreed as he tugged his sister's ponytail. "But she's cute."

"You're right about that, Todd. She is definitely cute!"

Chapter Twenty-One

Travis picked up Meghan bright and early Thursday morning. It was a nearly five-hour drive to Camp MiVoden, so they needed to get an early start since they would be making the round trip in one day. Christian music played softly on the Jeep's radio, which made for a nice relaxing drive. About an hour into the trip, Meghan adjusted her seat so she could lean back and rest. Within a few minutes, she was sleeping soundly. Travis quietly hummed along with the worship songs, feeling content and happy.

Dear God, even though I wish Meghan had not experienced the difficulties she has in her life, I am grateful You have protected her. Just as I am grateful You have always watched over me. Losing Angela and Levi was the most devastating thing I've ever experienced, and it nearly killed me. But You never let me give up, and You never left me to deal with it alone. When I thought I might lose Meghan, it brought back all those awful feelings again. I don't think I could survive losing her too. But You protected her from Danny, and provided an opportunity for me to admit my feelings for her. I know you brought us together, and I am confident in Your perfect timing she will hopefully realize and admit her feelings for me as well.

Meghan began to stir in the seat next to him, and Travis

glanced over to see if she was awake. "Hey, sleepyhead," he greeted with a smile. "You must have needed some rest. You've been sleeping for a couple hours."

"Really? It only seems like I've been asleep for a few minutes."

"No, you got in a pretty good nap. That's good because that stretch of the trip is a little boring anyway."

"I agree, which is why I should have stayed awake for you. If I'm driving that stretch by myself, I sometimes really struggle with staying awake. I'm sorry I fell asleep and couldn't keep you company."

"That's okay. It gave me some time to think and meditate. There's a rest area coming up in a few miles. Did you want to take a break and stretch a bit?"

"I've apparently already had my break," Meghan answered with a chuckle. "But let's stop anyway. I'm sure you could use a break and we can both stretch our legs."

Once at the rest area, they used the opportunity to take a short walk and get some fresh air. They would soon be entering the more forested area, so the scent of pine trees could already be detected in the air. Meghan took a few minutes to give Kaci a call to make sure they were all on the same schedule.

As they walked back to the Jeep, Meghan told Travis about her phone call with Kaci. "Kaci said she's all packed up and ready to go whenever we get there. She loves going to camp and loves working with the kids, but she's usually ready to come back home by the end of the summer."

"And no doubt Mom is ready for her to get home too," Travis said teasingly.

"No doubt! I have to admit that I miss her when she's gone. I've gotten kind of used to having her around."

"She will be amazed at how much work you've gotten done

on the house since she left. She probably won't recognize it."

"Oh, she'll recognize it alright. She made a point of telling me that we have talked about it so much, and done so much preliminary planning that she would be able to recognize it right away. She did ask me to let her pick out the paint and carpeting for her bedroom though. She wants to paint it herself. And she wanted to pick out the paint color for the family room as well. So those things will be on the agenda in the next couple days, I'm sure."

"By the time she gets back and has a chance to regroup, and you take her down to get the paint, you should be able to resume a normal schedule again."

"I certainly hope so. All this sitting around is making me fat and sassy!"

"Well," he said much too quickly. "Maybe a bit sassy!"

"You be careful there, mister, or I'll be putting you to work painting and laying carpet!"

"Hopefully you have a paintbrush that fits my hand," he replied jokingly. He then opened the car door for her, gave her a soft kiss on the forehead, and began whistling as he walked around to the driver's door.

* * *

True to her word, Kaci was ready to go when they pulled into the parking lot in front of the administration building. Meghan got out of the Jeep and hurried over to give her daughter a big hug. A very long hug.

"You look great, kiddo! The sun definitely agrees with you. Boy, have I missed you!"

Kaci laughed as she gave her mom another hug and said, "I've missed you too, Mom. I've gotten used to having you around."

Travis looked from Kaci to Meghan, shook his head, and chuckled softly. They were most definitely two peas in a pod. He bent over and picked up her duffle bag in one hand and her sleeping bag in the other. "Is this little pile all your things, Kaci? You don't travel like most girls."

"Hi Pastor Harmon," Kaci greeted. "I like to travel light. It makes packing and unpacking a lot easier! I learned that from Mom. The two of us can go on a trip for a week and only need one bag apiece. And our pillows, of course." She then grabbed her pillow. "We have to have our pillows!"

Kaci grabbed her backpack, and Meghan picked up the remaining small duffle bag then they stowed everything in the back of the Jeep. "Do we need to sign you out, kiddo?" Meghan asked.

"Yeah, safety procedures, you know."

"I figured as much," Meghan responded as she headed toward the building. "I'll be back in a minute then we can hit the road."

As soon as Meghan was out of earshot, Kaci turned to Travis and asked, "So, how is Mom doing? Really. I know she will sugarcoat things, so I want to get the straight scoop from you."

"Todd's right," Travis replied. "Not much gets past you. But I don't think you need to worry. Your mom is doing great. Todd and I had our hands full making sure she obeyed Dr. Patterson's orders, but we all survived."

"I bet that was fun!" Kaci said with a laugh. "Mom does *not* like to sit around doing nothing! She's like a caged animal if she's forced to take a break and relax!"

"That's an understatement!" Travis agreed. "You'd have thought we were torturing her those first three days when she wasn't allowed to go over to the house! She was finally able to work over there for a few hours the past couple days, and she was in heaven. She doesn't really like the fact that we won't let her be over there working by herself though. She's one independent lady!"

Kaci laughed. "I hope you're not just now figuring that out!"

"No, I figured that out the first time I met her!"

"Did Mom get a restraining order against Dad?"

"Yes, she did. That wasn't a pleasant battle either. But your Uncle Todd and I refused to back down on that one. She wasn't happy about it, but I think she realized it was something that needed to be done. I think she was more concerned about what you would think than anything else."

"I know," Kaci replied in understanding. "She always thinks of me before she thinks of herself. But Dad can be violent at times, especially when he's drinking. I saw a lot of that growing up. She doesn't need to deal with that."

Travis put his arm around Kaci's shoulder and said, "You're a remarkable young lady, Kaci. Your mom is very lucky to have you."

"I'm the lucky one. Mom is amazing. She works so hard all the time and never asks for anything from anyone. She deserves the best of everything. She deserves that house. She has worked really hard for it, and I can't wait to see her face when it's finally finished, and we can move in. Then maybe she can relax a little."

When Meghan stepped out of the administration building, she looked across the parking lot and loved what she saw. Travis was standing next to Kaci, with his arm around her shoulder.

They look so natural together, she thought to herself. *They look like any other father and daughter at camp. He's such a good man. He would be a great father.*

Her thoughts were interrupted when Kaci yelled playfully across the parking lot. "Come on, Mom! A girl could starve out here. It's lunchtime!"

"Well, we certainly can't have that!" Meghan replied as she approached. She looked at Travis. "I suppose you're starving too?"

"Yes, ma'am!" he replied.

"Can the two of you wait about twenty miles? There's a great family restaurant in the little town just down the road."

Kaci agreed excitedly. "Michael's has the best food! And incredible peach pie!"

"Well, Michael's it is then," Travis agreed. "Load up, ladies. I believe there's a slice of peach pie that has my name on it!" He opened the doors for both of the ladies and gave Meghan a quick kiss on the cheek before closing her door. Kaci didn't miss it and smiled at him. He winked at her, then closed the door, leaving her smiling in the back seat.

* * *

Travis watched patiently as mother and daughter perused the paint chips like two kids in a candy store. After much debate, Kaci finally settled on a pale sea mist green for her bedroom, and a soft gray-brown tone that reminded her of the sand on the beach. Both good choices, and typical of Kaci's taste. When it was time to pick the color for the carpeting, Meghan guided her daughter to the neutral tones, knowing full well the room would be repainted at some point.

As they left the hardware store, each carrying a bucket of paint, Kaci asked, "Can we start painting my bedroom today, Mom?"

Meghan looked to Travis before answering. "I need to see what your Uncle Todd's schedule is first."

"Maybe Pastor Harmon isn't busy," Kaci said, looking

hopefully at Travis.

"I am at your disposal for the entire afternoon," Travis replied, grinning.

"Yay!" Kaci yelled excitedly. "We can paint my bedroom first because then we can schedule delivery of the carpet. Since we will be laying the tile ourselves, we can paint the family room while the bedroom carpeting is being installed."

Travis couldn't help but laugh out loud. "Meghan, you have created a miniature planner just like you!"

"It does tend to run in the family," she said with a chuckle.

Before long the three were spreading drop cloths and prepping Kaci's bedroom for painting. The way they tackled the task at hand, an outsider would think they had been working as a team for years. The ceiling had been painted at the same time as the ceilings in the other rooms, so Travis got to work with the trimming, while Kaci and Meghan took rollers to the walls. In no time at all, the room was finished. Kaci was eager to get started on the family room, which was the last room in the house yet to be painted. Knowing that Meghan was still technically on light duty, and it was already midafternoon, Travis suggested they get the family room prepped and ready to go, but save the painting for the next day.

They were just finishing the prep work in the family room when the front door opened, and Todd walked in. Kaci ran over to Todd and gave him a hug. "Hi, Uncle Todd!"

Returning the hug, Todd gave a little jerk on her ponytail and said, "Hey, munchkin. I heard you got back from camp yesterday, so I figured you would probably be over here working already."

Kaci grinned at her favorite uncle and stated proudly, "We just finished painting my bedroom. You should see it. It's beautiful!"

"Lead the way, kiddo. Let's check it out." As he passed

Meghan, Todd gave her ponytail a tug as well. "Hey, sis, glad to see you made it back okay. I see it didn't take you long to get a crew over here."

"This was Kaci's idea," Meghan explained. "Once we had the paint buckets in hand, there was no putting it off until another day."

Todd looked skeptical because he knew his sister. But Travis backed up her story. "She's right about that one, Todd. We just finished Kaci's room and that kid was ready to get started on the family room!"

"Yeah," Todd said in understanding. "That poor kid is just like her mother!"

Meghan reached out to slap Todd on the arm, but he side-stepped just as Kaci yelled from the top of the stairs. "Come on, Uncle Todd! You were going to look at my room."

"On my way, kiddo," he said chuckling. "Yep, just like her mother!"

Chapter Twenty-Two

The last few days of summer gave way to early fall where the slightly cooler mornings reminded everyone that winter wasn't far away. Meghan loved the Indian summers around Hope. Fall was in the air, but the weather was still nice and warm during the day and into the early evening. It was her favorite time of the year. School was back in full swing and, with it, all the extra-curricular activities around town. Soccer fields, tracks, and football fields were busy places in the afternoon as parents returned to juggling the schedules of work and busy kids.

Meghan had wasted no time getting back into her routinely hectic lifestyle. Since bringing Kaci home from camp, Meghan had thrown herself into working on the house, working at the construction company, and doing design work on the side. True to their words, Todd and Travis made sure Meghan was never at the house alone. Until school started back up, Kaci and her mom worked side by side finishing the house. All the hard work that had gone into their dream was beginning to pay off. The house was nearly finished.

Meghan pulled her Jeep onto the property, seeing that Todd was already there talking to the landscaper. In the past few weeks, they had poured the sidewalks, planted trees and shrubbery, put in underground sprinklers, and paved the driveway. The sod was being laid today, and that would finish the landscaping. Meghan leaned against the Jeep and stuck her hands into the front pockets of her Levis. She smiled, knowing the completion of her dream was so close she could almost smell it. That's how Travis saw her when he parked his pickup beside the Jeep.

"That doesn't look like the smile of someone who will be laying sod all day," Travis joked as he leaned over to give Meghan a kiss.

"You're right," she agreed, returning the kiss. "It's the smile of someone who can almost taste victory. We're almost there, Travis. I can't believe it, but the house is almost finished. There's no way I could have done it without your help. And Todd. You two have been nothing short of a gift from God."

Travis put his arm around Meghan's shoulder and held her close. "God has certainly been spreading gifts around. A year ago, I never could have imagined the changes He had in store for me. God is good."

"All the time," Meghan finished with a smile.

Todd stopped at his pickup to take off his jacket then continued down the driveway toward Meghan and Travis. "I hope you two plan to do more than lean against the Jeep today. There's plenty of sod to go around."

"Well, then," Travis replied enthusiastically, "the sooner we get started, the sooner we'll get it done!"

The three pulled on their gloves and headed over to where the landscapers were beginning to pull rolls of sod off pallets. They were completely unaware of the dark pickup parked down the street, just outside the restrictions imposed by the restraining order.

* * *

Danny sighed as he sat the binoculars on the seat beside him. He had to find a way to talk to Meghan. To explain. To ask her to forgive him. After all, she's a Christian. She has to forgive him. But he knew Todd well enough to know that he would never allow him to talk to her. He didn't really want to take a chance of breaking the restraining order, but he saw no other way. It looked like they were finished laying sod and the landscapers were getting ready to leave.

I guess it's now or never, he thought to himself. *I just hope I don't end up sleeping in a jail cell tonight.* Danny took a deep breath, started the truck, put it in gear, and pulled slowly out into the street.

* * *

Travis noticed that Meghan had suddenly turned very pale, and he thought maybe she had overdone it today. "Are you okay, Meg?"

Meghan didn't reply. She simply pointed toward the street. Travis looked in the direction she was pointing and saw the dark pickup stop on the street in front of the house.

"Todd," he called. "It looks like we have a visitor."

Todd had been washing the last of the dirt off the sidewalk with a hose and looked up when he heard Travis. He immediately started toward Travis and Meghan, mumbling under his breath the entire way.

He came up beside the others and said, "What is it going to take for that guy to get the message?" Travis was standing on one side of Meghan, and Todd stepped up to the other side. Both men stood with their feet planted shoulder-width apart and their hands on their hips. There was no way Danny was going to get near

Meghan.

Danny slowly opened the door of his truck and got out. He looked toward the house and immediately began to rethink the wisdom of his actions. The two men were imposing forces, and it was obvious they had no intention of letting him near Meghan.

Before moving away from his truck and setting foot on her property, Danny called out to them. "Todd, I just want to talk to Meghan. I won't touch her. I just want to talk to her."

"If you think you're ever going to get close enough to touch her again," Todd said matter-of-factly, "you're crazier than I ever thought you were."

"Can I come over there, so we don't have to scream? Please? I just want to talk to her."

Todd and Travis exchanged glances then looked at Meghan. She nodded ever so slightly.

"Okay, Danny," Todd said. "You have five minutes. And keep in mind that we can and will call 911 if you get out of line. Although I'm pretty sure we can take care of things before they get here. So, keep that in mind."

"I will," Danny replied as he slowly walked toward the threesome.

As Danny approached, Todd and Travis instinctively moved in front of Meghan. "Can I at least look at her when I talk to her?" he protested.

"She can hear you just fine," Travis stated. "Just say what you have to say then leave."

Danny let out a heavy sigh. "Meghan, I'm sorry. It was an accident. I didn't mean to hurt you. It was just an accident. You know I would never hurt you deliberately."

"Yeah, right," Meghan said under her breath.

"Lying isn't going to help your case any, Danny," Todd advised. "She has ended up in the emergency room on more than one occasion because of you. I would suggest you try to be honest for once in your life. Say what you need to say then leave."

"Meghan…" Danny tried again. "I'm sorry. You have no idea how badly I felt when I saw you lying on the floor bleeding because of me."

"Yeah," Travis interjected with muffled anger. "You felt so sorry that you took off and left her lying there instead of getting help."

"I know, and I'm sorry about that too." Danny looked between the two men in an attempt to read Meghan's face. "I had been drinking and was feeling sorry for myself. Sorry for the mess I've made of my life. Sorry that my drinking cost me my wife and daughter. Sorry for all the times I hurt you, physically and emotionally. I realize there's nothing I can do that will make up for that. But I need you to know that because of that accident, it forced me to make some changes in my life. I haven't had a drink in over a week. And I hope that, with God's help, I'll never drink again."

Danny let out another heavy sigh as he tried to regroup. "Meghan, I know I can't undo the damage I've done to you and Kaci. I wish I could, but I know I can't. I also wish we could start over again." Danny looked straight at Travis as he continued. "But I also see that's not possible. You have moved on. Even though I wish things were different, I'm really happy that it looks like you have found someone who deserves you. You deserve the best, Meghan. You always have. You just never got it from me. Not because you didn't try. You did everything you could. I just wasn't able to give you what you deserve. Maybe this guy can. I hope so. I also hope that you will allow me to try to rebuild my relationship with Kaci. I know I've never been the dad she deserves, but maybe we can find a new starting point and move forward. I would like to try. But that's up to you. And to Kaci.

That's all I wanted to say, so I'll go now. Again, I'm really sorry about everything. And I hope someday you will be able to forgive me."

Danny turned to walk back to his truck just as Meghan stepped out from behind Todd and Travis. "Wait, Danny."

He stopped and slowly turned to face Meghan. She no longer seemed to be afraid of him. Her face had regained its color, and the spark in her eyes had returned. "You're right, Danny," she began. "You will never be able to undo the damage you have done to me and Kaci. Some of those wounds are pretty deep." Travis stepped up beside her and put his protective arm around her shoulder. "You're also right in realizing that your chances of starting over with us are nonexistent. That's never going to happen. The best you can hope for is that Kaci will allow you to apologize to her and maybe move forward. But that's entirely up to her, and you *will* apologize to her before you even ask if there's any chance of a future relationship. You owe our daughter that much."

"I know," Danny agreed contritely.

"You're also right about something else," Meghan continued as she looked to Travis. "I have moved on. And I plan to continue moving on with my life. Hopefully to the life God has in mind for me, a happy and contented life. Because you see, Danny, God has great plans for me. He knows my potential, and He knows my heart. He wants me to have all the joys of my heart, and He will be with me every step of the way."

"I'm really glad, Meghan," Danny said honestly. "You deserve it."

Danny turned once again to leave, and Meghan called out to him one last time. "Yes, Danny, I forgive you. And I really hope someday you will find peace and can start to rebuild your life."

"Thanks," Danny replied with a wistful smile. "I hope so

too."

The three stood in silence for a few moments as they watched Danny drive down the street. Todd was the first to break the silence. "Well, that wasn't at all what I expected."

"Me neither," Meghan agreed. "Do you think he was sincere about it?"

"I don't know the man, other than the few negative encounters we've had recently," Travis offered. "But his remorse seemed genuine to me. Most of the time it takes a tragic or upsetting event to convince people it's time to make some changes. Maybe that's what it took for him. Unfortunately."

Meghan looked at Todd. "Do you think we can remove the restraining order?"

"He has a lot of history, Meg," Todd answered. "All of it bad. That isn't going to disappear because of one seemingly heartfelt apology. He gets points for the apology, but I think we need to give it a little more time and see what he does."

"Okay," she said reluctantly. "I suppose you're right. What do I do about Kaci? I don't want him trying to contact her when I'm not around."

"For what it's worth, Meg," Travis offered. "Somehow, I don't think you're going to have to worry about that. I think he will try to contact either you or Todd before he makes any attempt to talk to Kaci."

"I think Travis is right, sis. The restraining order keeps him away from both you and Kaci. I suspect he will contact me if he really does intend to try to make things right with her. What do you say we call it a day? It's been a very long day. Physically and emotionally. Do you think you'll be okay tonight? You and Kaci can stay at my place if you want to."

"Thanks, Todd," she replied. "But I'm fine. I just want to go home, take a long hot shower, and curl up with a good book. I think Kaci was planning to make spaghetti for dinner tonight. Do you guys want to come over for dinner?"

"You know, sis, that sounds a lot better than whatever I can scrounge up in my fridge at home."

Travis wasted no time accepting the offer as well. "I agree with Todd. If you're sure it's okay with Kaci, and she was fixing enough. I can bring over some ice cream for dessert."

Meghan laughed. "Kaci always fixes lots of spaghetti whenever she makes it! I have no doubt there will be plenty. Why don't you guys go get cleaned up and plan to meet over at the apartment around six-thirty. I'll let Kaci know to set a couple extra plates at the table. She'll be thrilled!"

Travis walked Meghan to the Jeep then pulled her into his arms. "I'm real proud of you, Meghan."

She looked at him quizzically, not quite sure what he was referring to.

"You stood up for yourself with Danny and told him exactly what you expected from him as it relates to Kaci. You didn't let him off the hook. And you made it very clear that things are over between the two of you. There is absolutely no chance of reconciliation. I was glad to hear you say that. But what I'm most proud of is the fact that you told him you forgave him. That's a big step, Meghan. And that's not always easy. He hurt you deeply over the years and a lot of people would have a hard time with forgiveness."

"Just because I forgive him doesn't mean I'll ever forget the damage he has done to me and Kaci."

"Just because you forgive someone doesn't mean you accept their behavior. And it doesn't mean their behavior is excusable. It simply means you will no longer allow their behavior to destroy you. You are ready to move on with your life. That's a huge step, Meghan. It's very liberating."

"I suppose you're right," she said smiling. "You are a very wise man, Travis," she said as she got into the Jeep. "And I wise man will not forget the ice cream when he shows up for dinner tonight."

"I won't forget," he replied as he leaned over to give her a kiss. "You might not forgive me for something like that!"

The sound of her sweet laughter as she backed down the driveway put a smile on his face and in his heart.

I told you that you would know when your heart was healed, and you could move on. It's time. The thought didn't surprise Travis this time. He knew God was right. As always.

I know, God. Thank you for not allowing me to give up. Thank you for helping me to wait on Your timing. And thank you for bringing Meghan into my life. You always know what's best for me. I won't let her get away. I'm going to marry that girl. Even after a long day, Travis walked to his pickup with a spring in his step and a song on his heart.

Chapter Twenty-Three

Meghan stood in the front yard of their new home with her arm around Kaci's shoulder, looking toward the house. The Indian summer was now a distant memory as the crisp mornings were causing the ground to be covered with beautiful fall leaves. Luckily, no snow had fallen yet, even though Thanksgiving was only a few days away. She and Kaci had been packing up their apartment for the past week, and today was moving day. At least the beginning of the move. Todd and Travis had loaded furniture into their pickups this morning, and the Jeep was loaded with boxes.

"Well, kiddo," Meghan began, "it looks like we did it. We finished our dream home. There's still work ahead of us, but the bulk of it is now behind us."

"It looks great, Mom!" Kaci agreed with obvious excitement. "I can't wait to get moved in and get my room set up."

"It will be a busy weekend, that's for sure," Meghan stated. "It would be nice to have things fairly well organized before Thanksgiving, but we'll do what we can. If we can get all the furniture over here today, that will be a big step in the right direction."

As if on cue, Todd and Travis pulled up out front and were

now backing down the driveway. Todd stopped alongside Meghan and lowered the window on his pickup. "I think it would be better to take most of the furniture into the house from the back deck. We could open the French doors that way, and it would give us more room to maneuver things."

"Whatever you guys think would work best," Meghan agreed. "That's probably a good idea. Kaci and I can take the boxes from the Jeep in through the front door so we won't get in the way while you're moving furniture. Do you think you and Travis can move the furniture by yourselves? Kaci and I can help if you need us. A lot of it has to go upstairs."

"We'll be fine, sis," Todd assured her. "A couple guys from the shop will be here in a few minutes to help. You girls get the boxes out of the Jeep then go ahead and go back for more boxes. Don't worry about the furniture. We'll get it."

"You know which rooms everything goes in, don't you?"

"Yes, we do," Travis said as he walked up beside her. "We purposely loaded all the bedroom furniture first. That way we can get all the furniture upstairs before we run out of gas."

By the time Meghan and Kaci had hauled all the boxes into the house from the Jeep, the guys had unloaded Todd's pickup and were working on Travis's pickup. Once the guys from the shop showed up, things went quickly. Meghan had just gotten back to the apartment when the men showed up with empty pickups, ready for the second load. It was definitely true that "many hands make light work."

Much to Meghan's surprise, by the end of the day, her apartment had been completely emptied. Everything was now at the house. The men had put together both beds and arranged all the bedroom furniture. They had also arranged all the furniture in the living and family rooms, as well as the dining room. They were even able to get Kaci's piano into the family room, which had been no small feat.

Just as the chairs were being placed around the dining room table, finishing the last of the furniture, the doorbell rang. Meghan looked at Todd and Travis and said, "I wonder who that could be."

"I'll get it, Mom," Kaci offered as she headed toward the front door.

She returned a few moments later carrying boxes containing four large pizzas. "Dad brought pizza for everyone!" she explained. "He went back to his truck to get the drinks."

Danny walked in toting a cooler filled with ice and an assortment of soda, juice, and iced tea. By way of explanation, he said, "Kaci told me you would be moving today. I figured by the end of the day you would all be too tired to cook. Pizza is always a good answer for moving day."

Tied to the handle of the cooler was a plastic bag containing paper plates, napkins, and a few forks he brought from his place. Kaci laughed as she handed one of the forks to her mom. "I see Dad remembered you eat your pizza with a fork, Mom. You're such a goofball. No one eats pizza with a fork!"

"Hey, wait a minute!" protested Travis. "I'll take one of those forks."

Kaci rolled her eyes. "Don't tell me you eat pizza with a fork too?"

"I do today," Travis laughed. "I wouldn't want your mom to be the only goofball in the house!"

They all enjoyed a laugh at Meghan's expense, but she didn't seem to mind at all. It had been a good day. Lots of friends and family had made the move go smoothly. Tomorrow they could concentrate on unpacking. Even Danny had managed to be helpful without being intrusive. As she looked around the dining room table and listened to the various conversations and friendly banter, she realized just how lucky she was. Very lucky, indeed.

* * *

Meghan had been right. It turned out to be a very long weekend. They spent their first night in the house, sleeping in their own beds, thanks to Todd and Travis. By the end of the day, they were too exhausted to do any unpacking. The unpacking would have to wait. They needed to go over to the apartment to clean so they could get completely checked out and get their deposit back. As Meghan and Kaci walked up to the front door of their apartment, they were surprised to see the door partially open. They were even more surprised to hear music coming from inside. Meghan cautiously pushed the door open, and they walked into the living room.

"Hello?" she called out.

She heard faint laughter over the music that appeared to be coming from the kitchen. Kaci looked at her mom and said, "That sounds like Mrs. Gilbert's laugh."

Meghan looked confused as she replied, "I think you're right."

About that time, Shannon Gilbert walked around the corner. She reached out and gave Meghan a friendly hug before joking, "Isn't that just like you to show up when the work is nearly done!"

Again, Meghan looked confused. Kaci called out from the kitchen, "Mom, you're going to want to come see this."

Shannon took Meghan by the arm, and they walked toward the kitchen. Leaning against the kitchen counters were four other women, all wearing smiles. The women stepped away from the counters, revealing a very large centerpiece, done in fall and winter colors.

"What is all this?" Meghan asked in surprise.

Doris replied with excitement, "We came over to surprise you. We cleaned the entire apartment and brought a new centerpiece for your dining room table at the new house. New house, new centerpiece. It makes sense, don't you think?"

"It certainly does! It's beautiful!" Meghan replied in agreement. She gave each of her friends a big hug. "But how did you know I would be here today? And how did you get in?"

Shannon laughed, shaking her head. "Are you serious, Meg? We've all been friends long enough to know how you operate. You were able to empty the apartment entirely yesterday, so we knew you would want to get it cleaned today so you could cross that off your list. And that sweet brother of yours let us in. We need to find a wife for that boy! He's quite a catch!"

"Oh no!" Meghan replied quickly. "You're not the first one of my friends to suggest that. Todd has made it very clear that I am to stay out of his love life!"

"Hmmm, I think there's a loophole," Shannon said with a grin. "He said you were to stay out of his love life. He didn't say anything about your friends."

"Well," Meghan said as she smiled. "You little matchmakers just leave me out of it!"

The ladies started toward the door, and Doris waved her hand dismissively. "Yeah, yeah. Don't you worry. We won't tell you a thing."

Meghan simply shook her head, knowing the little band of matchmakers probably already had some unsuspecting young lady in mind.

As they headed to their car, Shannon said, "Everything is finished over here. Now you can go home and work on something more important. Like unpacking."

"Thank you all!" Meghan replied. "I don't know what I'd do without such great friends." Meghan turned to Kaci and said,

"Well, kiddo, it looks like we're done here. You can help me load that beautiful centerpiece into the Jeep, and I guess we can go home and start the unpacking."

Kaci sighed. "Home. That sure has a nice ring to it, doesn't it, Mom?"

"Yes, it does. Home in time for the holidays. We have certainly been blessed."

* * *

It required a lot of work, but by the time Thanksgiving arrived a few days later, Meghan and Kaci had the house looking fabulous. All the unpacking had been done, pictures were up on the walls, and the decorating was complete. It made a huge difference that Kaci was out of school for Thanksgiving break, so the two of them worked together to get the house ready for the holidays.

Meghan had decided to make Thanksgiving a low-scale affair so they could concentrate on having a big Christmas in their new home. She and Kaci cooked a traditional Thanksgiving dinner, with all the trimmings, but scaled it down for four people.

Todd and Travis joined the girls for Thanksgiving dinner. They enjoyed a relaxing meal then watched a football game on the television in the family room. Travis had just finished getting a nice fire going in the fireplace when Meghan brought out a tray with plates of pumpkin and Dutch apple pie.

"With all the work you've been doing for the past few days, you managed to find time to bake two different kinds of pie?" Travis asked in amazement.

Todd chuckled. "She didn't really have a choice, Travis."

"Oh, really?"

Kaci was the one who jumped in to clear up the confusion for Travis. "Uncle Todd is right. Mom didn't really have a choice.

You see, Uncle Todd insists you must have pumpkin pie with whipped cream for Thanksgiving. It's almost sacrilege if you don't! Mom doesn't really care for pumpkin pie, so she always makes Dutch apple pie too, because that's her favorite."

"Ah," Travis said in understanding. "So, what that really means is that I get to eat a slice of both kinds of pie because they are my two favorite pies!"

Todd nudged Travis with an elbow as he reached for a piece of pumpkin pie. "Don't tell Meghan, but they are both my favorites too, so I manage to sneak a piece of both when she's not looking."

"You're not so sneaky, Uncle Todd!" Kaci laughed. "Mom has known for years that you always manage to eat some of both."

"Well, then, if it's not a secret, sis, hand me a piece of that Dutch apple pie!"

"Don't you think you should at least finish eating the piece of pumpkin pie you have in front of you first?" Meghan asked, grinning, as she sat down a second piece of pie.

"Why?" Todd asked innocently. "I have two hands, don't I?"

"Now you sound just like Dad! I guess the nut doesn't fall far from the tree!"

"That would be an apple, my dear sister. You know I don't like nuts in my desserts. And neither did Dad."

"Just eat your pie, little brother, or I'll cross your name off my Christmas list!"

"I guess I'd better be nice to you then. You're the only one who likes me well enough to get me a Christmas present. And I suspect that's only because we're related!"

"Don't worry, Uncle Todd, I'll always give you a Christmas present. But that might be because you happen to be my only uncle. Hmmm…"

Travis enjoyed the closeness Meghan and Kaci had with

Todd. He loved the way they kidded around with each other without hurting feelings. They shared a tight bond, and it was heartwarming to see. So many families missed out on that. "I'm beginning to get the impression that a good sense of humor must be a Byers family trait. I think I missed out a bit by not knowing your dad."

"Yes, you did," Meghan agreed. "Dad was the ultimate prankster. He loved a good joke better than anyone. And he had the best sense of humor."

"He sure did," added Todd. "I will gladly accept any comparison to Dad. He was quite a man."

"And he always spoiled me at Christmas!" Kaci said with a smile. "That's one of the things I remember about Grandpa. Christmas was his favorite time of year."

Things got quiet for a moment as they each reflected on their own memories. "How does your family normally celebrate Christmas?" Travis asked out of curiosity. "Do you have certain traditions you like to follow, like opening one gift on Christmas Eve or something?"

Todd laughed out loud when he heard Kaci gasp. "If you think it's almost sacrilege not to have pumpkin pie for Thanksgiving, just try suggesting opening a Christmas gift on Christmas Eve! Go ahead, buddy, live dangerously!"

"I do believe I might have stumbled upon a tightly held Christmas tradition," Travis said, laughing. "I think I will use my better judgment and not open that can of worms."

"You're right about that," Meghan said with a smile. "Dad was always adamant that Christmas gifts are supposed to be opened on Christmas morning. Not Christmas Eve. Not even one gift. And there was a very particular way of opening gifts. Todd and I grew up with that tradition, and we carried it on with Kaci since we normally had Christmas at Dad's house."

"Now I'm curious. What is this 'very particular way of opening gifts' that you mentioned? Doesn't everyone open gifts the same way?"

Todd and Meghan exchanged glances before Todd commented, "He has so much to learn, sis. You're going to need all the help Kaci and I can give you."

Meghan looked at Travis as she replied, "That's okay, he's a quick learner."

"It's not really anything mysterious," Kaci began to explain. "Grandpa just never liked the idea of it being a free-for-all. He didn't want everyone opening gifts at the same time. That way no one could see what anyone else got for gifts. It needed to be done in an orderly fashion. Right, Mom?" Kaci asked, looking to her mom for confirmation.

"That's right," Meghan agreed. "When I was a kid, I assumed it was because of Dad's engineering background. Everything he did was done in a logical and orderly fashion. But his reasoning made perfect sense. How could you see what anyone was getting for Christmas if it was a free-for-all?"

"Okay, let me see if I've got this right," Travis began. "There are definitely no Christmas gifts opened on Christmas Eve."

"Right!" Kaci confirmed.

"All gifts are opened on Christmas morning. In an orderly fashion. Absolutely no free-for-all."

"You're right, sis," Todd chimed in. "There might be some hope for him yet. He does appear to be a quick learner."

"Thanks, Todd," Travis replied, as he pretended to ponder his next statement. "So, explain to me, if free-for-alls are not allowed, just exactly how do the gifts get opened?"

Meghan smiled, happy in the knowledge that Travis felt comfortable with her family. "One person at a time opened gifts. There was no set rule on who went first or anything like that. It just had to be one person at a time. That way people could see what gifts that person received. Then another person opened all their gifts. We simply went around the room until everyone had opened their gifts. It's really probably no different than the way most people do it."

Travis laughed. "I would venture to guess there are probably more free-for-alls on Christmas morning than you imagine!"

"Could be," Meghan said. "That's just not the way we do it."

"Since we're obviously on the topic of Christmas," Todd interjected, knowing the answer to his question before he asked it. "What's the plan for this year, sis?"

Meghan's face instantly lit up. "Kaci and I were discussing that last night. We obviously are planning to have our first Christmas in our new home. In fact, we're going to start decorating this weekend. And, Todd, we would really like you to join us, of course. You're welcome to spend Christmas Eve here too if you'd like."

Turning to Travis, Meghan asked, "What do you normally do for Christmas, Travis? Will you be going to spend it with your parents, or will you be in town? If you're in town, Kaci and I would love to have you join us."

"Dad told me the other night on the phone that he and Mom are coming to Hope for Christmas. In Mom's words, at least according to Dad, 'That boy seems to have forgotten his way home, so we will go to him.' So, they will be coming here. Dad said it's really because Mom wants to hear me preach again."

"That's great!" Meghan replied excitedly. "We would love to have you and your parents join us for Christmas! Please invite them! Or, maybe you had other plans?"

"How can I say no to that face?" Travis said as he leaned over to kiss her cheek. "I'm sure they would be thrilled to come. I'll call them tonight."

"Fantastic!" Meghan said with a huge smile. "It's going to be the most wonderful Christmas!"

"I have no doubt," Travis agreed as he pulled her close. "God is good."

From across the room, Kaci added, "All the time."

Chapter Twenty-Four

Kaci ran downstairs Christmas morning, belying the fact she was a teenager. She couldn't help it; she always acted like a kid at Christmas. But she had good reason for being excited this morning. When she looked out her bedroom window, she discovered her prayer had been answered. There was a sparkling blanket of fresh snow covering the ground. She raced into the kitchen, nearly toppling Todd over as he walked to the breakfast bar with a mug of hot cocoa.

"Whoa, there, munchkin!" Todd said as he protected his mug. "I don't really want to wear hot chocolate first thing this morning."

"Oh, sorry, Uncle Todd. But did you look outside? It snowed last night!"

"Yeah, I noticed that first thing this morning. In fact, I have already shoveled the sidewalks."

"Thanks, Todd," Meghan said as she entered the room. "Who votes for breakfast then gifts, or gifts then breakfast?"

Meghan looked from Kaci to Todd, trying to keep a straight face, but failing miserably. "Yeah, right, that was a pretty silly question, wasn't it? It's always been gifts first, then breakfast. No sense changing traditions now, right?"

The three headed into the family room, where Todd had already started a fire in the fireplace, when the doorbell rang. Meghan opened the door to let in their guests. "Mr. and Mrs. Harmon, I'm so glad you were able to join us this morning. I was hoping we would be able to make a day of it."

Travis gave Meghan a kiss before his mom had a chance to wrap her in a motherly hug. "Dear, I have asked you to call me Dottie. There's no reason for formality. It was so nice of you to invite us. Travis has told us so much about your house that we simply couldn't wait to see it!"

"I just came for the breakfast," Dennis Harmon joked as he gave Meghan a hug and kissed her on the cheek.

"As you can see, Meghan," Travis interjected, "Dad cuts right to the chase."

"That's okay," Meghan replied. "I like a man who knows what he wants!"

"I came prepared to wait," Mr. Harmon said with a grin. "Travis explained to me that gifts are opened in a very particular manner, and there will be no breakfast until after the gifts are opened. And speaking of gifts, Kaci, why don't you take this bag of goodies and go scatter them out under the tree before the chaos begins."

Kaci was happy to oblige as she took the bag and immediately began searching for just the right spot for each gift under the tree. Finding a perfect spot for each package, she stood back to survey the scene. She admitted silently that everything was perfect. Mrs. Harmon came up behind her and put her arm around Kaci.

"Kaci, my dear, I believe this is the most beautiful Christmas tree I have ever seen! And the arrangement of the packages is perfect. The way you have mixed up the colors and patterns of the wrapping paper shows you have a real eye for design."

Kaci beamed with pride. "Thanks. I wanted everything to look perfect. Especially since it's the first Christmas in our new home!"

"You have definitely succeeded. Everything looks amazing! Where did you find such a gorgeous tree?"

"A friend of Grandpa's has a tree farm. He raises the most beautiful noble firs. Mom and Uncle Todd used to go there with Grandpa every year to cut their Christmas tree. So that's where we have always gone. It's a lot of fun. We make a day of it because it's up close to the mountains. We get to wander through the tree farm and pick out a tree then we cut it down ourselves. Uncle Todd always goes with us so we can haul it back in his pickup." Kaci leaned over to whisper a secret to Mrs. Harmon. "Uncle Todd says he only goes so we can use his truck. He won't admit that he has as much fun as we do out there. He's like a little boy." Mrs. Harmon and Kaci giggled at their shared secret.

Travis had his arm around Meghan's waist as they stood back watching his mom and Kaci. Meghan looked up at him and smiled, just as she heard a commotion coming from the kitchen. A moment later Todd and Dennis came up behind them carrying trays filled with mugs of hot chocolate and pastries.

"If we're just going to stand here all day, instead of opening Christmas presents," said Todd, trying to muster all the indignation he could, "then Dennis and I decided we would need some nourishment."

Dennis set the tray of pastries down on a table along the wall then reached for the tray of hot chocolate Todd was carrying. Todd started passing around mugs of hot chocolate as people were finding places to sit. Meghan noticed Kaci sit in the middle of the sofa next to Dottie, and they immediately started whispering back and forth. She had always felt bad that Kaci grew up essentially without a grandma, so it was nice to see Dottie seemed to slide right into that role without hesitation.

"You know, sis," Todd began, "I can be as patient as the next guy, but if we don't get started on the gifts pretty soon I will die of starvation! Especially since I can smell that turkey cooking in the oven!"

"Okay, okay, let's get started. I wouldn't want Todd to starve to death! Kaci, why don't you help your Uncle Todd pass out the gifts, then we will have our guests open their gifts first."

Kaci jumped up eagerly, always willing to help pass out the Christmas presents. They made a good team. Todd retrieved the gifts from under the tree, handed them to Kaci, who delivered them to their owners. In no time at all, Mrs. Harmon was ready to begin. She was astonished to discover she had several gifts to open. Since they were planning to celebrate Christmas with Meghan, Travis brought his gifts over to the house as well. His parents each had a couple gifts from Travis, as well as the gifts from Meghan and Kaci.

By the time the gifts were all unwrapped, there was a sizable pile of wrapping paper in the middle of the room. Todd was as happy as a kid in a candy store since he received an assortment of tools. He usually got tools as gifts, but that's what he wanted, so it was easy to please him. Travis's parents made huge brownie points for their gift of a new tool belt. Dottie loved the necklace from Meghan and the handmade scarf from Kaci. Dennis told Kaci he had needed a new wallet for a long time, but just never got around to getting one, so he wasted no time putting her gift to good use. Kaci received a book and CD from Travis's parents, as well as several wonderful gifts from her mom, Travis, and Uncle Todd. Meghan and Travis each received several gifts, but particularly treasured the gifts from each other. Meghan gave Travis a new Bible with his name engraved on the leather cover, and Travis gave her a beautiful sterling silver cross necklace with a small diamond in the center.

Everyone pitched in to clean up the after-Christmas debris and get breakfast started. Dennis took charge of a large frying pan, insisting with a grin that he made the best scrambled eggs on the planet. Travis began frying some bacon and sausage links, and Dottie found an apron and started pouring pancake batter onto the griddle. In the meantime, Todd was hauling a bag of trash out to the dumpster, leaving Meghan and Kaci with nothing to do except set the table in the dining room.

Before long everyone was seated around the table, anxiously waiting to dig into the feast before them. "Travis," Meghan began, "would you mind asking a blessing on the food before we get started?"

"I would be happy to," he agreed. "Our Dear Heavenly Father, we come before you this Christmas morning as we celebrate the birth of Your Son. This has been an incredible year. You have blessed us all beyond anything we could have imagined. You made it possible for Meghan and Kaci to have this beautiful new home. You have blessed Todd's business with a level of prosperity he didn't think possible. You have blessed my parents with a comfortable retirement and good health. And you have brought Meghan into my life, allowing me to heal and love again. For all these things we are forever grateful. But the biggest blessing of all is the gift of Your Son, Jesus Christ, our Lord and Savior. We ask that you bless this bounty before us, allowing it to nourish and strengthen our bodies. We ask these things humbly in the name of Your Beloved Son, Jesus Christ. Amen."

Meghan quietly echoed "amen" as she leaned over and gave Travis a kiss, thinking she had to be the luckiest woman in the world. The clatter of dishes and the blending of conversations soon brought her back to earth. This was exactly what she had been dreaming of for years. A happy home, filled with people she loved, her laughing daughter enjoying life, and a good man at her side. Life couldn't get much better than this.

Thank you, God. For everything.

* * *

The entire day was filled with the makings of unforgettable memories. Four snowmen adorned the yard, evidence of a snowman-building contest. Todd had insisted he could make a better snowman than anyone. Kaci immediately rose to the challenge, as did Travis. Not to be left out, Dennis reminded them that he had been building snowmen since long before any of them were born, so he got to work to prove his point. Meghan and Dottie watched from the back deck, sharing easy conversation and joining in the laughter. They had been blessed with a beautiful day, full of sunshine, and they took full advantage of it. As dinnertime approached, the ladies were called on to judge the snowmen and announce the winner.

"I was afraid this was going to happen," Meghan chuckled. "How are we supposed to pick the best snowman?"

"Diplomacy, my dear," Dottie replied with a smile. The two women circled around all four snowmen, appearing to be carefully considering the merits of each. They then huddled up, waving their arms and whispering furtively as if struggling with a consensus. Dottie walked over to Todd's snowman.

"The winner of the biggest snowman goes to Todd!" She winked at Todd and said, "The hard hat was a nice touch."

Todd had barely started his victory dance when Meghan piped in. "Don't get so excited just yet, little brother. The winner of the most stylish snowman goes to Kaci! None of you guys can compete with the matching hat and scarf her snowman is wearing."

"Yes!" shouted Kaci in victory.

Dottie then walked over to Travis's snowman. She circled around it again, nodding the entire time. "The winner of the most creative snowman goes to Travis! The bear was a very clever idea."

Travis pumped his fist in the air in victory then gave Kaci a high five.

"Hey, wait a minute," Todd protested in laughter. "This was a snowman-building contest. Not a bear-building contest! I call foul!"

Dottie walked over and patted Todd on the arm. "We make the rules, we make the dinner, and the decision of the judges is final. Deal with it!"

Dennis interrupted the laughter. "Hey, what about me?"

Meghan walked up to Dennis and said, "We didn't forget about you. The winner of the most traditional snowman goes to Dennis! It's kind of nice to see an old-fashioned snowman, complete with the carrot nose."

"Stick with the tried and true, I always say!" Dennis replied with a chuckle.

Travis walked up behind his dad and put his arm around his shoulder. "Is that what you always say, Dad?"

"Well, that and 'let's eat!'" he replied, laughing.

* * *

After enjoying a wonderfully traditional Christmas dinner, followed by dessert and conversation in the family room, Dottie pointed to the piano in the corner and asked, "Who plays the piano?"

"Kaci does," Meghan replied.

"I do, too!" Dottie said. "Kaci, do you have any Christmas

music? Maybe we could play together."

"I have some in the piano bench! That would be fun!"

For the next hour, the house was filled with the sounds of laughter, piano music, and singing. Meghan was surprised at the beautiful baritone voice Dennis had, and by how well Travis's parents harmonized together. Even Todd, who normally didn't like to sing around others, joined in with his smooth bass and surprised himself by how much he enjoyed it. All too soon, the long day began wearing on everyone as muffled yawns began to emerge. Dennis and Dottie were the first to gather their things and head out, with Travis right behind them. Todd took Meghan up on her offer to spend the night and was soon snoring softly in the recliner. Meghan put a blanket over him, knowing he probably wouldn't bother going up to the guest bedroom.

As Meghan and Kaci headed upstairs, Kaci turned and looked at the lit Christmas tree in the family room. "Mom," she said. "This has been the best Christmas ever."

Meghan put her arm around Kaci's shoulder and agreed. "I think you're right, kiddo. This has been the best Christmas ever."

Chapter Twenty-Five

The pace of winter seemed uncharacteristically slow to Meghan, but she was content. She and Travis saw each other nearly every day. She found that she now had time to enjoy reading a book occasionally, which she had not been able to do for a very long time. Not since she began working on the house project. Things at the construction company typically slow down a bit during winter so she was able to spend more time on her design work during the day, which freed up some of her evenings. She was beginning to discover that she liked the slower pace and wondered how she had ever managed to juggle everything she did before. She also returned to church. She had been attending sporadically for a few months, but now she and Kaci went nearly every weekend. Her spiritual life was growing, and she began to understand how much she had missed that part of her life.

All in all, life was good. Danny had been working to repair his relationship with Kaci, so she was agreeable to spending time with him occasionally. Yet at the same time she was developing a tight bond with Travis. Meghan was happy to see that. She thought back to the first time Kaci met Travis and how they had an immediate connection. There was no way she could know at the time what a big part of their lives Travis would become. Now she couldn't imagine, or even bear to think, what their lives would be like without the presence of that Godly man.

You are such a gracious God. So much of my life was in shambles. I didn't know what I needed. But You did. You knew what I needed and who I needed. I am eternally grateful You placed Travis along the street across from my property that day. Thank you, God. For everything. Meghan got out of the recliner and started across the room to add another log to the fire. A very clear message popped into her head that put an instant smile on her face.

He needed you every bit as much as you needed him.

Before she finished stoking the fire, Meghan heard a vehicle pull into the driveway. Looking out the window, she saw Danny drop Kaci off. He had taken her to lunch then a movie. Kaci came in, took her coat off, and hung it on the coat tree just inside the door.

"Hi Mom," she said as she gave Meghan a hug. "It feels nice and cozy in here. I love having a fireplace."

"Me too, kiddo. Did you have a good time with your dad?"

"It was okay," she replied unenthusiastically.

"Where did you go for lunch?"

"His idea of lunch was grabbing hot dogs at a hot dog stand."

"Seriously? He made it sound like he was going to take you out for a nice lunch before the movie."

"Yeah, I know. It was just as well, I guess. Between eating the hot dogs in the truck on the way to the theater, and watching a movie for a couple hours, it meant he didn't have to talk to me much."

"I'm sorry, kiddo."

"It's okay. He just doesn't get me. We have nothing in common. He doesn't understand me at all and has no clue what things I'm interested in. It makes it hard to carry on much of a conversation. I've known Travis for less than a year, and he understands me a lot more than Dad does."

"Travis makes more of an effort than your dad does. He makes a point to ask about what's going on in your life. There's no way your dad can relate to you if he has no idea what's going on in your life."

"I know. Dad and I are never going to be close. I've learned to accept that. I'll spend time with him once in a while, but we're never going to have any kind of quality relationship. And that's okay. Hey, is Travis still coming over for dinner tonight? He said he would read through my essay for Bible class and give me some input."

"Yes, he is. In fact, he should be here shortly. Oh, and he mentioned something about possibly going sledding tomorrow. That is, if you're interested."

"Of course, I'm interested!" Kaci exclaimed with excitement. "Is Uncle Todd going to come with us?"

"Why don't you call and invite him. I'm sure Travis wouldn't mind at all."

"Yay! Tomorrow is going to be so much fun!"

Meghan had mixed emotions as she watched her daughter run up the stairs. On one hand, she was thrilled that Kaci had something to look forward to tomorrow because she enjoyed spending time with both her uncle and Travis. On the other hand, she was very disappointed that Danny never seemed to take a genuine interest in their daughter. He put on the outward appearances of being a good dad, but never really invested much time and effort into developing a relationship with her.

"Oh well," Meghan said quietly. "It's his loss because Kaci is a great kid. A parent couldn't ask for a better daughter. And she deserves so much more than he is willing to give. I'm glad she has Todd and Travis in her life as good male role models. Thank you, God."

* * *

Travis barbecued hamburgers on the back deck, even though it was February and there was still snow on the ground. Kaci had the idea of turning their dinner into a picnic. She spread a blanket on the floor of the family room, strategically placed directly in front of the fireplace so they could soak up the warmth. By the time Meghan and Travis walked into the family room with the tray of burgers and bags of chips, Kaci had an entire picnic set up, complete with plates, utensils, and napkins.

"This looks like fun," Travis said with interest.

"Mom and I used to have picnics like this a lot when I was little," Kaci explained.

"That's true," Meghan confirmed with a smile. "There were many times we barbecued a nice dinner then ate it picnic style on a blanket on the floor."

"What a great idea!" Travis agreed as the three found their spots on the blanket.

After a brief prayer of thanks, they dug into the burgers and ate in silence for a few moments. "Kaci, I mentioned to your mom that I was thinking about going sledding tomorrow. Is that something you might be interested in?"

"Absolutely! Mom told me about it when I got home. I already called Uncle Todd and asked if he wanted to come. I hope that was okay."

"Sure. The more the merrier," Travis said.

Once the picnic was over, Meghan began taking things back to the kitchen, leaving Travis and Kaci to look over her essay. When she returned to the family room, she found them curled up on the sofa with Kaci looking over Travis's shoulder as he read her paper.

"This is quite good, Kaci," Travis said as he nodded his approval. "What were the guidelines for the assignment? Was this your idea?"

"We were just told to write anything we wanted as long as it was about Jesus living in our world."

"What made you decide to write it from the perspective of Jesus being a newspaper reporter? That's a unique idea."

"Thanks," Kaci replied beaming. "I just thought about the way reporters look at things going on around them, and they sometimes see things differently than most people. So, I thought it would be interesting to see what Jesus would see as an outsider walking through our town."

"Well," Travis said proudly, "I do believe you nailed it."

"Thanks! Mom liked it too, but sometimes I wonder if that's just because she's my mom."

Meghan sat down beside Travis on the sofa before replying. "No, kiddo, it's because you are a good writer, and you have some very clever ideas. And maybe a little bit because I'm your mom," she added with a smile.

"Hey," Kaci said as she jumped up from the sofa. "Do you guys want to watch a movie?"

Travis and Meghan looked at each other then nodded. Before long, the three of them were curled up together on the sofa watching a Hallmark movie. About two-thirds of the way through the movie, Meghan looked over and saw that Kaci was fast asleep, snuggled up against Travis. He had his arm around her in a protective hug. Meghan nudged Travis and pointed to her sleeping daughter. He simply smiled as if it was the most natural thing in the world.

* * *

"Come on, Uncle Todd! Hurry! We have to beat Mom and Travis to the top of the hill!"

"I'm coming, kiddo! Slow down! I didn't know it was going to be a race," Todd replied laughing.

It seemed like they had barely parked the truck before Kaci hopped out and grabbed her sled from the back. Travis and Meghan were just pulling into the parking area, as Todd hoisted the toboggan out of the pickup.

Calling to Travis over his shoulder as he started up the hill, Todd said, "You two better hurry. Kaci is on a mission to leave you guys in the dust. Or the snow, as the case may be!"

"Well," Travis replied, accepting the challenge. "We can't have that! Come on, Meg, let's go!"

It was no surprise that Kaci was the first to reach the top of the hill, but she not so patiently waited for her uncle. He joined her moments later as he pointed partway down the slope, indicating they were getting a good head start on the others.

"Okay, kiddo, let's go!"

Kaci did a graceful dive with her sled and was on her way, snow flying in all directions. Todd let her get a little way down the hill before he slammed his toboggan into the snow. Then he jumped on and gave what could only be referred to as a war whoop as he jetted down the hill. It wasn't long before Travis and Meghan were streaking down the hill behind them. Laughter, yelling, and whoops of excitement soon filled the air as the four made their way down the hill, just to haul their sleds back up the hill and do it all over again.

The morning and early afternoon flew by as they made many trips up and down the hill. They all agreed, after one final run, to succumb to exhaustion and hunger. Travis started a fire in the fire pit, while Meghan and Kaci brought the cooler from the truck.

Todd retrieved the camp chairs from his pickup, and in no time at all they were sitting around the fire, roasting hot dogs and marshmallows. Between the fire and the thermos of hot chocolate Meghan brought along, they were soon dry and warm.

As the sun began to drop in the sky, the temperatures began to fall as well. It had been a long day, but one that had created many new memories. While Travis and the girls took their belongings back to the trucks, Todd doused the fire then joined the others in the parking area.

"Well, gang," Todd said. "What say we head back and call it a day."

"That sounds like a great idea," Meghan agreed. "I'm exhausted."

Travis helped Meghan into his pickup, then she slid over next to him when he got in on the driver's side. He leaned over and gave her a kiss before starting the truck and falling in behind Todd on the road.

"This was another great day, Meg," Travis remarked as he turned the radio on for some soft background music. "And hopefully there will be thousands more that are just as great."

Meghan didn't reply. She simply snuggled in close and smiled. Glancing at the incredible sunset in the rearview mirror, and seeing this amazing woman beside him, Travis knew without a doubt that God was directing his life.

God is good. All the time.

Chapter Twenty-Six

Springtime had always meant two things to Meghan – tulips and baseball. Even as a small child, there had been an unwritten competition to see who spotted the first tulip in their massive yard. Every fall, her dad planted more tulips without telling either her or Todd where he planted them. In doing so, he unwittingly fueled their natural competitive drive. It was a friendly competition, but a competition, nonetheless. As she got older, Meghan made sure her little brother was able to find the first tulip occasionally. Once that first tulip had poked its head out of the cool dirt, they anxiously waited for it to bloom and tried guessing what color it might be. By the time all the tulips were in full bloom, they had the most colorful yard in the entire town.

There was never any doubt Meghan and Todd bonded over tulips every spring, but an even tighter bond was formed over baseball. George Byers lived and breathed baseball, and he instilled a love of the game in both his children. As soon as the spring weather allowed it, they were outside playing catch, hitting pop flies, and honing their baseball skills. When the Hope Angels, the local AAA minor league team, started practicing, Meghan and Todd could usually be found clinging to the fence along the third baseline. Besides coaching Little League baseball, their dad was one of the umpires for the Angels' home games, so the Byers kids spent a lot of time at the ballpark.

Even as an adult, Meghan never lost her love of the game. She and Todd took Kaci to the ballgames every year. So, the advent of spring meant the beginning of baseball season. And this year, Meghan had every intention of making up for lost time. Even though Todd had taken Kaci to most of the Angels' home games last year, Meghan had only made it to one game. Work on the house kept her so busy that she had a hard time justifying the time away. This year would be different. She had already put Travis on notice that they would be attending all the home games. Luckily, Travis also loved baseball, so he didn't consider it a sacrifice to go to ballgames with Meghan and Kaci. In fact, as he pulled into their driveway, he was not surprised to see them both sitting on the porch swing waiting for him. And, of course, they had their baseball gloves with them. Just in case.

As he got out of the pickup, Travis smiled and said, "I see my two favorite girls are ready to go to the ballpark."

"It's the first home game of the season, Travis," Kaci stated obviously. "Where else would we be?"

"Where else, indeed," Travis said as he leaned down to give Meghan a kiss. "Let's go so we can catch some of their batting practice."

Neither the weather nor the Hope Angels disappointed the baseball fans. It was a beautiful spring day, perfect for watching a ballgame. The Angels took an early lead in the second inning, but it was not a blowout. The lead went back and forth throughout the game, leading up to the Cardinals being one run ahead when the Angels came to bat in the bottom of the ninth inning. Their leadoff batter got a double, but the second batter flew out to center field. That brought up a promising young rookie just signed by the Angels. He took the first two pitches as called strikes. He adjusted his helmet, squared his feet, and sent the third pitch soaring over the right field fence. The Hope Angels just won their first home game of the season and, in Travis's mind, that was a sign of many good things to come. Right here on this ball field.

* * *

Travis sat in his pickup outside the jewelry store, thinking back to the first time he met Meghan. That seemed like a lifetime ago. He had to admit that he was intrigued by her right from the beginning. She was a hardworking, independent woman who was about as far from traditional as a woman could get. Maybe that was what drew him to her. There was no doubt she could take care of herself, but he felt such a strong need to protect her. He never wanted her to be afraid again. He never wanted her to feel like she had the weight of the world on her shoulders. And he never wanted her to doubt his love for her.

You said I would know when it was time to move on, God. I still miss Angela so much it hurts at times, and that makes it hard to let go. But I think she would want me to be happy. Meghan makes me very happy, and I love her like I never thought I'd be able to love again. And I love Kaci as if she were my own daughter. So maybe it's time.

Travis got out of his truck and walked into the jewelry store, knowing full well that he was stepping into his future. A future he was very much looking forward to.

Nearly two hours later, he emerged from the store carrying a small bag. Once he was back in his truck, he took the small box out of the bag and opened it. He was not surprised it had taken him so long to pick out the ring. He wanted it to be just right, and it had to reflect Meghan's taste. She didn't go for the big gaudy jewelry that screamed "look at me." She preferred a simpler, yet classy style.

The only jewelry he had ever seen her wear, and she wore it all the time, was a simple gold band that was her grandmother's wedding band and a small gold cross on a chain. So, he was fairly confident she would like what he picked out. It was a two-toned wedding band, gold and white gold. Across the top of the band was a row of small diamonds. It would go perfectly with what he was planning to use as an engagement ring. He had his grandmother's gold wedding band that had a similar row of small diamonds across the top. The two rings would complement each other nicely. Most importantly, they were both low-profile rings, so Meghan wouldn't feel the need to take them off when working. He grinned as he recalled the image of her operating a bulldozer, and knew his life was never going to be boring.

The next step would be paying a visit to Byers Construction. He had a very important question to ask Todd.

* * *

Todd was on the phone discussing a delivery when Travis walked into his office. He motioned for Travis to have a seat while he finished the call. Instead, Travis paced. Todd watched him with curiosity as he paced back and forth across the office. The faster he paced, the bigger Todd's smile became. Obviously, Travis had something important on his mind.

When Todd hung up the phone, Travis happened to be pacing away from him, so he leaned back in his chair and crossed his arms over his chest. And he waited. Wearing a smile that indicated he planned to have some fun with Travis.

"So…" Todd began slowly. "It appears that you have something on your mind. What's up?"

"We need to talk," Travis replied nervously.

Todd simply smiled. "I assumed as much since you are pacing in my office."

"I went shopping this morning," Travis began.

"Okay. And you feel obligated to share your grocery list with me?"

"No… no," Travis stammered. "I didn't go grocery shopping."

"Did you go shopping for a new truck?"

"No," Travis replied as he began pacing again.

"Well, buddy, I can't help you. If you didn't go shopping for either food or a new truck, I have no idea what else a man would shop for. You're going to have to give me more to work with than that if you expect me to participate in this conversation."

"I went to the jewelry store," Travis said with a sheepish grin, assuming that would explain everything.

"You do know, don't you, that you can get a new watch a lot cheaper at the department store."

"No, no, no!" Travis said in exasperation. "I didn't buy a watch. I bought a wedding ring!"

"You don't say!" Todd replied, still not quite ready to let him off the hook. "What do you need with a wedding ring?"

"I'm going to ask your sister to marry me," Travis replied as he pulled the small box out of his jacket pocket. He opened the box and sat it on the desk in front of Todd. "What do you think? Do you think she'll like it?"

"What, no big diamond?" Todd tried, unsuccessfully, to look shocked.

"Uh, no. I didn't think she'd like a big diamond. That doesn't seem to fit her personality. Do you think I made a mistake?" Travis was suddenly unsure of himself.

Todd finally decided to take pity on Travis. He picked up the box and looked at the ring, nodding his head in approval. "You did good, buddy. This is exactly her style. She doesn't go in for flashy jewelry."

Travis let out such a heavy sigh of relief that Todd couldn't help but laugh out loud. "So, when do you plan to ask her?"

"At the Angels' next home game. Before the game. Todd, do you think she'll say yes?"

"Travis, my sister is crazy about you. Of course, she will say yes. She loves you. She has for a long time."

"I hope you know that I love her, too," Travis stated.

"I know you do. I'm the one who pointed it out to you, remember?"

Travis laughed. "Oh, yeah!"

Todd walked around his desk, leaned up against the front of the desk, and folded his arms across his chest. "I like you, Travis. I think you're a great guy. Not a bad carpenter either. And I have no doubt Meg is crazy about you. Kaci has gotten pretty attached to you as well. I know I joke around a lot, and I love giving people a bad time. But if you don't treat my sister and niece like they deserve to be treated, or if you ever hurt either of them, I guarantee you will be answering to me. I wasn't thrilled when she agreed to marry Danny, and we all know how that turned out. But Dad gave his blessing, so there was nothing I could do. Dad isn't here now, but before he died, I promised that I would look out for her and protect her. And that's exactly what I plan to do."

"Todd," Travis began. "I appreciate the way you protect your family. That's one of the many things I like about you. But you don't have to worry about Meghan or Kaci. I plan to spend the rest of my life watching out for them. I love them both and will do everything in my power to keep them safe and happy."

Todd stepped away from his desk and approached Travis. He reached out his hand and smiled broadly. "Well, then," he said as he shook hands and slapped Travis on the back. "Welcome to the family!"

"Thanks, Todd! I assume that means I have your blessing, then?"

"You sure do. I have a question, though."

"What's that?"

"Normally people go to their pastor to perform a marriage ceremony. Who does the pastor go to when he wants to get married?"

"As long as it's okay with Meghan, I'd like to ask my dad to perform the ceremony."

"I didn't realize your dad was also a minister. You went into the family business, huh?"

"I guess you could say that," Travis replied, laughing. "Dad is a retired pastor. I haven't even mentioned it to him because I want to make sure it's okay with Meghan first. As long as she's agreeable, I know Dad would love to do it."

"Well, congratulations, Travis. Seriously, I mean that. Meghan deserves someone like you. And so does Kaci."

"Thanks, Todd. I'll take care of them. I promise."

"I know you will. I've seen it already. You've been taking care of them for months."

* * *

"Hey, Mom," Kaci yelled down the stairs. "Do you care if I ride to the ballpark with Uncle Todd? He's going to the game today too."

"Sure, that's fine," Meghan agreed. "Travis and I are going to go early to watch batting practice."

By now, Kaci was downstairs and heading to the kitchen to grab some snacks for the game. "Yeah, I think Uncle Todd was planning to go early too. He said he would swing by to pick me up in about half an hour.”

It was all Kaci could do to contain her enthusiasm. Ever since Todd and Travis let her in on the little secret last week, she had been just bursting at the seams with excitement. As much as she wanted to spill the beans, she was even more thrilled to be included in the conspiracy. Todd had offered to pick her up from school a couple times, which was not out of the ordinary, so they had an opportunity to meet up with Travis to work out the details. As near as they could tell, Meghan remained completely clueless.

Todd pulled into the driveway, while Kaci was helping her mom water the potted flowers on the deck railing. He got out of his truck and walked toward the house. “You about ready to go, munchkin?”

“Sure! I just need to grab my backpack and glove then I’ll be ready to go.”

“I hope you packed some extra snacks in your bag. I get hungry during ballgames, you know.”

“Uncle Todd, you know you always get at least two hot dogs whenever we go to the ballpark, so I’m pretty sure you won’t starve!”

“You’re probably right, but I don’t want to take any chances!”

Kaci ran into the house to grab her things, then gave her mom a quick hug before heading to the pickup. “We’ll see you at the game, Mom.”

“Okay, kiddo. Travis should be here shortly, so we won’t be far behind.”

As a casual afterthought, Todd said as a reminder, “Don’t forget to bring your glove, Meg. Remember, today is the day they let the fans help shag fly balls in the outfield during batting practice.”

“Oh, that’s right! Thanks for the reminder! See you guys at

the park."

Todd put his arm around his niece's shoulder as they walked to the truck. He looked at her and winked. She grinned and whispered, "This is going to be awesome."

* * *

When Travis pulled into the parking lot at the ballpark, they could see that the Angels were just getting ready to start batting practice. Meghan loved that they designated several home games each season as fan participation days. They not only allowed the fans to shag fly balls, but they also let some of the younger kids act as bat boys and girls during batting practice. Meghan looked around to see if she could locate Todd and Kaci. There weren't a lot of people at the park yet, so it was fairly easy to find them. Once they connected, they headed over to sign the necessary waivers then started toward the outfield.

"How about we go to center field today? We usually do left field," Todd casually suggested.

"Sounds good to me," Travis agreed. "This is my first time, so I'll just follow your lead."

"Sure, center field is fine," Meghan added.

Kaci looked around the outfield as they approached the middle of the center field area. "There doesn't seem to be a lot of people here today. There are only a couple over in left field, and we're the only ones in center so far."

"That's okay by me," Meghan said. "I like it better when it's not so crowded, and it saves more fly balls for me!"

Kaci laughed as she replied, "Mom, you really are a die-hard baseball fan!"

They all shared a laugh just as the announcer came over the PA system to let people know to stay alert because batting practice was ready to begin. The batters were doing a great job spreading out their hits so the fans in the outfield all had an opportunity to catch some. Meghan, Todd, and Travis had all caught several. Kaci was still waiting for her very first professional fly ball catch. One was coming directly toward her. The others stepped away to give her sole opportunity to make the catch.

"Stay with it, kiddo," Meghan encouraged. "You got it, you got it. Watch it all the way into your glove."

With a loud slap, the ball slammed into the pocket of her glove. Kaci immediately closed her mitt around the ball, just like she had been taught. She jabbed her glove high into the air in triumph and yelled, "You're outa there!" She ran over to her mom, holding the precious treasure tightly in her glove. "I did it, Mom! I finally caught a fly ball from a professional baseball player!"

Meghan gave her a proud hug, and both Todd and Travis gave her a high five.

"Hey, kid!" the batter yelled out to Kaci. "Keep the ball. Bring it to me at the end of batting practice and I'll sign it for you. Is that your mom there with you?"

Kaci yelled back, "Yeah, it is!"

"Okay, Mom," the batter said loudly. "This one's for you!"

The batter smacked a high fly ball. Meghan kept her eye on it from the moment it left the bat. It was going to be a fairly easy catch, but she would have to run slightly toward left field. She stretched her arm above her head, and the ball landed in her glove with a satisfying slap. She reached into the pocket and pulled the ball out.

That's odd, she thought, noticing writing on the ball. She rolled the ball over in her hand and discovered the words "Will You Marry Me?" She seemed confused as she looked toward the batter. With his bat, he pointed back in her direction. Meghan turned toward center field and there, down on one knee, was Travis holding a ring out to her.

Meghan slowly walked toward him, cradling the ball against her chest. She looked down at him with tears in her eyes. Travis reached up to take her hand as he stared deeply into her eyes and asked simply, "Meghan, will you marry me?"

She replied just as simply, "Yes, Travis, I'll marry you."

She dropped her glove to the ground, and he slid his grandmother's wedding ring onto her finger. He stood up, wrapped his arms around her, and kissed her tenderly. Cheers erupted all around them. Meghan looked around, having momentarily forgotten where they were. She looked back at Travis and blushed slightly, never liking to be the center of public attention.

No longer able to restrain herself, Kaci ran over to her mom and gave her a big hug. "I was in on the secret! Travis has been planning this ever since the last home game!"

"Hey!" Meghan said in surprise. "You knew about this and didn't tell me? You normally can't keep secrets from me."

"Right?!? But this was a big secret! Travis and Uncle Todd swore me to secrecy!"

Meghan looked over at her brother and smiled. She then picked her baseball glove up off the ground, took Travis by the hand, and said, "Uh, let's get out of center field." Wearing big smiles all around, the four quickly made their way toward the first baseline then headed towards the stands.

Chapter Twenty-Seven

Several days later, Meghan was still walking around with a permanent smile on her face. Her life had suddenly gotten very busy, but she didn't mind at all. There were lots of plans to be made and details to be worked out, but it was so exciting that she found she enjoyed it. It helped that Kaci absolutely loved planning things. It didn't matter what it was, if it involved planning and details, she was all over it. Even as a young girl, she planned her tea parties down to the last detail. So, she was definitely in her element when it came to helping with the plans for her mom's wedding. And she had a lot of great ideas, things that Meghan never would have considered.

The one thing that Meghan was insisting on was that it be a fairly low-key wedding. Since this was the second wedding for both her and Travis, she didn't see the need for a big elaborate ceremony. She told Kaci that pretty much any other ideas she had would be open for consideration. On the flip side, Kaci also had one detail that she would not budge on. Her mom would be getting married in an actual wedding dress. Not in Levis. Meghan had mentioned that she would be perfectly content wearing Levis and a nice top. Kaci nearly fainted at the idea! So, apparently wearing jeans was out.

Meghan was in the kitchen preparing a few snacks because Travis's parents and Todd would be coming over shortly to discuss the wedding. Kaci was sprawled out on the floor of the family room, poring over bridal magazines. She was having way too much fun planning this wedding! Travis and Meghan had decided on a fall wedding, so Kaci was researching decorating ideas that would incorporate all the beautiful autumn colors. When Meghan first mentioned they had decided to get married in the fall, Kaci's initial reaction was one of panic. That only left a few months to shop for the dresses, find the venue, and work out the apparently thousands of other details involved in planning a wedding. Meghan just smiled and allowed Kaci to run with it. She wasn't too concerned with the details, and Kaci was more than concerned enough for the two of them, so everything evened out.

"Kaci," Meghan called from the kitchen. "Would you please help me take the snacks out to the family room? Everyone should be here in a few minutes."

As they carried the trays to the family room, Kaci asked, "Mom, do you think Mr. and Mrs. Harmon will let me call them grandma and grandpa?"

"I don't know kiddo. I never thought about that. What do you want to call them?"

"I've never really had any grandparents for most of my life. It would be nice to have someone I could call grandma and grandpa."

Meghan gave her only child a hug and replied, "It sure would. I guess we'll have to ask them at some point."

At that moment, the front door opened, and Travis called out, "Knock, knock. Anyone home?"

Travis walked in, followed by his parents, just as Meghan and Kaci came around the corner. He immediately leaned down to give Meghan a kiss, then gave his future stepdaughter a hug.

Dottie wrapped Meghan in a tight hug and said, "Congratulations, dear! I'm so happy for both of you! Welcome to the family!"

"Thanks, Dottie," Meghan replied just as Dennis Harmon leaned in to give her a kiss on the cheek.

"Your brother is right behind us," Dennis said.

"Hi, Mr. and Mrs. Harmon," Kaci greeted with a smile.

Dottie gave Kaci a big hug before saying, "Kaci, honey, why don't you just call me Grandma Dot. We're going to be family soon, so we might as well dispense with the formalities!"

If it had been possible, Kaci's smile grew even wider. "I'd like that a lot, Grandma Dot!"

Not to be outdone, Dennis stepped in with a hug of his own for Kaci. "And you can just call me plain old grandpa."

Kaci giggled as she replied, "You don't seem plain or old! So, I'll just call you Grandpa."

Dennis laughed out loud and said, "This one's pretty sharp, son. You're going to have to stay on your toes!"

Todd stepped in the door behind Dennis and said, "You guys weren't planning to start this party without me, were you?"

"Of course not, Uncle Todd! Everyone knows you're the life of the party!"

"And don't you forget it, kiddo!"

In no time at all everyone had settled in the family room, and Meghan noticed that Kaci had opted to sit on the sofa between Dennis and Dottie. Mother and daughter shared an understanding smile that Travis picked up on. He loved these two women with his entire being, and it made his heart swell to know they were happy. He sat down beside Meghan on the loveseat and put his arm around her shoulder.

"Mom and Dad," Travis began. "As you know, I've asked Meghan to marry me, and she said yes. But before I asked her, I checked with Todd, and he gave me his blessing. I guess being sharp runs in the family because the first thing he asked me, after he made it very clear that I would be answering to him if I didn't treat Meghan and Kaci right, was who do pastors go to when they want to get married. Meghan and I discussed it and have agreed that we'd like you to perform the ceremony, Dad."

Tears quickly formed in Dennis's eyes as he stood and walked over to Travis and Meghan. "There's nothing I would love more son." Father and son embraced in obvious love and admiration.

Meghan stood and gave Dennis a hug as he kissed her on the cheek. "Are you sure you're okay with this, Meghan? I would be honored to perform the wedding ceremony, but I want to be sure you're okay with it."

"Dennis," Meghan replied in all sincerity, "there's no one I would rather have do it than you."

"Thank you, dear," he replied, nearly overcome with emotion.

"As long as most of us are already standing," Travis began. "I have another question to ask. Todd, as you know, I don't have a brother. But over these past several months you have become like a brother to me. I would be honored if you would agree to be my best man."

"Wow, really?" Todd asked as he got up from the recliner. "Of course, I will. After all, someone has to make sure you don't slip out the back door of the church!"

"You don't have to worry about that!" Travis assured him. "She's stuck with me now!"

Over the course of the next couple hours, many of the wedding details were ironed out. They had decided to get married in mid-October when the foliage was at the peak of its glory. The wedding would be held at Hope Community Church where Travis pastored, with his dad performing the ceremony. Todd would act as Travis's best man, and Kaci would be her mom's maid of honor. Kaci would work with a couple of Meghan's best friends to work out many of the little details. After the wedding, there would be an informal reception at the house. And Meghan would most definitely not be wearing Levis to the wedding! The reception, however, was a completely different story.

* * *

The next several weeks were a blur for Meghan. Springtime also meant the construction season was heating up, so she became very busy at work. At least the house project was finished, but that time was quickly taken over by wedding planning. Kaci was having the time of her life working out all the little details, and Meghan pretty much gave her free rein. She had a strong suspicion that her low-key wedding was going to blossom into a much larger affair than she had anticipated. Particularly since Todd had given her a five-thousand-dollar check from Byers Construction to help with wedding expenses. Meghan and Travis had both argued that it wasn't necessary, knowing full well that Todd would get his way. Todd's logic was that their dad would have done it if he were still alive, thereby making it nonnegotiable.

Because of Todd's generosity, Meghan decided to take Kaci and Dottie to Portland to go shopping for dresses. In her online research, Kaci had discovered a bridal shop in Portland that had a huge selection of dresses in stock, and also had an in-house person to do alterations. So, they made plans for a girls' weekend outing. That would provide an opportunity for the girls to spend some one-on-one time together and also take care of one of the primary wedding details. They would purchase the wedding dress, the bridesmaid dress, and the dress for the mother of the groom.

By the end of the weekend trip to the city, Grandma Dot and Kaci were best of friends. It seems that Dottie was also quite the planner and had a lot of great ideas for decorations. On the ride home, Dottie chose to sit in the backseat of the Jeep with Kaci so they could go over their checklist to see what kind of progress they had actually made. Besides the dresses, they had purchased the biggest share of the decorations for the reception and most of the miscellaneous things needed for the wedding. They also found what Kaci had described as "the most perfect" wedding invitations and got those on order so they would have them in plenty of time. The next order of business would be dragging Travis and Todd down to be fitted for their tuxedos and giving some thought to the wedding cake.

But the one unfinished detail at the forefront of Meghan's mind was shopping for a wedding ring for Travis. She had asked Dottie to go along with her for some guidance. She did not want to inadvertently choose a ring that was too similar to what he wore when he and Angela were married. That's when a mother's input would come in very handy. Travis's parents would be in town for a few more days, so Meghan and Dottie were planning to get that done before she left town. Once she had Travis's ring in her hand, Meghan felt she would be able to relax a bit and let Kaci deal with all the final little details.

* * *

To no one's surprise, summer disappeared into early fall and the wedding was only a couple weeks away. Thanks primarily to Meghan stepping back and letting her daughter and future mother-in-law handle things, everything was wrapping up without any unforeseen glitches. Some of Meghan's friends had jumped in to help Kaci make decorations and centerpieces, and Dottie had offered to make the wedding cake. Much to Meghan's surprise, Dottie had worked in a small bakery before she retired and had quite a talent for cake decorating. The three men had managed to remain scarce during the majority of the wedding planning. Heeding the advice of the man with the most experience, both Travis and Todd listened when Dennis said, "Trust me, sons, just step back, stay out of their way, and keep your wallets open!"

Chapter Twenty-Eight

Standing in front of the full-length mirror in her bedroom, Meghan hiked up her wedding gown to reveal her favorite pair of cowboy boots adorning her feet.

"What do you think, kiddo? Do you think I can pull it off?" Meghan asked with a smile.

Kaci chuckled as she replied, "Mom, even if that look weren't becoming so popular, you would have no trouble pulling it off. It screams 'Country girl gets hitched!' Did you ever tell Travis you were planning to wear your boots?"

"No, I didn't. I don't think he'll mind."

"Considering how much trouble you had convincing him to wear a tux instead of jeans, I'm sure he won't mind a bit. If anything, he'll probably be jealous!"

"I'm sure you're right!" Meghan looked at her only child and said, "You look beautiful, Kaci. And I never could have done this without you."

"Thanks, Mom. You look beautiful too. Even wearing your boots."

Meghan's friend Becky poked her head in the door. "How are you ladies doing? The limo should be here in about twenty minutes to take you to the church."

"I think we're about ready," Meghan replied.

Kaci confirmed, "Dressed, hair done, makeup finished. I think our work here is done."

As they started toward the door, Becky held up her hand to stop them. She leaned down and lifted the hem of Meghan's dress. She looked up at Meghan and grinned. "Seriously, Meg? You're wearing your boots?"

"Sure," she replied, smiling. "Why not? Besides, Kaci said this look is very popular!"

Becky gave her best friend a hug and said, "You're one of a kind, Meg. That's a fact. I hope Travis knows what he's getting himself into!"

"He's just as bad as Mom is," Kaci explained. "If Grandma Dot and I hadn't protested, they would probably be getting married in a barn wearing boots and jeans!"

The sound of the doorbell broke into their laughter. "That's probably the limo driver," Becky said. "We should head down. I'm sure everyone else is already at the church waiting for your grand entrance."

"No doubt," Meghan said unenthusiastically. "Grand entrances are highly overrated. Well, let's go, ladies. We don't want to keep them waiting!"

* * *

Standing in the foyer of the church, Todd paced back and forth. He had been here earlier making sure he took care of the preliminary best man duties. Now he was nervously waiting to fulfill the second half of his dual role, walking his sister down the aisle. He briefly looked toward the ceiling when he felt Meghan put her hand on his arm.

"I know," she said in understanding. "I wish he was here

too."

"Dad would have been so proud to walk you down the aisle today, sis. And I'm sure he would approve of Travis."

"I think so," Meghan agreed.

"He also would have told you how beautiful you are. And he would have been right. You really are beautiful, Meg. Inside and out. I love you, sis."

"I love you too, Todd. I couldn't have asked for a better brother."

The traditional wedding march started inside the sanctuary, and two attendants opened the double doors. Meghan looked down the aisle to see Travis and Kaci standing with Dennis.

"Well, sis," Todd began. "It's time. It looks like you have a couple people waiting for you up there."

Todd leaned over and gave his sister a kiss on the cheek, then took her by the arm, and they started down the aisle, each sporting the trademark family smile.

As they neared the front of the church, Travis and Meghan locked eyes and smiled. Today truly was the first day of the rest of their lives.

* * *

A Year and A Half Later

Kaci slowly opened the door and poked her head into the hospital room.

"Mom," she began. "Can we come in?"

Meghan looked up with a smile on her face and replied, "Of course you can. Who all is here?"

"Me, Uncle Todd, Grandpa, and Grandma Dot."

Dottie poked her head around Kaci and said, "We couldn't

wait any longer. Are you up to having some company, dear?"

"Sure," Meghan agreed. "Come on in."

Travis stood to pull a couple chairs closer to the bed for his parents. The small hospital room filled up quickly, but no one wanted to take a seat. All eyes were on the tightly wrapped bundle Meghan was holding close to her chest. Travis reached over and carefully lifted his son away from her and held him proudly for everyone to see.

Kaci was the first to reach out for the tiny fingers. "Mom, he's got your nose."

Travis pulled off the little stocking cap and said with a grin, "He's got her red hair too!" Everyone laughed as Travis gently ran his hand over his son's tuft of bright red hair.

Travis looked at Kaci and asked, "Would you like to hold your baby brother, Kaci?"

Feeling a little unsure of herself, Kaci looked toward her mom. "Is it okay, Mom?"

"Sure. Why don't you sit in one of the chairs and hold him."

Kaci sat down, and Travis placed the baby in her arms. He immediately opened his eyes and looked right at her. Kaci's face lit up and she said, "He's got blue eyes."

Grandma Dot was looking over Kaci's shoulder at her grandson and said, "Most babies are born with blue eyes. It would be nice if his stayed that color because it's a very pretty shade of blue."

Travis sat back down in a chair at the side of the bed and took Meghan's hand as they both watched the family get to know their newborn son. Kaci passed him off to Grandma Dot, who reluctantly handed him over to Dennis after about fifteen minutes. Dennis eventually passed him to Todd, who had been patiently waiting his turn to meet his new nephew.

Todd seemed like an old pro as he stared into the baby's face and said, "Hey, little buddy. Are your mom and dad going to give you a name, or will I be calling you Rug Rat until you start school?"

"Rug Rat sounds like a perfectly fine name to me," Travis joked.

Meghan gave him a playful slap on the arm and said, "I don't think so! Honey, why don't you tell them what we decided."

"Yes, dear," Travis replied with a grin. "We narrowed it down to two choices and decided to wait until after he was born to make the final decision. His name is Joshua Christopher Harmon." Tears began to well up in Travis's eyes as he explained. "Joshua was the middle name of the son Angela and I lost." Dottie put her hand on her son's shoulder as she, too, felt the pain of loss. "Joshua means God is salvation. Christopher means Christ bearer. I imagine we'll probably end up calling him JC."

Kaci looked over at her baby brother and announced, "I'm going to call him Joshie."

Meghan smiled at the daughter who had obviously fallen in love with her new brother. "Joshie would probably work when he's a little boy. I doubt he'd like it much when he got older."

"He would let me call him Joshie, but probably not anyone else," Kaci said with certainty.

"You're probably right, Kaci," Travis agreed as he put his sleeping son back in Meghan's arms.

Dennis spoke up and said, "It looks like I need to be the voice of reason here and herd everyone out so Mama can get some rest. What time do you think you'll be home, son?"

"I'll probably be home in an hour or so," Travis replied. "I want to sit with Meghan for a while then I'll head out so she can get some sleep. The doctor said he would probably release them both in the morning."

Grandma Dot leaned over and placed a tender kiss on the

forehead of her grandson. "I love you, Joshua." She then gave both her son and her daughter-in-law a kiss on the cheek. "You have a beautiful little boy. Don't you worry about anything at home. We'll take care of everything and we'll see you tomorrow."

"Thanks, Mom," Travis replied as he gave his mother a hug.

Kaci was having a hard time letting go of her brother's tiny hand. She reluctantly gave him a kiss on the forehead and said, "Bye, Joshie. I'll see you tomorrow."

By the time everyone said their good-byes and Travis sat back down in the chair, he noticed that Meghan was already fast asleep. He reached over and took Joshua out of her arms, cradled him against his chest, and settled in for a little nap of his own.

* * *

Kaci had been staring out the living room window ever since Travis called to say they were on their way home. Dottie was busy in the kitchen fixing some snacks and tidying up after breakfast. Dennis and Todd were upstairs in the nursery, putting the finishing touches on the crib. Before they left for the hospital, Meghan had set up the bassinet in the family room, knowing they would be spending a lot of time there. Kaci had a small stuffed teddy bear sitting up in the corner of the bassinet, a gift for her baby brother.

"They're here!" Kaci yelled from the living room. Dottie came from the kitchen, taking off her apron along the way. Dennis and Todd hurried downstairs in time to see Kaci rush out the front door. It wasn't long before everyone was right behind her.

Travis came around to the passenger door of the Jeep and helped Meghan out, then opened the back door to retrieve his son, still safely tucked into the baby car seat. Todd grabbed the diaper bag and Meghan's overnight bag from the backseat. The entire entourage made its way to the house. After a significant amount of fanfare, everyone settled into the family room and fell into a series of conversations occurring simultaneously.

Kaci took up residence next to the bassinet and was gently rocking it. After several minutes, she finally spoke up and asked, "Shouldn't we try to be a little quieter? Joshie is sleeping."

Travis walked over and put his arm around Kaci's shoulder. "We don't want to get into the habit of being quiet around him all the time. He needs to get used to the normal sounds of the family. Otherwise, he won't be able to sleep unless it's quiet. And it's a pretty safe bet this home will not be quiet most of the time!"

"I suppose you're right," Kaci agreed. "This family does tend to get noisy at times."

Meghan relaxed back into the comfort of the sofa as she listened to the sounds around her. Her husband and daughter were bonding over a mutual love for this newest member of the family. Her brother and father-in-law were engaged in a game of chess, and her mother-in-law had moved a chair over next to the bassinet so she could stand vigil over her new grandson. This was what made Meghan feel complete. Their home was filled with the love of family.

Thank you, God.

Travis noticed that Meghan had fallen asleep on the sofa. Leaving his son in the care of the watchful eyes of his daughter and mother, he lifted Meghan's legs up onto the sofa. After covering her with an afghan from the back of the sofa, he sat down beside his wife and gently laid her head in his lap. He took in the scene around him and liked what he saw.

Thank you, God. You asked me to trust you, and I did. You told me I would know when I was healed and ready to move on. As always, You were right. You assured me I would be happy again. I am.

Epilogue

Meghan stood on the deck, scanning their large back yard, looking for her rambunctious three-year-old who had managed to disappear once again. Travis, her husband of nearly five years, rose from his chair and stood beside his wife with his arm around her waist.

"You worry too much, honey. The entire yard is fenced. He can't go anywhere."

"I know, but…" she began before she spotted the object of her search.

"Joshua Christopher Harmon, you get down from that Bobcat right now!"

The little boy had just managed to scramble up over the side of the Bobcat sitting next to the shop and plopped down in the seat. "But, Mommy," he protested. "I'm wearing my hard hat! Uncle Todd said I couldn't get on the 'quipment less I wore my hard hat!" In an effort to prove his point, he tapped down on the yellow plastic hard hat, knocking it down over his eye.

Travis laughed. "Like mother, like son. You have to admit, honey, he comes by it honestly."

"I know," Meghan smiled. "But it's been a while since I've had to deal with that." She looked over at her twenty-one-year-old daughter, who was home for the summer. Kaci was working an internship in the family construction business before beginning her senior year of college as a business major.

Travis ran his hand along Meghan's rapidly expanding mid-section. "Maybe you'll get lucky and this one will be a little girl."

Kaci stood next to her stepdad and said with a chuckle, "You know that wouldn't make any difference, Travis." Kaci headed toward the back yard, calling over her shoulder, "Don't worry, Mom, I'll get him."

As she approached the Bobcat, Kaci could see Joshua pre-tending to work the controls like he was plowing ground, making all the appropriate sounds just like any normal three-year-old would do. "Hey, Joshie, why don't we play baseball?"

Little Josh hesitated, his hands still on the controls. He rarely turned down time with his big sister, but working the controls on the Bobcat was hard to give up. "Can I wear my hard hat?" he asked.

"Sure, why not."

"Do I get to bat?"

"Of course, you do. Do you want to bat or just play catch?"

"Can we do both?" he asked hopefully, taking his hands off the controls.

"Anything you want, Joshie." Kaci reached up and rescued her little brother from the cab of the Bobcat.

He wrapped his dirty arms around her neck and said, "I love you, sissy."

That boy had a way of melting her heart. "I love you too, Joshie. Let's go find your bat and ball."

About that time, the side gate opened, and Todd walked into the yard.

"Uncle Todd!" Josh screamed as he ran full tilt toward his uncle.

Todd reached down and scooped him up like a football, packing the giggling boy toward the back deck. "Hey, Rug Rat!"

"I'm not Rug Rat, Uncle Todd," he giggled. "I'm JC."

"Is that so? What does JC stand for, Junior Cowboy?"

"No, silly. I'm Joshua Christopher!"

"That's quite a name for a little fella like you, don't you think?"

"That's why everybody calls me JC. Everybody 'cept Kaci."

"And what does Kaci call you?" Todd asked innocently.

"Joshie!" he replied excitedly.

"You don't say. Why does she get to call you Joshie? I think I'll start calling you Joshie, too."

"No, Uncle Todd! Just Kaci 'cause she's my sissy!"

Todd swung Josh up onto his shoulders as he replied, "Well, she must be a pretty lucky girl then."

"Yep! I love her!"

Travis and Meghan leaned against the railing of the deck as Todd, Kaci, and JC came toward them. Josh was bouncing up and down on his uncle's shoulders while simultaneously swinging his feet.

"Hey, sis," Todd greeted with a smile. "How are you feeling these days?"

Meghan laughed as she replied, "Probably better than you! That boy is going to kick a hole in your shoulder if you aren't careful!" Todd just smiled. He loved spending time with his niece and nephew.

Meghan turned to Travis. "Do you remember a few years ago you were telling me how God needs to scrape off our rough edges and polish us up?"

"That's right, I remember. We're all diamonds in the rough before God gets to work on us. Hey, maybe that's my sermon for this week!"

She pointed at her son and remarked, "Well, that little dust devil is a big lump of coal! He's going to need a chisel first!"

With JC still bouncing on his shoulders, Todd said, "Ah, sis, he's going to be okay. He's got good genes, remember."

"I got good boots, too, Uncle Todd!" he said, holding his feet out for Todd to see. "I got good jeans and good boots!"

Travis reached over and tugged on his son's foot as they roared in laughter. "You sure do, son!" Then he added, "You never know, Meg, that little tornado just might end up being a missionary someday."

~ The End ~